Honor's Lark

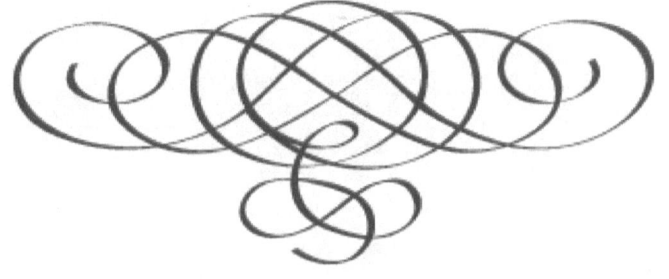

Rachel L. Hamm

DEDICATION

Like Honor, I have yet to find the love of my life. I've yet to have children, and don't know if I ever will. Also like Honor, I'm lucky enough to have some amazing nieces and nephews. This book is for them.

Gracyn, Lane, Addison, Baby Shan #3, and Emerson

Blood isn't the only thing that makes a family.

Love does, too.

TABLE OF CONTENTS

Chapter One: The Fairy Tale

Bonnie closed the door to her bedroom and leaned against it as she turned to face me. A picture of her four-year old daughter, Lang, and her lifemate, Caron, rattled on the wall. "What's the issue?" she asked.

"We are three, intelligent women," I said.

"I know that."

"You'd think that three, intelligent women would have something more to talk about than the current state of my love life."

"Calm down, Honor. We were talking about plenty of other things before Caron asked about your pull."

My stupid pull. It was supposed to be leading me to the one person who would love me as much as Caron loved Bonnie. I understood why my friends felt the need to ask about it, but that didn't stop me from being pissed off when they did. "I've told you and your mate several times that I don't want to talk about it."

Bonnie shook her head and gestured wildly around the room. Talking with her hands was a habit she'd had since childhood, and it had only grown more dramatic as we got older. "She was trying to be nice — to express an interest in you. Isn't that what you wanted?"

"I don't want her pity."

"She wasn't pitying you."

It took every ounce of self-control I had to stop myself from sighing. "Of course she was. 'So, Honor, have you felt any pull lately? Any at all?'"

"You're being a real jerk, Honor. Caron made you dinner and was trying to be nice, and how do you thank her? By pulling me aside and talking about her behind her back?"

"I just don't want to talk about my pull or my lark, okay?"

Her hands paused, palms facing me. "Fine. You choose the topic of conversation then."

"Fine."

"And apologize to Caron when we go back."

"Fine," I said through gritted teeth. I had been rude. I knew it. And I felt bad about it. Honestly, I did. But Bonnie and Caron didn't understand. How could they? I didn't know anyone who really and truly could.

I followed Bonnie back to the dining room, where Caron was pouring a glass of wine. She set it at my place and poured another. Bonnie took it from her and drank. Her eyes darted to me and I cleared my throat.

"Caron, I'm sorry. It was rude of me, taking Bonnie away like that. I know you can't exactly cook and watch after Lang at the same time."

Caron smiled, and filling her own glass, said, "It's fine. Come and sit before it gets cold."

"Can Honor sit next to me?" Lang asked. She bounced up and down in her seat and patted the chair next to her. Picking up my glass from the opposite side of the table, I made my way to her and plopped down. "Do I get some juice, too, Caron?" Lang asked, pointing to my wine.

"That's Big Girl juice, honey. You can have some when you're twenty." Caron kissed the top of Lang's head. "Did you turn the screen off when your show was over?" Lang nodded once. Caron gave her a cup of water, then took the seat originally intended for me. Bonnie sat to her right, in front of Lang.

"How was work today, sweetie?" Caron asked Bonnie as she passed around fried pork chops.

"You'll never believe what my boss said to me…"

I had already heard the story about Bonnie's boss's inappropriate comment regarding her time-off request. It wasn't a great story. "Lang, do you want some mashed potatoes?"

"Yes, please!"

I scooped a spoonful onto her plate and one on mine. "Gravy?" I asked. She bounced again in her seat, reaching for the boat. "Wait – if we do *this*," I built up the potatoes into a mound resembling a volcano, "then we can pour the gravy in like lava." She giggled and made me do the same on my own plate. Of course, after that she didn't want to eat because the "lava would melt her mouth." Oops.

We finished eating and Lang was sent to her playroom so the adults could clean up and consume a few more glasses of wine. Their dishwasher was broken, so I was assigned to drying duty.

"I know you don't like to talk about your lark, Honor, and I'm sorry I brought it up earlier, but I don't see you as often as Bonnie does. I just wanted to be supportive," Caron said, handing me a dripping plate. I glared at the dark brown mark on my left wrist. It had grown uglier and uglier to me over the years. The longer it went unfilled, the more I hated it.

"There are no updates to give. I haven't felt the pull in five years. I don't think he wants to be found."

"That's something I was wondering about. You always refer to your lifemate as a 'he,' but have you considered maybe it's a 'she?'" Caron asked.

Bonnie gave me a knowing look as I took another wet plate out of Caron's hands and began wiping. I cleared my throat. "When we were growing up, Bonnie and I would talk about finding our lifemates when we got older."

"I always knew mine would be a woman," Bonnie said.

"And I always knew mine would be a man," I added.

"I think it has something to do with the pull." Bonnie took the stack of dry plates beside me and shelved them in the cabinets above the sink.

Caron turned off the water. "Yeah, I knew you would be a woman when I found you, too, Bon. But if Honor's pull has faded now, maybe her assumption was wrong."

I shrugged. "Maybe, but I don't really think so."

"You never know," Bonnie said. She pulled a fresh bottle of wine out of the pantry and handed it to her partner.

"Let's talk about something else," I said, passing my glass to Caron and thanking her for the liberal portion she poured. Caron's generosity was one of the things I loved about her, but it had taken me a while to warm up to her. When Bonnie found her and they moved to Linhill, I felt abandoned. It wasn't either's fault, but Bonnie had always been my person. Until, suddenly, she was Caron's.

I followed them to Linhill, hoping its location in the center of my pull's erratic wanderings would lead me to my mate faster than drifting aimlessly. Needless to say, it hadn't. On the bright side, though, I was only an hour or so from the coast and the weather maintained a happy medium for most of the year. My friends chose wisely when they settled there.

Once the dishes were done and the bottle emptied, I helped Bonnie get Lang ready for bed. She was a stubborn little girl who did not like having her hair or teeth brushed, but between Bonnie and myself we managed to get it done and somehow coax her into her pajamas, too.

"Get under the covers and I'll tell you a story," Bonnie instructed.

"The Lark story!" Lang exclaimed.

Bonnie glanced quickly at me, but I shrugged again, so she nodded to her daughter and Lang hopped into bed.

"It's my favorite story, Honor! Is it your favorite, too?"

"Sure thing, kiddo." I moved to the door to give them privacy.

"Don't go! You have to listen to the story, too."

"No, she doesn't, Lang." Bonnie reached to the lamp on the nightstand and tapped the base, eliciting a soft yellow glow from the bulb. "Honor, turn out the light and shut the door behind you."

"It's alright. I can listen. It's such a good story, right, Lang?"

"Right!"

I leaned against the doorframe, arms crossed over my chest, while Bonnie situated herself on the bed beside Lang. A nurturing arm went around the little girl's shoulders; their backs sank against the headboard.

"A long, long time ago..." Bonnie began.

Lang clapped her hands. "There was a God named Paolo..."

"...and a Goddess named Pria. Paolo and Pria were very much in love and it saddened them that they did not have anyone else to share their love with. So, they created the Earth and filled it with people – people with big hearts full of love. Pria and Paolo wanted to make sure their people were as happy together as they were, so they designed each person a mate and gave each couple an unmistakable mark so they would know when they had found each other. A Love Mark..."

"A lark!" Lang squealed.

"That's right. Some pairs' marks are on their hands, or their legs, or..."

"Their stomachs!" Lang lifted her shirt to display hers.

"Yep, or their stomachs. And when you find your mate, your lark becomes a whole picture. Like a flower, or a star, or a..." Bonnie paused and waved her hand to Lang.

"Or a dog!" A chubby finger reached up and touched the black dog on Bonnie's neck.

"And you know you've found your lifemate because not only is your lark complete, but so are you."

"When will I find my mate, Bonnie?"

"I don't know sweetie. Someday." Bonnie kissed the top of Lang's head and helped her slide down until she was lying flat on her back, the covers tucked tightly around her. "Goodnight, I love you."

"Love you, too!"

I sucked in a breath and cleared out of the doorway. Bonnie was walking towards me, a horrible look of sympathy on her face. When she reached me, her arms engulfed me.

"You'll find him," she whispered. "The Gods do not want us to be alone."

"That's just a fairy tale," I said, but hugged her back tightly and hoped with all I had that she was right.

I stumbled into work the next day a half-hour late, thanks to the copious amounts of wine at Bonnie and Caron's house. No one appeared to notice, though, as I slid into my cubicle and powered up my computer.

"What day is it?" I muttered to myself, opening the company-wide calendar. "Ah." Wednesday, the fifteenth day of the tenth month. A meeting for my division was listed at 10:00, so I printed the agenda and answered the most urgent emails in my inbox before heading to the lounge to grab a cup of coffee.

"Morning, Honor!" my teammate Alyscia said brightly as I added cream and sugar to my mug.

I yawned. "Morning."

"Did you hear the good news?"

I took a sip and shook my head. "What? Did Felix sit in paint again?"

"No, silly, I found him!"

"Found who?"

"My lifemate, of course! Look!" She pushed aside the collar of her shirt to reveal her lark, now a complete, leafy tree. The last time she'd shown it to me, too many pieces of the puzzle were missing and I hadn't been able to make out what it would eventually be.

"Oh. Great. Congratulations." It was a strange thing to offer congratulations on. It's not like she achieved some major accomplishment. Everyone found his or her lifemate eventually. Well, everyone except me. I walked away without asking for more details, though I could tell she was dying to share exactly how she found him and what he said to her when they met and how perfect they were for each other. My stomach was already queasy from the hangover – I didn't want to push it over the edge.

Besides, Alyscia was only twenty-one. She started at the consulting firm a few months out of school. What right did she have to be flaunting her lark? She hadn't been looking for a long time. Most people I knew found their mates at some point between eighteen and twenty-four.

I slumped into a chair at the end of the conference table, as far from the front of the room as possible, and gulped down my coffee, ignoring the bitter sting as it burned my throat. My co-workers filed in, bouncing to their seats like a bunch of toddlers. A few were even discussing Alyscia's lark at high volume. To listen to them, one would think it was the biggest news to hit Linhill all year. I blocked out the conversation by reading over the agenda for the meeting.

The leader of our division, Felix, walked in with another man I didn't know. The new guy was tall, at least a head taller than Felix, and dressed in an expensive-looking grey suit. They took seats at the head of the table and the babble in the room quieted as Felix arranged the agenda and glass of water in front of him.

"To kick things off today I want to introduce our new division manager, Sedric Eckland. He'll be taking over Maling's accounts now that she's been promoted and he'll also be responsible for evaluating the team over the next couple of months. Sedric, would you like to say anything?"

"I'm happy to be here and look forward to working with each of you." Sedric surveyed the room, taking a brief second to meet each individual's eye. When he reached me, I averted my gaze.

Turnover was common in our section. It was kind of a joke within the company: head to Division Four if you're looking for a life change. I was the longest-term employee at four years. The pool on how long Sedric would last was probably already forming in Divisions One, Two, and Three.

Once Sedric finished all of his eye contact, Felix made a check on his agenda and moved to the next topic. I sank as low as I could in my chair and rested both arms on the table in front of me. Being the senior member of the team at least gave me the advantage of already knowing most, if not all, of Felix's talking points. I tuned him out as easily as I'd tuned out the gossip regarding Alyscia and found my eyes focused on my own lark.

When I was younger, I loved that my lark was so visible — always right there on my wrist. I could look at it whenever I wanted. I could show it to my friends, my family. It was a source of comfort and hope. I spent hours tracing the pieces over and over with my fingers. Memorizing every line, every curve. Trying to figure out what picture it would form when I found my lifemate and it completed itself.

As Felix droned on, I found myself falling back into the old habit – using my right index finger to continually follow the outline of the lark. I didn't care what my boss was talking about. It didn't matter. I focused my energy on tracing and willing the damn thing to just go away already. I did what I was supposed to do – I followed my stupid erratic pull as long as it led me, but it led to nothing. Nothing. If I was going to be alone, I didn't want the horrible, ugly reminder of it staring at me day after day, week after week, year after year.

What were the Gods playing at, anyway? Giving humans these marks, determining destinies, but leaving me out in the cold wondering what I'd done wrong to deserve such loneliness and the constant reminder of it. And if it wasn't bad enough that I could see the damn mark every day, everyone else could see it, too. My co-workers, friends, and family saw the unfinished lark and their eyes filled with pity for poor, lonely, lifemate-less Honor.

"Honor?" Felix basically shouted. I straightened up. One glance around the table told me he'd called my name more than once.

"Yes?"

"Welcome back. Were you having a nice daydream?"

"I was. It's strange how your voice can lull me into fantasy land every time you speak."

His face reddened, probably with both anger and embarrassment. He'd never gotten used to my sarcasm and I knew he wanted to fire me on several occasions, but since my clients were so pleased with my longevity, the higher ups wouldn't let him.

"Did you want something from me?" I asked, putting a sweet smile on my face.

"Um, yes, well, since you've been here longer than the rest of the team, you'll be partnering with Sedric for a few weeks. He'll be going on your calls to shadow you and you'll be going on his calls to introduce him to Maling's clients. You know, show him the ropes. Do you think you can manage that?"

"Nothing in the world would give me greater pleasure." I wiped the smile from my lips and peered at Sedric. I expected eye contact again, but he was staring at my hand. No, not my hand. My wrist – my lark. Great, just great. I yanked my sleeve down and put both hands in my lap.

He looked up and faced Felix. "Sounds good. Anything else on the agenda?"

"No, we're done for today. Back to work, everyone."

I jumped from my seat and was the first person out the door. Practically running to my cubicle, I tripped on a loose piece of carpet and face-planted.

"Whoa – careful. Are you okay?" Sedric reached down and helped lift me while the rest of the departing members of my division looked on. I brushed myself off and wriggled out of his grasp.

"I'm fine." I could feel his stare on me as I stormed away.

I tried not to speak with anyone else for the rest of the day. Embarrassed by the fall, the meeting, and Sedric's eyes on my wrist, I couldn't face the normal around me. I didn't want my new boss to immediately know just how sad I was. It would make the weeks of having to work one-on-one with him unbearable.

"Good morning, Honor." Sedric approached me a few minutes after I arrived the next day. He loomed over the walls of my cubicle like a giant in one of Lang's fairy tales, seeming even taller than he'd been the day before. He didn't smile when he said 'good morning,' like most people, so at least we had that in common. I nodded to acknowledge his greeting and continued checking my email, the clunky bracelet I'd worn to hide my lark jangling as my hands moved over the keyboard.

"We should probably coordinate our agendas for the next few weeks."

I nodded again.

"Look, if you have some sort of problem with me, I can ask someone else to go with me to meet my new clients. But, you should probably remember that I'm your boss."

Classic management strategy – a threat right out of the gate. Except, he didn't say it like a threat. His tone hadn't changed at all. I glanced up from my computer. "I don't have a problem with you. But it really makes no difference to me whether you're my boss or not. Felix is my boss, too. He knows how I work and he knows I produce results. He lets me be."

"I'm not Felix."

"Good for you." I meant it with all sincerity. Good for anyone who wasn't annoying, pain in my ass, thinks-he's-clever-but-is-actually-an-idiot, Felix.

Sedric came around the side of my cubicle and leaned on my desk. I expected him to start yelling, or threatening my job, but when he spoke it was in a lowered, softened voice. "When did you lose him?"

"Huh?"

"Or her?"

"When did I lose who?"

He pointed to my wrist. "Your lifemate."

"What, I didn't lose…" I tugged at my sleeve to ensure the lark was completely covered and thanked Pria I'd had the good sense to put jewelry on that morning. The look on his face was so earnest. It wasn't just sympathy. It was like he understood the pain. "I didn't lose him."

His voice lowered even more. "Why were you so focused on your lark yesterday in the meeting? Did something happen to him?"

"No. We had a fight. A really big fight. My fault. I was feeling guilty."

"Oh." He straightened his back and adjusted his tie. "Sorry to have bothered you." As he walked away, I could feel sadness emanating from him. Like he'd harbored some kind of hope in approaching me. I'd never felt worse for lying in my life.

Chapter Two: Shattered Delusion

Dying weeds and fallen leaves were overtaking my yard. Formerly green patches of ground were yellow, straw-like, and coarse. "I should really hire a gardener," I muttered as I stuck my key in the lock. The front door swung open and I left my miserable lawn behind as I stepped into the cool house.

I didn't waste any time. A bottle of wine on the kitchen counter waited for me. Glass in hand, I stretched out on my sofa and turned on the wall screen. After a few seconds of fiddling with the menus, Valor's face popped up. I pressed 'call' and waited.

Real-time video replaced the photo of my brother as his living room came into view. "Hang on just a sec!" a shout came from offscreen. Valor jogged into the room and sat in front of his screen. "Honor!"

"Hey."

"You do realize it's after eleven here, right?" My brother looked good. Happy. He usually did these days, but it somehow still surprised me to see him smile. The brother I grew up with wore a permanent scowl, but it disappeared when he met his mate.

"Yep."

"And you still thought it a good idea to call?"

I shrugged. "I missed my big brother." I really did.

"You usually call on the weekend."

"I know, but I had a crappy day at work."

Valor pointed at his screen, indicating my wine glass. "I can see that."

"You're one to talk." He could name over a hundred beers by brand in a blind taste test – he won a contest only a year ago.

"Why was work so crappy?"

"New boss." I sighed and swirled the contents of my glass.

"Is he an asshole?"

"What makes you assume it's a he?"

"Fine – is she an asshole?"

"He's not an asshole." Another swirl, then a big sip. Okay, it was a gulp.

"What did he do to cause your rough day?"

I considered the question. My first instinct was to blame the guy's general existence, but that wasn't fair. Or accurate. "He didn't do anything. I caused it all by myself. As usual."

Val smiled knowingly. "You really need to work on that."

"Yep."

"What did you do then?"

Setting my glass on the coffee table, I leaned towards my screen. "I lied to the poor guy, about something stupid, and he was trying to be nice to me."

"I've always told you your pathological lying is going to bite you in the ass."

"Yeah, well, what kind of sister would I be if I listened to my brother's advice?"

"The smart kind?" He chuckled, slapping his palm against his forehead.

"Are the kids around? I think having my niece and nephew tell me how kick-ass and awesome I am will really make me feel better."

"We don't let them use the screen after nine."

"It's only five-thirty here."

"And it's eleven-thirty here."

Not willing to be defeated, I said, "I get Shyla, she's young, she needs her sleep. But Handor is fifteen! He's at that age where he can stay awake for three days straight and barely be worse for the wear."

"I can have them call you in the morning, before they head to lessons."

"What time is that?"

He grinned. "Seven-thirty."

"That's one-thirty here!"

"I guess you're just going to have to wait until the weekend then."

I slumped back into the cushions. "You suck."

"I know. Do you want to say hi to Mabry? She can stay up as late as she wants."

"That's okay. Your lifemate isn't my biggest fan."

"Maybe because every word you say to her is a lie."

"And pretty obvious ones. Honestly, if she falls for them, it's kinda her own fault."

Val groaned, but in a *gosh darn it, if you weren't my kid sister and so stinkin' cute, I'd kill you* kind of way. "I gotta go, Honor. But I'll make sure the kids call you this weekend, okay?"

"Okay. Love you."

"You, too."

The real-time video dissolved back into Valor's picture and I guzzled the rest of the wine. I missed my brother so much since he moved across the ocean to Esterland with Mabry – it was easy to forget we hadn't always gotten along.

It's no piece of cake growing up with a ten-year age difference. Our lifegivers, Hero and Gizella, already had the perfect offspring in Valor and hadn't planned on having any others, when, *surprise!* I showed up. They loved me, of course, and so did Valor, but it still took a long time before he stopped resenting me for taking over his turf and I stopped hating him for always being so perfect.

I never particularly liked Mabry, but she did improve my relationship with Valor. He became softer and gentler when she came into the picture. And though I could not have blamed her had she persuaded Val to never speak to me again – I once convinced her Val had a genetic defect that caused nocturnal involuntary urination – she actually encouraged him to spend more time with me.

Man. I really was a bitch.

Such reflection had me reaching for my glass, yet again, but my lips found it empty. I stood and headed to the kitchen. Instead of uncorking the wine bottle, though, I rinsed the glass with warm water and put it in the dishwasher. Leaning against the counter, I looked around my house. It was a small rental, but I liked it. The carpet was soft beige and the walls matched. I'd never bothered to paint, just like I rarely bothered with the front lawn. Those were the owner's problems.

There were a few pictures on the walls I'd hung right after moving in: my lifegivers, Valor and his kids, Bonnie with Caron and Lang. The ones I cared about. The only people I had to love.

My pantry doors were open, as they often were. I went in and out so frequently it never seemed to make sense to close them. I'd thought of taking them off the hinges, but had nowhere to store them. Plus, if I ever moved out, I wouldn't want the hassle of putting them back in.

I entered the pantry and grabbed a canister of flour. And one of sugar. I stuffed a bottle of vanilla into the crook of my elbow and went across the kitchen to the fridge. Eggs. Milk. Butter. Hmmm, cream cheese?

After spreading the ingredients on the counter, I set the oven to pre-heat. Bowls, beaters, and pans came out of cupboards. My favorite wooden spoon. I mixed from memory, having made the recipe so many times. It was simple. Like breathing. No need to think about it. In fact, if I started thinking too much, that's when things would go to hell.

A dash of cinnamon to top things off, then into the oven. While the cake baked, I scooped the remaining batter into a separate, smaller pan and set it aside. The next step consisted of melting a small brick of chocolate and the cream cheese together on the stovetop.

When the frosting was whipped, my stomach started growling. "That's what happens when you make dessert before eating dinner." I popped a frozen meal into the microwave and watched dumbly as the glass plate spun.

The food wasn't very good, but I knew the cake would be. I didn't taste it when it was ready, though. I placed it in a white cardboard box, sealed it with a gold sticker, and put it in the fridge. The smaller version followed. It was still early, but I went to bed and fell promptly asleep.

The halls were empty as I tiptoed to the third division's employee lounge. The coffee pot hadn't started brewing yet. I set the large cake box beside it and pulled a new stack of paper plates from the cabinets above. After pouring in some fresh grounds and pressing *On*, I left with the smaller box and crept to my division.

The coast still looked clear as I found Sedric's office, so I stepped inside without knocking.

"Good morning."

Shit! I nearly dropped the box, jumping in response to his voice. "What are you doing here?"

"Did you miss the nameplate on the door?"

"No."

"Well, then, that answers your question."

I tried to recover my breath and my dignity, straightening up to my full height. "I meant, what are you doing here so early?"

"I like to get a head start on the day. Why, were you planning on sabotaging my office or something? A little hazing of the new guy?"

"Yep, that's exactly what I was going to do. But you caught me. Damn. The plan's foiled. I guess I'll see you later." I had a foot out the door, but he was walking towards me.

"What's in the box?"

"Nothing." But he'd already taken it from my hands.

"The Dessert Fairy," he read from the seal. He broke it and lifted the lid to reveal a perfectly round miniature cake with chocolate cream cheese frosting. "That's a fairy I can get behind. Did you make this, Honor?"

"No."

"Is it from a bakery? It smells delicious."

"No, I didn't buy it. I don't know where it's from."

"Why were you bringing it here?"

I groaned and shut his door. "Look, you can't tell anyone, okay?"

"Tell anyone what?"

"That I'm the one who brings the desserts. I don't want anyone to know. I didn't think you'd be here so early, or I wouldn't have brought you that."

He held the box up, the seal facing me. "You call yourself the Dessert Fairy?"

"I don't. People around the office do. When I told my friend, Bonnie, about it, she made the stickers to seal the boxes with. We thought they were funny."

"They are."

"Okay, there you go. You aren't going to tell anyone it's me, right?"

"I won't say a word. But why don't you want people to know?" he asked.

"I don't do it for them. I don't need their thanks."

He nodded, looking at the box in his hands. "Why'd you make one just for me? Surely not to welcome me to the office. You didn't seem too pleased with my presence yesterday."

I shrugged and reached for the doorknob. I couldn't exactly say I'd made it to apologize for being such a bitch. Ours was a professional office, after all. As I walked out the door I said, "We can sync our schedules later today if you'd like. Let me know what time is good for you."

"How about over lunch?"

I nodded and picked up the pace heading back to my desk.

I shifted in my seat. One would think a swanky restaurant could at least afford chairs with cushions, but I guess not. "We could have eaten in the cafeteria, like everyone else."

"I got the sense you'd be more at ease away from our co-workers. You know, without an audience."

This guy. He was so... I couldn't figure out what he was. It was really annoying.

A server appeared with two glasses of water on a small, black tray. She set the drinks on the table in front of us.

"Thank you," Sedric said.

"You're welcome. Are you ready to order, or do you want a few minutes to look at the menu?"

"I'm ready. Honor?"

"I'll have the chicken parmesan." I handed my menu over.

"Excellent. And you, sir?"

"The shrimp scampi and a side salad, please. Thank you," he said.

The server jotted both orders on her notepad and collected Sedric's menu before smiling, nodding, and moving toward the kitchen.

"I like to spend one week in the office, then one week in the field. Starting Monday, I have appointments scheduled with two different companies in Campi," I said.

"Do you always alternate evenly, one week in, one week out?"

"I try to. It saves on travel time and enables me to keep up with paperwork and client needs."

"Would you object to being out of the office for a little while longer? I know you already have clients scheduled several months out, and we need to work in my new clients as well."

"Oh." I unfolded my napkin and spread it in my lap. We didn't have any food yet, but I needed to do something with my hands. "I suppose I don't really have a choice, do I?"

"Of course you do."

"The sooner we take you to your clients, the less time you have to shadow me, right?"

"Right."

"Then I guess that's what we'll do."

"You want to get rid of me badly, huh?" He didn't say it teasingly, or sarcastically like I would have, but matter-of-factly.

"I don't like having someone over my shoulder, that's all."

He nodded and we were silent for a minute. The server stopped by the table with Sedric's salad and he thanked her, then began eating. The salad was half gone when he said, "Does your lifemate travel for business, too?"

"What? Oh. No."

"Does he mind that you do? If so, I'll understand if you can't do the additional time. Is that what you were fighting about?"

I took a swig of water. "No. What makes you think that?"

"Zara and I used to fight about it. A lot. I took a different position after a while, one where I didn't travel. It helped." There was that damned sincerity again. It sort of made me hate him, but it made me hate myself more.

"My lifemate and I weren't really in a fight." My right hand instinctually traveled to cover my lark.

"If you weren't fighting and you didn't lose him, why were you so upset the other day?"

Why couldn't he let it go? I looked around the room, trying to decide what to say. There were other tables like ours – colleagues having a business lunch. But none of them seemed to be trying to force personal revelations from one another. What the hell – he wanted to be nosy, could he handle honesty? Most people didn't like it when I told the truth. "I've never found him."

He paused for a moment before setting his fork on the salad plate. When he peered at me, that same look of understanding was in his eyes. Not pity. Empathy. I didn't want him to speak. I'd heard all the platitudes before: *Don't give up hope, you'll find him when you least expect it. There's someone for everyone, keep looking. You aren't paying enough attention to your pull, let it lead you to him.*

Yet, somehow I knew Sedric would say none of those things. It was not knowing what he would say that scared me.

"May I ask – how old are you?"

Ah. So there it was. The pity would finally start once I told him my age. "Thirty," I said, holding my chin high and forcing myself to meet his eye.

"You don't look it, if that makes you feel any better."

"Not exactly." But the fact that there was still no pity in his eyes did.

"Your pull?" he asked.

"Stopped. Disappeared. I haven't felt it in years."

"Hmm." He leaned back in his chair, pushing his salad plate forward, and slowly stroked the inside of his left palm. "I may know why you haven't found him. I'm really sorry, Honor, but I think he died."

"I..." The heat radiating from my face could have melted all the ice in my water glass. The server walked up and set our plates in front of us.

"Enjoy!" she said.

Sedric cleared his throat, but I jumped from my seat before he could say anything, mumbling, "Excuse me," as I rushed from the table towards the ladies' room.

I locked myself in the largest stall at the end of the row and backed against the wall. I wanted to sink to the ground, feel the cool tiles on my hands and legs, but I was frozen. Someone flushed a toilet in the stall beside mine. Tears pooled in my eyes, but when the sound of the water stopped, I squeezed my eyes shut and wiped the salty liquid away.

I knew Sedric was right. Of course he was right. It was the only thing that made sense. Everyone had a lifemate. Everyone was paired. How had I never considered it?

Because I'd never known of anyone whose lifemate died before they met. And I was still holding on to hope that he was out there. It was too terrible to believe I would never meet him, so I hadn't let myself realize the truth.

My heart was empty. I'd been waiting so long for him. Hoping for him. Expecting him. And he was never coming.

When I returned to our table, I took my seat as calmly as possible and picked up my knife and fork.

"Honor, I'm sorry. I was too blunt."

"Not at all. I think you're right. In fact, I've suspected it for a long time," I said. Cutting into my chicken, I focused all my attention on the melted mozzarella and marinara dumped on top of the angel hair pasta on my plate. I knew the moment I looked up, I'd finally see pity in his eyes. The flecks of oregano dusting the cheese held no judgment.

"You seemed awfully upset."

"Well, I'm not. I don't want to talk about it, though." I stuffed a bite into my mouth and rebuffed his polite attempts at conversation throughout the rest of the meal. I knew it wasn't his fault, but he'd shattered my hope. My delusion, more like it. And I wasn't ready to forgive him.

Chapter Three: Ready For Answers

My brain operated on autopilot the rest of the day. I filled out and filed paperwork. Answered emails. Confirmed my schedule and travel arrangements for the following week, adding rooms and flights for Sedric. Sent receipts to accounting for reimbursement.

Through it all, my heart kept replaying Sedric's words. *I'm really sorry, Honor, but I think he died.*

I shouldn't have dwelt on it. After all, I'd just told Bonnie what an intelligent woman I was and how I didn't need my love life to validate my existence. Knowing I would never actually have a love life should have been liberating. But it wasn't. Because I could still see the damn lark on my wrist. There was no sense of finality or closure in learning that my lifemate was, in all likelihood, dead. In its place were a thousand questions, a million what-ifs.

What if we found each other before he died?

Would he still have died?

Would that heartbreak be better or worse than never finding him?

What if I had died instead of him?

What would he be doing now?

What was he like?

I hadn't bothered wondering since childhood what my lifemate would be like when I found him. That type of speculation had been Bonnie's specialty. I didn't worry about it because I knew whatever he'd be like, we'd be perfect for each other somehow, and he would love me.

Once I realized he was gone it seemed important to know what he was like, but impossible to think I'd ever find out.

I pulled box after box from the storage shed behind my house. None contained what I was looking for. But I hadn't thrown it away. I'd considered that, but in the end, sentimentality won out and it had been packed with the rest of my past. I should have labeled things better. Would I have placed it with books, important documents, or miscellaneous? Any seemed possible, but each of those boxes came up empty.

While restacking the unhelpful cardboard containers, I bumped into a small trunk in the back right-hand corner of the shed. The tan leather blended into the wooden walls, making it difficult to spot. I shoved the stacked boxes aside and squeezed myself into the corner. As soon as I gripped the latch, I could remember placing my old journals in when preparing for the move. Sure enough, once the lid was lifted, I saw three spiral-bound notebooks on top.

Pressing the books to my chest, I thrust everything beyond the door, then closed and locked it. The journals were my new source of hope. The beginning of answers.

"He's dead," I said when Bonnie opened the door.

"What? Who's dead?"

"My lifemate."

Her jaw dropped slightly, but she didn't say anything else as she stepped aside and let me walk past her into the house. I still clutched the notebooks.

"I realized it today. I was having lunch with my new boss-"

"Why were you having lunch with the boss? You never eat with your co-workers."

"Not the point. Focus. He asked about my lifemate because I lied to him yesterday, saying I'd had a fight with my mate and that's why I'd been out of it during a meeting."

She shook her head. "Honor…"

"Don't lecture me on the consequences of stretching the truth right now."

"Stretching the truth? Oh, that's rich."

"Anyway, so I told him I've never found my mate and my pull stopped years ago and he said, all matter-of-factly, 'I think he died.' And I realized, of course. Don't you think he's right? It's the only way to explain why it has taken so long to find each other and why my pull disappeared." I hung my purse and jacket in the mudroom.

"But Honor, people just don't die young or before they meet their lifemates."

"I thought that, too, which is why I probably never came to this conclusion before, but accidents happen. It's not entirely unheard of. I mean, yes, most people die of old age and natural causes, but that's not the only way people die."

Bonnie scrunched up her nose. She wasn't buying it until her eyes widened and she grabbed my hand. "Oh, Pria! Remember when we were kids and that boy in our class drowned? At the lake, on vacation with his parents, right? Do you think it could have been him?"

I walked into her living room, Bonnie at my heel. "No, we were only eight or nine then. I started feeling my pull when I was thirteen, so it couldn't have been him. But that's my point. That tragedy – that poor kid never got to meet his lifemate, either. So there's some other man or woman out there wondering what happened to him. They may never have felt a pull at all."

"I'd never considered it possible for people to die without finding their mate. That's heartbreaking."

"Yeah." I fell onto her couch, pulling one of its oversized pillows onto my lap.

"I'm really sorry, Hon. That was insensitive."

"No, you're fine. It *is* heartbreaking. I'm heartbroken. I never met the guy and I feel like I'm in mourning."

She sat beside me. "What's with the notebooks?"

"My journals from several years ago. I thought if I could pinpoint when I lost my pull, maybe I'd be able to narrow down when he died."

"Why? Are you going to try and find out who he was?"

I didn't say anything, but I didn't need to.

"Are you sure that's a good idea? If he's really gone, won't learning who he was make it harder on you? How will you move on?"

"Move on to what? There isn't another man out there waiting for me. The Gods pair everyone. One shot. That's all we get. Knowing has got to be better than not. I feel better now that I understand why I haven't found him."

"I don't want you to get hurt."

I tossed the pillow to the other end of the couch; Bonnie startled and reached for my hand, but I wouldn't let her take it. "I already hurt. Every day. You can't know, you can't imagine what it feels like watching all the happy pairings in my life. I love you and Caron, my brother and his mate, but it kills me a little inside. You have no idea what I go through waking up each day knowing how utterly alone I am."

Bonnie, close to tears and voice shaking, said, "You aren't alone. You have me."

"You have Caron and Lang. It's not the same. I wish it were, but it's not." I loved her for wanting to be there for me, but no matter how hard she tried, she would never be able to understand how I was feeling. I patted her knee. "Will you help me find him?"

She smiled. It was weak and forced, but it was there. "Yes, I'll do whatever you need. Where do we start?"

"With these." I plopped one of the journals in her lap and opened another. "Try and find any entry mentioning the pull. I remember it being very erratic and I wrote about it – how frustrating it was. That could be important."

"Should we look chronologically?" She turned to the middle of the book and ran her index finger down the page.

"Maybe, I haven't really thought it through, but I know the answer is here somewhere."

"We should get organized." Bonnie loved organization. It was one of the few things in life that gave her pure joy. While I scanned the pages of the two journals I still had, she gathered several sheets of paper, a clipboard, and a pack of multicolored pens and highlighters. "We should figure out where the books fall in order and use a different sheet of paper for each. Any time we see a mention of the pull, we'll write down the date and how you felt and where the pull was leading you. Then after we've looked through them all, you'll have all the clues neatly laid out."

"Ah, finally, your anal retentiveness is good for something!"

"It's good for a lot of things, you just don't know how to appreciate it."

"Touché."

Going through the journals created weird sensations. On the one hand, it was fun looking back at what I did that year – the trip to see Val and the kids and attending Shyla's dance recital, baking my first batch of raspberry scones, and interviewing for different jobs. On the other hand, it was draining. I was so unhappy most of the time. I should have expected that, but I'd forgotten the long passages where I detailed how unfair the Gods were being and how I wanted to get my life started like everyone else. Bonnie had already filled half of her page by the time I remembered to write anything down.

After rescanning the first third of the journal, I was able to find several significant mentions of the pull to add to my sheet. Bonnie was still plugging away, until suddenly, she wasn't. I heard a soft *thud* as she dropped the journal she'd been looking through on the coffee table. The couch bounced slightly as she stood.

"I know I said I'd help, but I don't think it's a good idea for me to be reading your thoughts," she said over her shoulder as she headed towards the kitchen.

"Bonnie, wait, what do you mean?" I reached forward and slid the journal off the table, placing it on top of the one in my lap. The entry she'd been reading was dated the fifth day of the twelfth month, 2008.

Saw Bonnie and Caron today. As happy as ever. More so, actually. Bonnie's pregnant. They've been working with fertility doctors for a while, apparently. I don't know why they didn't tell me. Okay, maybe I do.

I want to be happy for them, but I don't know if I am. I don't know if I can be. I can't help thinking it's not fair. Why do they deserve to be together, to have a child? All I've ever wanted is a family of my own: my lifemate and a house full of children. But I'm starting to wonder if that's ever going to happen. My pull has been more erratic than ever lately. Yesterday, I felt the need to head straight to Trenalda, but today, the pull is leading me to Sensory.

I stopped reading. The rest of the entry was probably more bitterness over my unfair lot in life and Pria-knows I'd had plenty of that. "Bonnie?" I rose and followed her into the kitchen, leaving the journals behind. She was at the stove, shoving a casserole in.

"Hey," I said.

"Caron and Lang are going to be home soon." She turned her back on me and opened the fridge.

"I wrote some really jerky things."

"You never thought I'd read them."

"I didn't, but that doesn't make them any less jerky."

A sigh escaped her lips. "It does a little." She faced me with a head of lettuce, two tomatoes, and a bag of carrots in her hands. "Help me make a salad?"

I accepted the produce and began to rinse the lettuce in the sink. "If it helps, I only meant what I wrote when I was writing it. I don't feel that way now and you know how much I love Lang, right?"

"Yes, I know you love us. I do know it. But you aren't very good at showing it." She handed me a bowl.

"I try…"

"No, you don't. I'm nothing but supportive of you and you can be so selfish sometimes. You never consider that anyone else can be in pain because you are."

"What?"

"Do you know how long it took for me to get pregnant with Lang?"

"I… um…" Turning off the faucet, I put the head of lettuce into the bowl and started tearing pieces off.

"We discussed it. I told you how difficult it was. For over a year."

I paused. "A year?"

"Yep. But when I complain, I see the wheels in your head working. You're thinking that whatever is wrong, it's not as bad as your life."

She was completely right. She knew me so well. Too well. "How do you even like me?"

"You bring me cupcakes." The left side of her mouth lifted into a half-smile.

"I'm really, really sorry."

"I know."

"From now on, just slap me over the head any time I'm not listening to you."

She laughed. "I can do that."

Chapter Four: Team Building

I glanced around the room. The employees in their sometimes stiff, sometimes wrinkled suits looked even less thrilled to be in the workshop than me. It was my job to lead it, theirs to attend, but we didn't have to be happy about it.

Sedric, at least, seemed to be enjoying himself. He sat in the back, an amused smile on his face as he spoke quietly with the owner of the company. I'd been consulting with Lampton, Inc. since my training ended three and a half years ago. The owner was a nice-enough man, but not the sharpest tool in the shed. Sedric was either really good at pretending to be interested in what could only be a torturous conversation, or he was a much better person than me. Either was probable. I didn't know him well enough to know which was more likely.

Clearing my throat, I stood and approached the head of the conference table. Sedric's gaze broke contact with the owner to follow my progress. Strangely, having him watching actually calmed my nerves.

I'd been public speaking as a career for over four years and I was pretty good at it, but I still felt like hurling every time I prepared to open my mouth in front of a crowd. Apparently my stomach didn't get the message that I was super talented.

Deep breath. Smile. Open mouth – speak.

"Hello, all! It's great to be back here in Campi at Lampton. For those of you who are new, my name is Honor and I'm a team-building specialist from Taylor & James Consulting. For those of you old-timers, it's good to see you again." My mouth stretched wider, but Sedric's turned into an unpleasant frown. I looked away from him.

"Today, we're going to perform some exercises to strengthen the communication in your team. Tomorrow, we'll discuss conflict resolution, and then we're just going to have some fun together. How does that sound?"

The group remained fairly quiet, but the boss raised his voice, "Sounds great!"

There were a couple of giggles. I groaned inwardly, but kept my fake smile in place. The company hadn't been as quiet the previous year. I scanned the room. There were a few familiar faces, but most of the attendees were new to me. "I know what you're thinking: Why do you need a team-building consultant? What am I going to tell you that you don't already know?"

Several people looked down at the pads of paper I'd placed in front of them. The rest looked around the room, as if trying to pin the doubt on the closest scapegoat. "In a lot of ways, you're right. Most of the concepts and techniques we're going to discuss are common sense. But, sometimes it takes saying those common sense things out loud for people to actually start using them."

More crickets. Tough, tough crowd.

"Let's start with an icebreaker." With false cheerfulness, I gave instructions and began the game. Sedric's frown was gone, replaced by something I couldn't quite pin down – boredom, perhaps? That's how I'd be reacting if I were in his shoes.

As the pack reluctantly carried out the icebreaker, I strode over and took the owner's now-empty chair beside my colleague. "I'm sorry if this isn't as exciting as you're used to."

He cocked an eyebrow. "What do you mean?"

"You look like you're about to fall asleep."

"Not at all. I think your presentation so far has gone very well."

"Oh." I turned my head to better observe the game. It was a strange thing for him to say – I'd barely done anything yet.

"I was surprised," he said.

"That I'd do a good job? Gee, thanks for all the confidence. So glad you're with me on all my calls for the next couple of weeks."

"There's no need for sarcasm. Wouldn't you be surprised that someone who obviously prefers to work alone is an expert on team building?"

The assembly's laughter spared me from answering. They had finished the icebreaker and the result, as usual, was a group thawed and ready to proceed with the day's workshop.

"So. Communication," I began once everyone had settled down, "is one of, if not the most important tool in a team's toolbox. Without effective communication, no matter how much you like and respect each other, the team will fall apart."

There was a derisive snort from one of the gentleman employees. I squared my shoulders so we were facing each other. "You don't agree, sir?"

"Fall apart? Those are strong words."

"They are. What is your name, sir?"

"Jensen."

"Okay, Jensen, I'll give you an example. Let's say the coffee machine in the lounge breaks one day. You go in, see that it's broken, get frustrated, and go back to your work. Then one of your co-workers does the same thing. And another. No one stops to fix the machine or alert the custodian. Each person who goes to get coffee and finds it broken ignores the solution to the problem. By lunchtime, you have an office of very irritated co-workers. The boss hands out an assignment. You are tired, you haven't had your coffee – you don't want to deal with it. Everyone else who hasn't had their coffee feels the same way. The assignment isn't completed. A client is upset. The company loses business."

Jensen snorted again.

"Yes, it is an extreme example, but do you understand the point I'm making? The Snowball Effect. How about another example?"

The owner nodded and even Sedric had a small smile of approval on his face.

"Jensen, what do you do when your boss gives you an assignment you don't understand?"

"I ask him for clarification."

"Exactly! By communicating your concerns to your boss, you collect essential information for completing your assignment. Now Jensen, if you were the team leader on a project and one of your co-workers asked you for information about their role, you would fulfill that request, right?"

"Of course."

"And why?"

"So they could do their job. If they don't do their job properly, it's more work for me."

"Yes, and as we all know, when one worker feels they are doing a disproportionate amount of work, conflicts arise and productivity is halted."

The owner nodded again. I wanted to sigh. It was so silly. Why anyone needed a consultant to explain such things was beyond me.

"Let's do another exercise. Everyone remember the whisper game?"

Several *yes's* and *yeah's* floated throughout the group.

"Perfect. I'm going to whisper in Jensen's ear the phrase written on this." I held up a white index card, the printed words facing me. "Remember, communication is key. We want the last person in the chain to be able to tell us exactly what's on the card. The *only* rule is you cannot say the phrase out loud for anyone else to hear. Everyone ready?"

Nods, murmurs of assent. I walked to Jensen's chair and cupped my hand around his ear, whispering as clearly as possible. He rolled his eyes as I finished the phrase, but moved to the person on his left and duplicated the process.

A few people later, a petite woman received the message. She turned to its giver and asked, "Can you please repeat that?"

"You can't do that!" Jensen cried.

"Why not?" I asked.

"It's against the rules."

"How is asking a question against the rules?"

"It's just… it's not allowed. You're supposed to whisper one to the other until it gets to the end."

I surveyed the group. "Who remembers what I said prior to starting the game?"

The woman who halted the proceedings raised her hand. I motioned for her to speak. "You said communication is key and the only rule was we couldn't say the phrase being whispered out loud."

"Exactly! This young lady understands the game perfectly. What's your name?"

"Penelope."

"Penelope, why did you ask him to repeat himself?"

"I only caught the second half of the sentence and if he didn't, the person at the end wouldn't have gotten the phrase correct."

I nodded. Comprehension dawned on Jensen's face. "Let's continue," I said.

The man sitting beside the young woman leaned over and repeated himself in her ear. She scribbled on a piece of paper in front of her and showed it to him. He nodded. She passed the paper to the person on her right. The next person read it and passed it on. As did the next. And the next.

It finally landed with the older gentleman on Jensen's right. He smiled as he read and held it up to me.

"Go ahead and say the phrase out loud," I said.

He read, "Honor is awesome and I wish I were as cool as her."

"Well, thank you!"

The entire group laughed, even Jensen.

"Great job, team! You were very close to the original message. Jensen, why don't you read it for us?" I handed him my index card.

"Honor is super awesome and I wish I could be as cool as her."

"We can assume the few small changes were made somewhere between Jensen and Penelope, but you didn't lose the meaning of the phrase, so I'd call that experiment in communication a success."

There were a few claps around the table and from the corner of my eye, I detected Sedric joining in the applause.

"Let's break for lunch and we'll start with one-on-one communication exercises when we get back," I glanced at the clock on the wall, "at one o'clock. Thank you, everyone."

Papers rustled, chairs scraped the floor as the employees began collecting their things and heading for the exit. When Sedric and I were the last two in the room he came up to me and asked, "Where would you like to eat?"

I preferred a silent, solitary meal. But he had the car so I was at his mercy. "Whatever you want is fine. I'm not very hungry."

We found a small deli a block away from the office building. It was prime real estate – the front windows overlooked the Campi River – but, even though it was noon, the shop was basically empty. Only two other customers sat at a table by the entrance.

"This does not bode well," I said, not really meaning to speak out loud. Sedric laughed. We received our food and took a table in the back corner.

"Seriously," Sedric started, "why team building? Communication isn't what I'd call one of your strong points."

I shrugged.

"Proving my point," he said.

"It's a job."

"It's your career. Shouldn't you enjoy your career?"

"Do you like consulting? It's your career, too."

"I do. I like traveling and meeting new people and I think communication is important in all relationships, not just business ones. I should have learned to apply it to mine a long time ago." He took a bite of his sandwich and fiddled with his fork, poking at the potato salad that came with the meal. After swallowing, he started again.

"What you told that team about communication is true and, like it or not, we're a team for the time being."

I tried to ignore him and sipped my soda. Sedric had no intention of dropping the subject, though. "If this is just a job to you, what do you actually want to do?"

"Construction."

He cocked an eyebrow again, but stayed silent.

"Prime Minister."

Still not a peep.

"Lion tamer for the circus?"

He laughed, but continued his quiet protest.

I relented. "I trained to be a dancer when I was young."

His upper lip twitched, but he held back his victory smile and waited. He left the choice up to me – sit in silence, or tell my story. Normally, I would have chosen silence. For any other co-worker, I would have sewn my lips shut. But he was right. Like it or not, we were a team. Damn it.

"I was good. Like, I won major amateur awards good. Was on track for a spot in the prestigious Fortune Ballet Company."

"What happened?"

"Broken ankle. Shattered, really. Four months in a cast. When it healed, my position had already been given to someone else and training to get back in shape was painful. All my hard work, years of classes and performances, down the drain."

"So you quit?"

"Not exactly. I wanted to keep going, but Fortune wouldn't open a spot for me and no other company wanted to take a chance on an injured dancer."

"Why not teach?"

"Why not stab myself in the eye with a pair of dull scissors?"

He held up a hand of surrender. "Baking seems like an odd hobby for a dancer. Aren't you only supposed to eat lettuce and spinach and not much else?"

"Baking for me has always been more about the process than the final outcome. Yes, I want it to taste good, but only because that means I perfected the recipe. The food itself isn't soothing, making it is."

"Hmm." Sedric tore off another bite of his sandwich and we chewed silently for several minutes. When we were both finished, he cleared our trays without a word. I could feel him staring at me while I examined a broken nail. Finally, he checked his watch and said, "Time to get back."

Chapter Five: Flat Tire

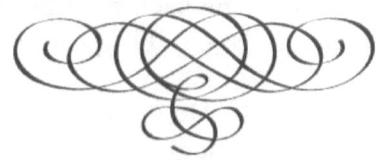

The workshop ended at three o'clock. The owner insisted his employees have the final hour of the day to return missed calls and answer emails. That was fine with me. I was with the company another day. One hour wasn't going to ruin my "hard work" with the group.

Sedric spent a few minutes taking leave of the owner while I packed my laptop, notebook, and icebreaker materials. Once the projector was secured in its case, I joined the two of them at the door.

"Ready?"

"See you tomorrow, sir." Sedric shook the owner's hand, they did that head nod thing men do, and then Sedric turned to me. We moved toward the door.

"Let me take that for you." He reached over to relieve me of the projector, but I stepped to the side.

"I've got it."

"Really, let me. It must be heavy."

"Not any heavier than it is when I'm doing things by myself."

"What were you saying in there about teamwork?" he asked.

"That it should be avoided at all costs?" I answered.

He chuckled, but let it drop and we walked in silence to the parking lot. I wasn't used to matching my strides with someone else and Sedric's long legs were difficult to keep up with, but I nearly ran into him when he stopped just a few yards short of the rental car.

I looked around him to see what caused the abrupt pause. "Oh, great. Just perfect." The back right tire was as flat as my chest during my dancing days. "I'll go in and call the rental company."

"No need," Sedric said. He popped the boot and started removing the false floor covering the spare.

"It's their car, their responsibility. They should bring us a new car. Or a new tire, at least. We can't drive around the rest of the week on a spare."

"You can call them and we'll wait a couple of hours here for them to show up, or I can change it now and we can call once we're back at the hotel, so we're waiting in the comfort of our rooms."

"I have some place to be."

"Even more reason for me to change it now." The spare was on the ground and he pulled the jack and some other tools I didn't recognize out of the trunk. He knelt on the asphalt beside the flat and examined it. A few seconds later, he removed his jacket and held it up. "Do you mind holding this?"

I took it and folded it over my crossed arms, shifting my weight every so often as I watched him work. Methodical. Like me in a kitchen. First, he rolled the sleeves of his crisp, white shirt up to his elbows. Then loosened his tie, holding it out to me as well. Silk, I realized, letting it slide through my fingers. Without the tie, he was able to open the top button of his shirt and free his collar. A few wisps of hair sprang out as if they'd been waiting all day to be released from their cotton prison. The jack was in place, secure under the frame of the car. His arms strained, rotating the wrench to loosen the lug nuts holding the hubcap in place. He always wore a jacket – I never would have guessed he was hiding such large muscles.

The air was humid and hot. I wanted to get in the car and turn the air conditioning on full-blast. I could hear rushing water all around us. The large presence of the river always struck me when I was in Campi.

The patter of footsteps sounded behind me. Good, a distraction. I turned and saw several of the employees from my workshop sneaking out of the building. Spotting me, one put a finger to her lips and winked. I nodded. Solidarity, sister.

When I returned my attention to Sedric, he had the flat off and was fitting the spare into place. Sweat dotted his upper lip as he replaced the lug nuts. He glanced toward me and smiled as he lowered the car. I looked away. I couldn't figure out why I'd been staring in the first place.

"All done," he said a few minutes later. He was at my side, collecting his jacket and tie. Once relieved of his effects, I stepped to the passenger door.

We were silent as he started the car and pulled onto the highway heading back to the hotel. I was actually kind of glad to have him there. I hate driving. Always have. I acted like it was a big sacrifice to let him take the wheel when we picked up the car, but really, I was happy. Almost four full days of no watching out for sudden brake lights, irritable stop lights and signs, and honking horns. Navigating unfamiliar cities and their confusing streets was always stressful, so letting him deal with it was an unexpected perk of being stuck with him.

"Are you meeting friends or family?" Sedric asked.

"Yes."

"Which one?"

"Oh. Friends." I found the directions I'd printed in my purse and unfolded the rumpled paper. "You can drop me off at the corner of West and Elm. It's only two blocks from the hotel. Right on the way."

"Are your friends driving you back or do you want me to pick you up?"

"Don't worry, I'll get a ride."

The car came to a stop along the curb outside the local library. Sedric looked past me, out the passenger window. "This is where you're meeting your friends?"

"Yep."

"I didn't know you were a reader."

"I'm not. And you don't know that much about me." Flinging the door open, I grabbed my purse and stepped onto the sidewalk. "I'll see you later." I shut the door on his goodbye. I was trying my hardest to show him I wasn't someone he wanted to get to know, but he refused to take the hint.

I moved toward the entrance as the rental car drove off. A couple of little kids scampered by, books clutched in their sticky hands. Their lifegivers held the door open for me to pass through.

Val often expressed his love of libraries and bookstores to me. The smell of books, the silent camaraderie of readers, the shelves stacked high, the creak of rolling carts moving down the aisles. It's all lost on me. Perhaps there is beauty in such things, but I'm incapable of discerning it.

I didn't dilly-dally absorbing the sights and sounds. One glance at a framed map standing to the right of the entrance showed the way to the help desk. "Excuse me?"

A young woman, in pigtails and a sweater much too thick for the climate, looked up from her computer at my approach. "Yes, ma'am?"

"I saw on your website that you have a news archive."

"We sure do. Do you have a library card?"

"I don't live here, but I filled out the guest form." It took a few seconds to dig the paperwork out of my purse, but the librarian was patient and took it with a smile when I placed it on the counter. As she scanned the contents, I pulled a five note from my wallet.

"There is a fee for a weekly guest pass."

I held up the note between my index and middle finger.

"You're well-prepared," she said, a bright smile plastered across her face. "Just a moment." She took the note and paperwork and disappeared into a room behind her desk. My fingernails drummed a pattern on the counter while I awaited her return. *Dra dra dra-dra-dra. Dra dra dra-dra-dra.* My stomach felt knotted. I almost couldn't believe where I was. A teenage boy queued up behind me, clutching a thick hardback to his chest. *Dra dra dra-dra-dra.*

Pigtails bounced back to the counter, a shiny pass the size of a credit card in her outstretched hand. "This will give you access to the computers and archives until next Tuesday. You'll need to drop it in this box," she pointed to a clear plastic cube to my left, "when you're done with it."

I took the card and looked around for another map.

"The archives are on the second floor, to the right, past the restrooms."

"Got it." I strode toward the stairs; the boy stepped forward with his book.

The second floor was empty. The movies, fiction, non-fiction, and children's sections were on the first floor. The second was all reference. Apparently, I was the only person in Campi in need of reference materials that night.

Pigtails' directions were spot on and I found the door to the news archives easily. There was a black metal square on the wall beside it, with a green glass panel in the center. I held my pass in front of it and the bar code scanned. *Click.*

I pushed the heavy door inwards and stepped into the musky room. There was a bookshelf immediately to my left with labels for *Today's, Yesterday's,* and *Last Week's* papers. Peering at the dates, I appreciated the masquerade – the papers hadn't been rotated in over a month. I continued past the shelf to the khaki-colored metal file cabinets. Each drawer was also labeled, but with a month and year. The cabinets crowded the perimeter, and two rows stood behind an empty table in the center of the room. I swung my purse onto the table and moved between the narrow rows. The timeline Bonnie and I created showed my pull pointing to Campi in the third month of 2008.

A layer of dust half an inch thick sat atop the cabinet and the drawer stuck when I pulled the handle. The knots in my stomach tightened. I yanked again. I stretched my hand – I'd been clutching the handle too tightly. What was I doing? What was the point? I braced myself and tried again. Third time was the charm. It popped open and more dust filled the room. Grabbing a stack of yellowed papers, I headed for the table and took a seat.

I didn't know what I was looking for. I wouldn't really know until I found it. I sighed. Quivering hands unfolded the top paper and perused the headlines. My notebook filled with scribbled clues. More than I needed, probably, but there would be no way of knowing until I visited more libraries in more cities.

I lost track of time inside the windowless archives and, as a result, was greeted with a dark sky and slightly-less humid air when I stepped out of the library. Street lamps flickered dull yellow light, but barely illuminated the block around the building. A couple exited behind me and walked across the street to a black SUV. Hand-in-hand. The taller man opened the passenger door for the shorter one. My eyes stung as I turned and walked in the direction of the hotel.

Chapter Six: Have Another Drink

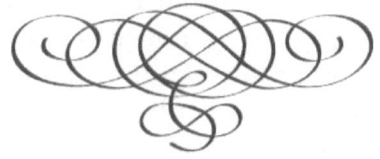

The one great thing about my job is staying in hotels. I racked up so many loyalty and rewards points that whenever I traveled for personal reasons, rare as it was, my stay was always free. And I loved hotels. Being away from home felt like being away from myself for a little while, and that was always a welcome vacation.

The pillows and bedding in that particular hotel were stark white and fluffy. Very soft. I sunk into them, closing my eyes and wishing I was a different person. For only a moment. The hotel magic wasn't working.

The clock on the bedside table read 8:42. Later than I'd planned, but not too late. I found the remote hidden in a dresser drawer and turned on the screen. The menus were different than the ones at my house, and it took two minutes to figure out how to place an outgoing call request. But once it went through, it didn't take long for Bonnie to answer.

"Hey!"

"Hey, Bon. How was your day?"

"Pretty great, actually. Yours? How was your flight?"

"Same old, same old. It doesn't even feel like autumn here yet. What was so great about today?" I asked.

"Hold on one second, Caron's putting Lang to bed." Bonnie drifted off-screen, but I could hear her footsteps as she moved to Lang's door, then hushed tones as Caron joined her in walking back to the living room. Once they were both visible in the screen, Caron burst forth a rapturous squeal.

"I'm pregnant! We're going to have another baby!"

Bonnie grasped her mate's hand and the smiles on their faces were bright enough to light the night sky.

"Oh, wow. Congratulations, you guys." I gulped. "I didn't know you were thinking of having another kid."

Caron nodded, her enthusiasm threatening to leap through the screen. "We've wanted a second child for a while now, and I've always wanted the experience of being pregnant. Since Bonnie had it with Lang, I got to do it this time."

"That's really awesome, Caron. You must be so excited." The understatement of the year, but I wasn't sure what else to say. I could sense Bonnie scrutinizing my every move and word; I wanted to show as much support as possible, even more than I felt.

"Like you wouldn't believe. I wish we didn't have to wait the next twenty-eight weeks to meet this little one, but I know it is going to be an incredible experience, feeling the baby growing inside me."

"We told Lang last night," Bonnie said. "You should have seen her. She cannot wait to be a big sister."

"She'll be a good one," I said.

"Yeah, she will."

"We've been dying to tell everyone, but our doctor said to give it a little time – to make sure it stuck, you know?"

"That's smart."

A muffled cry broke through Caron and Bonnie's smiles. "That'll be Lang," Bonnie said. "She's been having nightmares."

"Oh, I forgot to turn on her nightlight," Caron said, glancing over her shoulder.

"Go and take care of her. I'll see you guys when I'm back in town."

"Okay, bye."

"Congrats, again." My voice was too high. Bonnie was sure to notice it, but she didn't say anything.

"Thanks." They hurried away and I fumbled with the remote for a few seconds before achieving a blank screen. Sinking back into the pillows, I took a few deep breaths. I needed to be supportive. I couldn't be selfish. Breathing wasn't working. The pillows weren't working. Pretending I was someone else wasn't working.

A minute later, I knocked on Sedric's door. "Nice to see you got back safely," he said.

"Want to go downstairs to the bar with me?"

"The bar?" He looked at his watch. "Why?"

"There's alcohol there."

He hadn't stepped out of his room or invited me in. He just stood there, door slightly ajar, looking at me as if getting a drink at nine in the evening was the most ludicrous thing he'd ever heard.

Why had I bothered? "Never mind. I'll go by myself."

"No, I'll come. Let me grab my wallet." The door closed briefly, then he reappeared and we headed for the elevator. "Thanks for asking me."

"It's a little pathetic to drink alone. In public."

He laughed. "Why do you need to drink all of a sudden?" The lift dinged and slid open. We stepped inside.

"My best friend's lifemate is pregnant. It's their second child."

His eyebrows scrunched together. "So, it's a celebratory drink?"

"I guess it should be, but that's not what I had in mind."

"Aren't you happy for them?"

Was I? I couldn't really tell. I started speaking aloud, trying to work out my feelings, completely forgetting the fact that Sedric was standing right next to me. "Yes. Absolutely. And at the same time, no. Not really. But I will be – hopefully – by the time I see them again. I need to get used to the idea."

Lobby level. Doors opened. Sedric motioned for me to exit first. The bar wasn't crowded. It was Monday night, for Pria's sake. I took a stool at the middle of the counter and Sedric sat to my left.

"Why aren't you happy for them?" he asked as we waited for the bartender to acknowledge us.

Good question. "I am."

"But you're not."

"Right."

"Why?"

"What'll it be, folks?" the bartender asked, stepping toward us looking bored.

"Gin and tonic," I said.

"Whiskey, top shelf," Sedric said. I faced him, an eyebrow raised. "I only drink the best. It's not worth it, otherwise," he explained.

"It all does the same thing."

"Top-honor universities and community colleges do the same thing – educate – but I guarantee the experiences of attending those types of school are different."

"Touché."

He smiled. "Back to your friends. What's going on?"

I didn't want to tell him, but I couldn't hold it in anymore. Part of me thought if I said it out loud, I'd get over it. "I'm a train wreck, that's what's going on. Bonnie and I had a little fight the other day about me being unsupportive and selfish, and as soon as I hear this news, the only thing I can think about is how unfair it is."

"How so?"

"They have each other. They have a kid already – a great kid, I love her. I have no one. And like you said at lunch last week, I never will."

"I didn't say that."

"You said my lifemate is dead."

The bartender set my drink on a white, cocktail napkin in front of me. I took a gulp and relished the cold liquid streaming down my throat. Almost as good as baking a pie.

"If your lifemate is dead," Sedric started, but paused as the bartender set his glass in front of him. "If he is dead, that doesn't mean you'll always be alone."

"What else would it mean? Anyway, that's why I needed a drink. Because I had the wrong reaction to great news and that made me really depressed and it was too much to take today."

Sedric raised his glass to his lips, but instead of tipping it back, he let it linger and inhaled the rich smell of the dark, amber liquid. The satisfied sigh when he finally swallowed made me think he was on to something with his top shelf theory. "What about your other friends, the ones you were visiting? Did you have a good time with them?"

"I wasn't visiting any friends."

"What were you doing, then?"

I rolled my eyes. "You ask more questions than any woman I've ever known."

His comeback was instant. "You tell more lies than any man I've ever known."

"Look at us, debunking stereotypes." I smiled and Sedric looked like he wanted to, but instead he swirled the liquid in his glass. "I may be a liar, but I usually give myself away eventually. That makes it better somehow, I think."

"Whatever you need to tell yourself." Smirking, he took another teensy sip of his whiskey. "You aren't going to tell me what you were doing, then?"

"Research." I drained the rest of my drink and let the glass plunk onto the counter. The bartender looked over at the noise and made a motion to come closer, but I waved him away. One drink was enough to clear my head, but a second would lead to a third, a third would lead to a fourth, and a fourth would lead to an even meaner version of my usual self, and Sedric didn't deserve that bitch.

His curiosity and banter seemed satisfied for the time being and he did accept the bartender's gesture for a second drink.

"Did you have a chance to speak to your lifemate when you got back?" I asked, watching him savor another sip. He set the glass down and slowly turned to look at me, wrinkles forming on his forehead as he scrunched his nose.

"No."

"Why not? Does she work in the evening or something?"

He didn't answer, but the wrinkles deepened and his hand twitched as he reached for his drink again. A flash of black on the inside of his palm arrested my senses. His lark. I couldn't make out what it looked like, but the glimpse reminded me of our first lunch – he stroked his palm when he told me my lifemate was dead. Apparently, I only needed the one drink to enter full-on bitch mode.

I put my hand forward, but paused. He wasn't looking at me anymore. I reached out again and let my fingers hover for a few seconds. Comforting was not a strength of mine. Apologizing definitely wasn't. With a deep breath, I let my hand land softly on his arm. His head swiveled, the glass still at his lips.

"I'm sorry, Sedric. I can be a little self-absorbed, but I'm sure you've picked up on that. Did she pass away?"

He nodded.

"I know you've already told me, but what was her name?"

He downed the rest of his drink and the glass hit the counter with a clink. "Zara."

"Pretty name."

A sigh.

My hand felt stiff on his arm and I guessed he could sense my discomfort, so I removed it. He looked to the spot on his arm it vacated, but didn't speak, so I ordered him another drink.

Chapter Seven: Guilty Conscience

The drive to the office park the next morning was awkward. It wasn't the silence. We were usually silent. It was the undeniable guilt hanging in the air. Sedric refused to make eye contact with me. I couldn't blame him. Because it didn't directly affect me, I'd ignored the signs that his lifemate was dead.

Every time I opened my mouth to ease the tension, I lost the words. I'd come up with something in my head, but realize how wrong it would sound mere seconds before I actually said it. I tried considering what Bonnie or Caron would say to him, but without their natural sincerity, their comments would mean nothing.

Sedric pulled the car into a spot a few rows from the entrance. He turned off the engine. I opened my mouth one more time, but before I could whisper another apology, Sedric cleared his throat.

"I appreciate you not talking about last night."

What? "You're welcome?"

"It's been hard for me, the past couple of years. The looks. The sympathy."

"I know the feeling." Boy, did I ever.

"I thought you might."

"I guess we'll make a good team after all," I mumbled.

He laughed. "I never doubted we would."

"Would you like to go to dinner tonight, or do you have more research to do?" Sedric asked as we packed my presentation materials at the end of the day.

"I have more research, but we're here two more nights."

"Dinner, then?"

"Dinner sounds nice." And it did. Maybe he was rubbing off on me, or maybe the guilt hadn't worn away yet.

"What are you in the mood for?" Sedric unlocked the car and opened my door for me.

"I haven't had a good slice of pizza in a long time."

"Really? That's a staple of my diet. It's practically its own food group."

"If you have it all the time, we can do something else."

He closed my door and walked around the front of the car, getting in on the driver's side and putting the key in the ignition. Before starting the engine, though, he turned to me. "It's like you're a completely different person. You're being so kind and accommodating. I should have played the dead lifemate card a lot sooner."

I rolled my eyes. Sedric could actually be kind of funny, but I didn't want to let him know that.

He started the car and continued, "Pizza sounds good to me, so no need to martyr yourself."

"But didn't you know that's my goal in life?"

"I guessed as much. I drove past this little hole-in-the-wall place yesterday, looking for a convenience store. We can try that, if you'd like."

"If it was a hole-in-the-wall, how did you see it driving past?" I asked.

"Don't underestimate my stomach's ability to find food."

I laughed. What was happening? Was I actually enjoying the company of my co-worker? My boss, actually. I didn't see that coming. "Besides pizza, what other foods does your stomach know how to find?"

"Mmmm, pasta, steak, chicken wings. Anything with cheese. Foie gras. Crème Brûlée."

"You're a man of varying tastes."

"I think it's important to try everything at least once."

Not a philosophy I lived by, but Sedric and I were as opposite as night and day. He chatted on about food, restaurants, and cooking techniques as we drove through the city. I found myself listening instead of tuning him out. He was articulate, but not annoyingly so. He was intelligent, but didn't shove it down my throat. He was everything I disliked about people, but I didn't dislike him.

"This pizza is absolutely amazing!" A string of melted cheese connected my lip to the heavenly slice in my hand, and Sedric laughed at me, but I didn't care. It was the best meal I'd had in weeks.

"I can't believe you wanted to go plain cheese. That's amateur hour," he said.

"Sorry, dancer's habit. Light on toppings and the number of servings. But you made the right call – this barbeque buffalo whatever stuff is delicious."

"Like I said, don't doubt me when it comes to food."

"Never again." I bit once more into the crispy crust and sighed as I pulled the bite into my mouth. A small chunk of chicken fell from my slice onto the table. I debated picking it up and popping it into my mouth, but didn't want to gross Sedric out. I still had some self-respect, after all.

He wiped his lips with a napkin, then reached for the pie to grab another slice. "You never told me how your research went last night."

"Just fine."

"What are you looking for?"

Geez, could he be any more like a lifegiver? I glanced over my slice at him, trying to figure out his age. He didn't seem too much older than me, and he hadn't mentioned any children, so maybe the smothering thing was just a personality flaw. I took another bite, hoping my silence said *mind your own business* less rudely than my actual voice would have.

"You know, maybe I can help," he said. I added can't-take-a-hint to my inventory of his personality flaws. "I'm pretty good at research. That's what I did after Zara asked me to stop traveling."

My ears perked up like a dog's hearing his master's footsteps coming up the drive. I hated research and wasn't particularly good at it. If Sedric was willing to help, I'd be able to find my lifemate a lot faster. Still, I didn't know if I could trust him with something so big. "What kind of research did you do?"

"Why should I tell you mine when you won't tell me yours?"

"Touché." I tasted my beer.

"Is that your favorite word?"

"One of them." I sensed his gaze on my hands as I held the frosty glass to my lips. What did he want from me? Hadn't he realized yet that I wasn't the warm and fuzzy type? "Stop that," I said.

"What?"

"Staring at me. Your psychological tactics won't work on me."

"Sure they will." He grinned, taking a huge bite.

"I don't back down easily."

"I didn't think you would."

"And apparently you don't either."

"Nope." He reached for another slice while cramming the crust of the former one in his mouth.

"Geez, what are you – a trash disposal? You've eaten half the pie."

"My lifegivers say I'm a growing boy."

"Sure, twenty years ago."

"Just because you eat like a bird doesn't mean I have to."

"Of course not." I finished my slice and sipped casually on my beer while he continued his takedown of the pizza. The silence at our table only magnified my awareness of the chatter surrounding us. At every other table, couples and families sat talking over their days, fighting, sharing their happy or unhappy lives. I missed Bonnie and Val. But, even with them, I wouldn't feel the connection the groups around us had. Sedric didn't notice – he blocked out the other patrons like I'd blocked out our co-workers during the meeting where we first met. He probably did that a lot. I would if I were him. He used to be part of one of those happy couples. Now he was stuck here with me. Poor guy.

"I've decided to tell you what I'm researching."

He stopped chewing and dropped the slice onto his plate. I cleared my throat and focused on the bridge of his nose – the closest to direct eye contact I would allow. He swallowed. "I thought you didn't back down."

"I don't. Let's consider this more of a peace offering."

"If that's what you need to tell yourself."

I liked saucy Sedric a lot better than stoic Sedric, but I wasn't about to tell him that, so I glossed over his comment and got straight to the point. "The other day, you told me my lifemate probably died."

He nodded.

"I'd never considered that before and haven't really stopped thinking about it since."

"I didn't mean to trouble you or stress you out."

"I really should have realized it on my own. I just-"

"-didn't want to admit it to yourself."

My cheeks grew warm. "Exactly."

"I get that."

"Yeah, well, anyway, I want to know who he was. I need to put it to rest, but I can't. Not without knowing."

He frowned in concentration, glanced around the room, and ran his hand over his chin. "Do you think it will help?"

"I've already been through this conversation with my best friend. I don't need you trying to talk me out of it, too."

He put his hands up in surrender and I saw his full lark for the first time. It took up his entire left palm, even bleeding onto the bases of several fingers, but I couldn't tell what it was supposed to be. I'd never seen a completed lark so indecipherable. Then he put his hands down and I didn't have the courage to ask about it.

"So, your research is trying to find him, then?"

"Yes."

"What have you done so far?"

He listened patiently as I explained going through my journals, and Bonnie helping me create a timeline of clues.

"Bonnie's the best friend?" he asked.

"Yes."

"The one who's pregnant?"

"She's not pregnant, her lifemate is."

"Ah, got it."

I rolled my eyes. "Not the point. Geez, you would probably get along great with her. You both seem to focus on the inconsequential details."

His voice took on a stern tone I hadn't heard him use before. "If we're going to be working together for a while, I assume I'll be hearing about these people in your life. I just want to keep them straight in my head."

"Oh." *Well, damn. Does this restaurant serve foot-in-mouth?*

"Please continue." He waved his hand across the table.

"Um, well, this city was on the timeline – my pull was drawing me here, to Campi, during the third month of 2008. When I was at the library yesterday, I was looking through the local newspapers, trying to see if there were any events happening that my lifemate would have gone to."

"You aren't looking for obituaries?"

"No, he didn't die here."

"How do you know that?" he asked.

"The pull was leading me to Eribank when it suddenly stopped."

"What are you hoping to learn from the newspapers, exactly?"

"Bonnie and I figured that maybe he traveled for his job, or something. So, I'm looking for anything that could explain that. Conventions, tours, sales, anything that draws people in from other regions."

"What if he did something like us – consulting? You wouldn't find that in the newspapers."

I sighed. "I know, but it's the only thing I could think of to try and narrow the search so when we get to Eribank I won't have to investigate every single death."

He snapped his fingers. "I tell you what, while you're doing that, I'll look into companies like ours. See if I can find employee travel lists and cross check them with your timeline."

"You'd be able to do that?"

"Absolutely."

"How? Are you a hacker?"

He laughed. "No, you just have to know the right people. I used to do marketing research for companies all over the world."

"Wow. I don't know what to say."

"Thank you?"

"No, that's not it." I tried to hide my smile, but couldn't contain it for very long. Sedric laughed.

"It wouldn't kill you to say thank you."

"It might – better not risk it."

"You know, I've always found saying 'thank you' to be very cathartic. Liberating, in fact. It evens the score."

Maybe for him. I found it made people expect me to be nice all the time. "Do you want to come with me to the library tomorrow, or would you prefer to work on your own?"

"I'll come with you."

I relaxed my shoulders and leaned back in my chair. It probably wasn't a good idea to get Sedric involved in my crazy scheme, but I needed help. He picked up the half-slice on his plate and stuffed it into his mouth. I took a deep breath. "Okay, sounds like a plan."

The library was quiet when we walked in the following night. Pigtails was still stationed behind her desk, but she was flipping through a magazine and not paying attention to the patrons.

"This way." I pointed to the stairs and Sedric followed me. The second floor was as empty as it had been on my first visit – we didn't see a single person between the staircase and the door to the archives. I scanned my guest card and Sedric pulled open the door. He waited for me to pass.

"This is it. I hope you're not allergic to dust."

"I'm not." He sat at the table and pulled a laptop out of his bag while I wandered back to the filing cabinet with the third month's papers and pulled a new stack to work on.

"What's the internet password?" he asked, as I sat across from him.

"Oh, it's on the card." I slid it to him.

After a moment of silence, he said, "I think we're breaking the rules."

I was already scanning the headlines. "Huh?"

"The pass says one card per person."

"It's not like they check."

"We're using the library's resources. I should go and get my own card."

I peered at him over the paper and grinned. "Let me guess — you were teased a lot in school."

"What do you mean?"

"Goody-two-shoes, brown-noser. Follows directions and rules so strictly, you'd think you'd written them yourself."

He ignored me and started typing, but didn't say anything else about getting a second pass. We worked independently. The only sounds in the room were Sedric's keystrokes and my rustling papers. I liked it. That kind of noise is peaceful. No urgency, no desperation, no frustration. Sedric looked up for a moment and our eyes met. He smiled, so I turned away, but realized I'd been smiling first.

"What are you finding over there?" he asked.

"There was a big gaming convention in town for a couple of weeks, a touring performance of a well-reviewed play, and some little things. You know, book readings, bands playing, stuff like that."

"A wide spectrum."

"Yeah. I'm starting to think this isn't really going to help."

"Like you said, it's about narrowing down the choices later on, right? Process of elimination."

"Do you think I'm chasing the wind?"

He paused his typing and suddenly his hand was on mine, squeezing. Then it was gone. "Yes, but that's not to say it shouldn't be chased."

"Was Zara like the wind for you? Needing to be chased?"

"I don't know if I would say it like that."

"How would you then? How did you find each other?"

He closed his laptop and stood, stretching his arms high over his head, fingertips grazing the ceiling. "We were nineteen. Our pulls led us to this little town. Neither of us had family or friends there, but there's a school. I'd been looking through pamphlets and fliers for months, trying to decide where to go. My pull had been faint until that point. When my lifegiver brought home a brochure for Glassden College, suddenly, my entire body felt ready to fling itself out the window and fly there. You know that feeling."

Actually, I didn't. My pull had been strong in those erratic years – strong enough I knew where it was leading me, but never so strong that all doubts were cast aside.

"I arrived on campus, knowing she was there. Every nerve in my body screamed it. My lark grew hot – it actually stung, like sunburn. It was intense."

I gulped. "Sounds like it."

"My lifegivers were moving boxes into my dorm room and my pull told me to find the campus bookstore, so I left them and found it. I didn't need a map or anything, my pull guided me the entire way."

"She was there."

He nodded. "Just out front, a bag of books in her hands and a scared look on her face. It was overwhelming – the pull. And when our eyes met, my lark burned. Hers did too, she told me later. I tore my eyes away from hers to look at it, and found it had changed."

"The picture filled in."

"Yeah. A sun. She was not the wind, she was the sun." He sank into his chair, as if telling the story had exhausted him. Maybe it did. It exhausted me. The passion, the urgency. That's why the power of the lark stayed with me – stories like that. I'd witnessed and heard many accounts, but never experienced it for myself.

I wanted what I couldn't have.

"Hey, Sedric?"

"Yeah?"

"Thank you."

A cute half-grin crept up the left side of his lips. "I think I've done all I can do for the night. How about you? Want me to look through some of these papers?"

"No. I'm at a good stopping point. It could all be worthless, anyway." But I hoped it wouldn't be.

Chapter Eight: We're Not Good

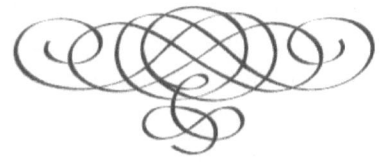

"What are your weekend plans?" Sedric asked. It was Friday afternoon and we were sitting at the gate, waiting for our plane to board and take us home for a few days.

"Dinner tonight with Bonnie and Caron."

"The best friend and the pregnant lifemate?"

"That's them."

"Are you feeling better about their news?"

"I haven't really thought about it. I'm sure I'll be fine with everything, eventually." Hopefully. But knowing me, it would take a while.

"Good." He opened his book and removed the bookmark, setting it on his thigh.

"What are your plans?"

"I don't have any."

"Why not?"

He gave me a piercing look, as if I should know better than to ask, but even though his lifemate was dead, that didn't mean he couldn't have friends. I did. And really, of the two of us, who was more likely to have friends?

"Why don't you come to dinner with me tonight?" The words were out of my mouth before I could stop them. What had I just done? It was bad enough I'd opened up to Sedric about my dead lifemate and trying to find him, now I was inviting him to meet my friends?

"Are you sure?"

There was the out. I should have taken it, but the longer I looked at the bookmark on his leg, trying to say no, the harder it was to open my mouth and let the word spill. Instead, I thought how nice it would be to have a buffer between Bonnie and myself at dinner. I didn't want to have to pretend to be supportive, when I still wasn't a hundred percent. "Yeah, why not? I appreciate your help and patience this week."

"Thank you, I think I'd like that." He nudged my elbow. "As long as your friends are nothing like you."

I laughed. "Don't worry, they're much nicer than I am. You won't leave any worse for the wear."

Standing on Bonnie's front porch, a pie in my hands and Sedric beside me, I tried to ease my irrational nerves. I wanted Bonnie to like Sedric and it seemed just as important that he like her. But why? Sedric was nothing to me – just a co-worker. My boss, for Pria's sake.

"What are you waiting for?" His voice shocked my system. I faced him with what must have been a blank expression because he said, "Are you going to knock, or should I?" It wasn't said angrily or out of frustration. A simple question. Why did it seem anything but?

I reached forward and rang the doorbell. The patter of Lang's small steps and their dog's clumsy gait came closer until Lang's cherub face smashed against the front window.

"Honor!" The sound was muffled between her mouth and the glass, but there was no denying the happiness in her voice. Sedric raised an eyebrow.

"Some people like me," I said, waving to Lang.

"I never doubted."

But I do sometimes, I wanted to say. Lang was too little to know who I really was. She only knew me as the crazy aunt-like figure who brought her junk food and toys. Of course she liked me.

The door opened and Bonnie stepped forward to hug me, but stopped abruptly when she saw Sedric. "Honor, I didn't know you were bringing someone." She put her hand to her mouth. "Oh, Pria! Were you wrong? He wasn't dead! This is your mate?" She seized Sedric's hand, flipping it over to check for a lark matching mine. If his face was any indication of my own, I turned as red as a strawberry.

"Bon, no. No!" I stepped between her and Sedric, allowing him to pull his hand away from her grasp. "This is my boss – Sedric. Didn't you get the message that I invited him?"

"We literally just got home twenty minutes ago, I haven't checked the screen yet. Making dinner." She took a step back, but before she could invite us in, the dog bounded through the opening and jumped onto Sedric. The black and white mutt tried licking Sedric's face, but the man was too tall for him.

"Down, Skitzo, down!" Bonnie leapt forward and attempted to grab the dog's collar, but he was hopping and shaking all over and wouldn't pause in his effusions to give her a chance. Sedric's arms swung about as he attempted to keep the animal at bay, but nothing was working until sweet, little Lang appeared in the doorframe.

"Bad Skitzo," she said, her index finger wagging. The dog settled down onto all fours and turned to her. He burrowed his head into her armpit.

Over her daughter's giggles, Bonnie said, "You can see who the Alpha Dog is in our house. I'm really sorry about that, Sedric. I would have locked him in the laundry room if I had known you were coming. He doesn't do well with strangers."

"No harm done," Sedric said, though from my vantage point, the front of his impeccably tailored pants looked ruined with scratch marks and dirt.

"Caron, can you come and help me with the dog?" Bonnie yelled into the house. Thirty seconds later, Caron was shaking Sedric's hand before wrestling Skitzo away from Lang and steering him off to banishment in the laundry room. With the doorway finally cleared, we all entered and I handed Bonnie the pie.

"What kind is it?"

I hung my purse on the coat rack in the mudroom to the left of the doorway. "It's a new recipe I'm trying. Raspberries, blueberries, strawberries, and chocolate."

"Decadent."

"You know how I work."

"I'll put this in the oven. Why don't you show Sedric the dining room?"

"Me, too, I'll help!" Lang said, grabbing one of my hands and reaching for Sedric's. Though obviously surprised, he let her chubby fingers grip his. "You're a big boy," she said.

"I know."

"Are you mean? Most of the big boys in my class are mean to me."

"He's very nice, Lang. That's why I brought him," I said.

Sedric stopped, causing Lang and I to pause as well. "I'm not just your annoying co-worker, then?"

"You're that, too."

"Come on, you guys!" Lang struggled to pull us forward. "I'm hungry." We let her lead the rest of the way down the hall. Caron came in behind us, rubbing her hands together.

"Oh, Sedric, we should have shown you the bathroom so you could wash your hands after Skitzo. Come with me."

Sedric let go of Lang's hand and followed Caron out of the room. Lang crossed her arms over her chest, her mouth pouting. "I wanted to show him."

"You can show me," I said. "We need to wash up, too, don't we?"

"You know where it is, Honor."

I was surprised she didn't throw in a "duh" with the rest of her sass.

Bonnie entered through the far door, across the room from us, carrying a platter of grilled chicken breasts. She set it on the table and approached Lang and I. "What's going on, Honor?"

"He's being nice to me, so I thought I'd invite him to dinner."

"No other motives?"

"Of course not." But there were. I didn't want to be alone with Bonnie and Caron. Not until I could be completely and totally supportive. I didn't want to fake it. They deserved better than that. "Why would you ask that?"

"It's not like you to be so altruistic."

"Hey!" Of course she was right. Man, I hated myself sometimes. Bonnie's frown pierced me. "You know me too well."

"That's always been our problem." She laughed, so I did too, but of course she was right again. Too bad it couldn't really be a joke.

Caron and Sedric entered, chatting amicably. It figured he was the type to make friends easily. That was a good thing for me. I wanted him to take all of Bonnie and Caron's attention so they didn't discuss the happy news, but it still annoyed me.

"Can the big boy sit next to me?" Lang asked, skipping to him and grasping his hand again.

"His name is Sedric, sweetie," Bonnie said.

"Lang, I'm hurt. You don't want to sit next to me?" I asked, trying to suppress a grin and look as sad as possible. But Lang was queen of the fake pout and she didn't buy mine for a second.

"I sit next to you all the time, Honor."

"Yeah, Honor," Sedric teased. I wished I had something to throw at him.

We sat around the table – I was opposite Lang and Sedric, while Bonnie and Caron each took an end seat. Just one happy, weird family. Plus my boss.

"Sedric, Honor was telling us you're shadowing her for a few weeks," Bonnie said, passing the chicken plate to him.

"Yeah, I've been out of the business consulting field for several years. She's helping me get back in the swing of things."

"What did you do before?" Caron asked.

"Market research."

"Like surveying teenagers and finding out what kind of shoes they'll convince their lifegivers to buy?" Bonnie was busy cutting Lang's chicken into bite-sized pieces, but still managed to carry on an intelligent and polite conversation with a complete stranger. I'd never taken the time to appreciate what a nurturing person she was. Even when we were kids, she was always the one playing with baby dolls and nursing boo boos.

"Among other things," Sedric answered.

"Why the switch?" Bonnie asked.

"My mate didn't like all the traveling I was doing as a consultant. The research position enabled me to work from one place, most of the time."

"You told me you worked all over the world," I said.

"I said I worked with companies all over the world. My position involved setting up focus groups and analyzing the results. I had agents in the field."

"How did you convince your mate to let you start traveling again?" Bonnie asked.

Sedric chewed slowly on the piece of chicken in his mouth, his face screwed up in a way that clearly indicated he didn't want to talk about Zara's death. Why hadn't I told Bonnie? If I had, she would never have brought it up. She wasn't an insensitive jerk. Finally, he swallowed. "I didn't have to convince her."

I glared at Bonnie, wishing telepathy was a real thing. I urged her, in my head, not to press the issue, not to make him say the words. Praise Paolo, she caught my eye! She must have seen the urgent request, because she moved on. "Do you like to travel?"

Sedric smiled and raised his water glass to his lips. After a sip, "Yes. I love moving about, seeing other regions. I've never felt right standing completely still. My lifegivers always laugh at me, because I'm a homebody who likes to be anywhere but home."

Caron laughed. "How does that work?"

"When I'm here, I like to stay around the house, working in my shop or on my cars, but when I'm traveling, I do it all. I want to see everything."

"Sounds like the best of both worlds," I said.

He met my eye. "I like to think so. I like contradictions – things that shouldn't fit together, but do. I've always been into puzzles and challenges."

What was he doing – interviewing for a job? Or a permanent place at our table? He sounded like a pageant queen.

"Bonnie, is there any wine in the cellar or pantry?" I asked, pushing my chair back to rise.

"Yeah, I'll go with you to grab it."

We excused ourselves, and as we walked away I heard Sedric asking Lang about her school and what she liked about it.

In the cold cellar, I went immediately to the wall of wine and selected a Pinot Noir Bonnie had introduced to me a few months before. I examined the label and wondered if it would go well with the chicken.

"Seriously, Honor, what's going on?"

"His mate died a couple of years ago."

"Oh." She paused. "That's really sad. What happened?"

"That's all I know. He doesn't seem to like talking about it. The sympathy."

"I wish you would have told me before it came up."

I handed her the bottle for approval. "I didn't think about it. And honestly, it's kinda his own fault – he brought her up in the first place."

"Honor! How can you be so insensitive?"

"I'm not. I feel bad for the guy," I said.

"Is that why you invited him – out of pity?"

"No. Maybe a little. He's been helping me find out who my lifemate was and you know it isn't easy for me to express gratitude. Out loud, anyway."

Bonnie nodded. "You really need to work on that."

"I'm trying."

"So, that's it?"

I studied the wall of wine. "Yep."

"No other reason?" She handed the bottle back to me.

She had a lot of wine. Why did she need so much? I was the only person who came over on a regular basis. "Nope."

"Honor."

"Bonnie?" I looked back to her. She was frowning.

"Are you sleeping with him?"

"What! Of course not. He's my boss. And he had a mate."

She glanced at the ceiling. "He doesn't anymore, and he's still young. I'm sure even if you haven't thought about it, he has."

"He has not. You know I don't sleep around."

"Not anymore."

I took a step back. "Whoa."

"I'm just saying, there were a few years there where, if you met any man without a mate yet, you, well, weren't so prudent as you are now."

"It's really easy for you to judge, isn't it? You found Caron when you were twenty. Do you think you would have been so pure if you'd been older?" I brushed past her and climbed the stairs. It was completely unfair of her to say that. Sure, I'd met a few guys at bars and gone home with them, or them with me, but how could she know what it was like to go to bed alone every night? One-night stands were better than nothing.

She was completely wrong about Sedric, though. The thought had never crossed my mind to take advantage of him like that. Sure, I had needs, and I'm sure he did, too, but he was in as much pain as I was. Hooking up with him would only hurt us both. I would never be Zara for him, and he'd never be a mate for me.

"Where's Bonnie?" Caron asked when I entered the dining room and took my seat. I placed the wine in front of me in the center of the table.

"I think she went to get a corkscrew." Plausible enough, until she came in without one.

"Where's the corkscrew?" Caron asked. Bonnie squinted at me, then turned on her heel to get one from the kitchen.

"What were you guys talking about?" I asked Sedric, not very happy with Caron. It wasn't her fault Bonnie had pissed me off, but that's what happens when people are bonded. They get treated as one person. And isn't that what they wanted, anyway?

"Oh, Lang's school, Caron's work. Nothing you don't already know all about," Sedric said. Like I was concerned I'd missed something. I wanted to tell him I didn't really care, that I was just trying to be polite, but that wouldn't have bern very polite. Maybe I should have cared. Or at least acted like I did. Fake it 'til you make it, and all.

Bonnie came up behind me and jammed the corkscrew into the cork. She pulled the bottle closer and began twisting. When the cork popped out, she immediately filled my glass, right to the brim. An olive branch of sorts. I took a large sip.

All was not forgiven, but I was the one who got upset she was happy for having a baby, so I guessed I shouldn't throw stones.

I let the others carry the conversation through the rest of dinner. Bonnie and Caron had so many questions for Sedric, it was almost ridiculous. They didn't stray back into lifemate territory, though, so it couldn't do any harm to let them get to know each other. He was my boss, and I did have to spend several more weeks with him. I didn't care what he thought about me, but it could only make our time together more pleasant if he saw me in a nicer light. Having Bonnie and Caron as friends certainly produced that result. He looked at me several times with a smile in his eyes that clearly said, "See, I knew you weren't as bad as you like to make everyone think." If only, Sedric. If only.

When the plates were cleared, I went with Caron into the kitchen to help with the dishes. Bonnie took Sedric and Lang into the family room to pick out a game to play.

"He's a very nice man," Caron said, turning the faucet on. The stupid dishwasher was still broken.

"I know. That does seem to be the word to describe him, doesn't it?"

"There are a lot of other words I could use, but I thought nice was the most neutral."

"You don't like him?" I tried to keep the shock out of my tone, but seriously, how could anyone not like Sedric?

"No, I like him very much. I just assumed you wouldn't want me to lavish praise on him."

Huh? "Why not?"

"I thought it would make you uncomfortable."

"Why?"

She handed me a wet plate and motioned to the dishtowel hanging on the wall. "I think he likes you, and whenever people like you, you shut down."

"I do not."

"Of course you do. It took you three years to warm to me, and I only liked you because Bonnie did. I didn't know anything about you except that you'd been loyal to Bonnie your entire lives."

"To be honest, I didn't warm to you because you took Bonnie away from me, not because you *liked* me."

She dropped the plastic sippy cup in her hand and it splashed into the water, sending droplets onto her shirt. I handed her the towel. "I had no idea. That didn't even occur to me. Although," she picked the cup out of the sink and began scrubbing it with a sponge, "that makes more sense, I guess. Should I say, *I'm sorry*?"

I laughed. "Of course not. You didn't do anything wrong. You found your mate. I should be the one apologizing. What did I expect, that you'd stay away because she already had a woman in her life?"

"Yeah, that probably wouldn't have gone over too well."

"I'm really sorry, Caron. I've been such a bitch to you. You've never deserved it."

"It's okay, you weren't that bad. And I sorta get it. If I were in your shoes, I'd probably act the same way."

I shook my head. "No, you wouldn't. You're a decent person, fundamentally. And I guess I'm just not."

"Don't say that."

"It's true. I've never done the right thing. I've always been waiting, thinking that when I found my mate, he'd make me a better person. I'd be happier and kinder because I'd have love. But he's not coming, and even if he was, he can't magically turn me into a person I'm not."

Caron turned off the water and dried her hands. She put her arms around me. We'd never hugged before and it was awkward, yet, at the same time, supremely comforting. I found myself saying, "Thank you." I guess it wasn't going to kill me after all.

Sedric and Bonnie had a board game set up on the coffee table when Caron and I joined them in the family room. Lang assigned pieces to everyone. "You get to be pink, Honor," she said, handing me the fuchsia cube. I settled on the floor next to Sedric. She choose purple for herself, blue for Sedric, "because boys are blue," red for Caron, and green for Bonnie.

About fifteen minutes into play, Lang burst into tears over some small injustice she considered catastrophic not just to the game, but to her life. Caron and Bonnie tried to soothe her and explain the importance of good sportsmanship, but she continued to howl and bemoan the unfairness of it all. Bonnie hoisted her off the floor and took her out of the room. Caron followed.

"Looks like it's bedtime," I said.

Sedric's gaze followed my friends, then turned to me. "How do you know them?"

"Bonnie and I grew up together. We've been friends since we were five."

"Really? That's impressive."

"Impressive?"

"The friends I had in childhood are spread out all over the world now. Followed their larks to different regions."

"After Bonnie found Caron, they came here. My pull stopped, my lifegivers passed away, and my brother's mate doesn't like me much, so I moved here, too. Bonnie's the closest thing to family I have, most of the time."

He pointed to a framed photo on the wall showing the four of us exchanging gifts for Paolumbo. "You spend holidays here?"

"Some. I'll go to Val's for Priamus."

"That's your brother?"

"Yep. 'Val' is short for Valor. My lifegivers had a thing about courage," I said. Hero thought giving us names like Valor and Honor would instill strong values in us. There were plenty of times I wanted to ask him if it worked, but he died before I found the nerve.

"I guess they passed that down."

"Oh no, I could care less about it."

"You're courageous every day."

"What?"

He blushed and stood. He moved as far away from me as possible without actually leaving the room. What was he talking about? How was I courageous? Lying and generally being rude to everyone I encountered seemed the opposite to me. I was the biggest coward I'd ever known.

"So, you met Bonnie when you were five..."

"Yeah," Bonnie said, walking into the room and plopping onto the couch. "In ballet class."

"He doesn't want to hear the story," I said.

"Sure I do." He smiled and sat on the other end of the couch, facing my friend.

Bonnie continued, "I was absolutely terrible. You have no idea. Like, you think, no five-year old can truly be terrible at something like that because no five-year old could actually be good, but I was horrendous."

"You're exaggerating, Bon."

She brushed hair out of her face. "One day after class I'm huddled in the corner, just crying my eyes out because I don't understand what the teacher has been trying to get us to do, when Honor walked over."

"And that's it," I said.

"Honor was the best in the class. Truly gifted. Did you know she was a professional ballet dancer?"

"I never made it to the pro stage."

"Okay – almost a professional dancer. Anyway, she walked up to me and asked why I was crying. I said, 'Because I'm no good.' She put her arm around me and said, very seriously, 'Well, that's okay.' Something in my five-year old heart really appreciated that she didn't lie to me and say I was doing well. She said it like it was. It was okay that I was doing poorly."

"She hasn't lost that blunt edge," Sedric said.

Bonnie smiled. "No, she hasn't. It's one of the things I love about her."

"Okay guys, let's get back to the game," I said. Caron was still off with Lang, but hearing Bonnie say such nice things about me got me all antsy. I still wanted to be mad at her. She knew, and wasn't allowing it.

"It's really a kids' game. Now that Lang's in bed, what's the point?" Bonnie picked up the players' pieces and tossed them in the box.

"I'm actually pretty tired. Jet lag, you know," Sedric said. "Would you mind if we called it a night?"

"Not at all." I stood and pulled down my shirt where it had bunched up in the back.

"It's so early," Bonnie protested.

"Thank you for having me." Sedric shook her hand. "I'm sorry it was a surprise. I hope it wasn't an inconvenience."

"Not at all. It was nice to meet you."

Caron appeared. "Are you leaving?"

"Yeah," I said. "We're both tired and Sedric has to drop me off at my house still."

"You know you can always stay here."

"I want to get home. I haven't slept in my own bed in a week."

"Well, thanks for coming!" Caron reached for a hug and it felt more natural this time. When she released me, she did the same to Sedric. That it did not feel natural to him was evident. His face blushed deep red and his arms were stiff at his sides. Just when it looked like he was relaxing into the embrace, she stepped back.

"Um, thank you for having me," he said.

"Anytime. I hope you'll come back — we always love company and making new friends."

He hesitated, looking at me. What did he want me to say? *Yes, please hang out with my friends all the time? No, stay away, they're mine?* I couldn't give him the reassurance he was looking for.

"Thank you, Caron, I had a lovely evening," was what he came up with.

We moved toward the door, Bonnie and Caron on our heels. I picked my purse off the coat rack and reached for the front door's knob, when Bonnie touched my elbow.

"Are we okay?"

I should have brushed the night off my shoulders and forgotten what Bonnie said in the basement. But that would be too easy. And when did I ever make things easy on anyone? I moved to the side and lowered my voice. "Do you still think I'm a slut?"

She matched my level. "No! I never said you were. You're overreacting. That's not what I meant."

"Okay, what did you mean, then?"

Sedric was chatting loudly with Caron, deliberately trying not to hear my conversation with Bonnie. I made a mental note to bring a cupcake to work for him on Monday.

Bonnie said, "I know how much pain you're already in, and then you throw in searching for your mate and becoming friendly with your boss. You're setting yourself up for disaster."

"If that's how you see it, then no. We're not good." I stomped to the door, flung it open, and bolted.

Chapter Nine: Suck It

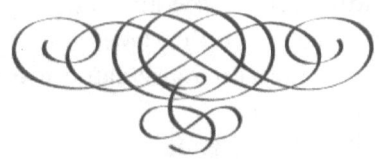

The second I stepped in the door, I wished I was back on the road. My eyes strained under the fluorescent lights of the offices of Taylor & James Consulting. Hadn't I read studies proving that bright lighting actually hindered productivity? I hated the building. I hated the job. Why was I there? When I started, I assumed it would be temporary – a placeholder until I could figure out what I wanted to do with the rest of my life. But it was four years later and I had no exit strategy. I couldn't convince myself it was temporary any longer.

If I hadn't broken my ankle I would have been on tour, not squinting under harsh lighting, trying to adjust the glow of my computer monitor. My plans were bigger, but as usual, fate, or the Gods, or whatever decides those things, had different ideas.

When the glare from the monitor was slightly more bearable, I opened my email to start catching up on the backlog. Sedric and I spent an hour or two every day we were on the road answering important emails and checking in with the office, but those messages that could wait, did. I couldn't justify ignoring them any longer, though.

"Hey, Honor!" Alyscia's bubbly face popped over the front of my cubicle. "Welcome back! How was your week on the road?"

"Just fine."

"What's our new boss like?"

"Like every other boss, a pain in the ass." I didn't mean that, but she wouldn't believe me anyway. Alyscia was the type who only saw the good in people. Even me. She was an idiot.

"Did you see the Dessert Fairy came today?" She held up an apple cinnamon cupcake.

"Oh, yeah? I'll grab one later."

"The Fairy outdid herself this time. They're amazing. This is my second one. Shh. Don't tell anyone."

"Your secret's safe with me. Now, if you don't mind, I have a lot of work to do."

"Okay, see you later." Her head bobbed down the hallway and I watched as she peered into Sedric's office. I couldn't hear what she said or his response, but she stood there for at least five minutes. What could she have to say to him that would take so long? She didn't know him – he'd been at the office a total of four days before we went on the road.

She was heading my way again, so I turned my eyes to my keyboard, hoping to discourage conversation as she passed. It didn't stop me from hearing her say to Felix as he crossed her path, "Did you see Sedric got his own special cupcake? The Dessert Fairy has never brought me anything like that."

"Me either. Someone's sucking up." His voice was right above me. I turned my chair so I wouldn't see him even accidentally in my periphery. I didn't want to deal with Felix. Of course, I never wanted to deal with him, so it was nothing new.

"Good morning, Honor."

"Sure it is, Felix."

"How was your trip? Are the good folks at Lampton going to be renewing their contract?"

"I can't see why they wouldn't. You know I'm the best you've got, and they know I'm the best in the business." Ugh. I wanted to vomit in my mouth. What did it say about the company that I was the best they had, when I didn't give a shit about what I was doing?"

"Well, lucky for you, Mr. Eckland's reports from the road were in your favor. You know you're on thin ice, right?"

"Sure I am, Felix. Keep telling yourself that if it makes you feel better."

"I'm going to have to report your attitude on your yearly review."

"I'm shaking in my swivel chair."

"That's all – get back to work."

"I never stopped working. You're the one wasting time." Since I hadn't turned to look at him, I couldn't see the sneer on his face, but I knew him well enough to know it was there.

"I definitely won't miss him if I ever get out of this place," I muttered.

I'd been through twenty emails – most of them mundane, easy answers. But number twenty-one was a newsletter from Fortune Ballet Company. My almost-life. I scanned the contents. In the middle of the page, Irina's face blocked out the left column. She was the lead in *Life and Death*, my favorite ballet. I didn't know they were planning on performing it, but I guess I hadn't paid as much attention to the newsletters as I thought. It wasn't my destiny anymore.

Irina was a year younger than I, but we'd trained together for the last ten of my dancing years. She had graceful limbs and technical precision, but her passion for the art never showed. She was always right below me on the ladder – never the principal, always the understudy. When I injured my leg, she took the place in the Company that should have gone to me. But I had no idea she'd worked her way up the ranks to the lead in the best ballet on the planet. I thought she was still a lost face in the chorus.

Could that have been me? My heart and soul went into every dance I performed. Even when my technique was shaky, my coaches said they couldn't take their eyes off me. I thought when I went into the Company I would have a small chance of making it into the program, but if Irina made it, did that mean I would have been a shoe-in?

I moved my cursor on the screen and the link at the bottom of the message glowed blue. Click. A box popped up. *Are you sure you want to unsubscribe?* Yes.

I spent the rest of the morning plodding through my inbox. I had a date with a stack of paperwork on my desk after lunch. When the clock struck noon, I grabbed my purse out of my bottom desk drawer and bee-lined for the cafeteria.

I wanted to avoid Sedric. Snatches of gossip made their way to my ears throughout the morning, and half of it was about Sedric's special dessert. How could I have been so stupid? I didn't want the office talking about us, and this was like handing them exactly what they needed to jump to the wrong conclusions. It was stupid of me to bring cupcakes my first day back when they wouldn't have received any at all while I was gone, but it was simply moronic to bring a special set just for Sedric and leave it on his desk for anyone to see. Maybe part of me thought he'd be smart enough to keep it out of sight, but mostly, I wasn't thinking at all.

Trays hitting tables, forks scraping plates, and ice clinking as drinks were dispensed made up the sounds of your standard, office-building cafeteria. We shared the ground floor with nine other companies, which made for interesting lunchtime groupings. The sales team from Siebert's Shoes sat with the do-gooders from We C.A.R.E, a non-profit organization working with the elderly. Investment bankers in their thousand-note suits hobnobbed with the dental practice from the second floor. I found a table in a corner alcove away from the entrance and sat by myself, hidden from any Nosy Nellies, but ready to observe them all.

Sedric came in ten minutes later with Alyscia and Felix. They went through the line and Sedric selected a hamburger and fries, Felix, a bowl of fruit salad, and Alyscia, a granola bar and bag of salt & vinegar chips. They chose a table a few yards away from me, but my spot served its purpose and they had no idea I was there.

Sedric's voice: "Alyscia, did I hear correctly – you found your mate recently?"

"I did! This is actually my last month with the company. During the Priamus break I'll be moving to Freyacre – that's where he lives."

"He didn't want to move here?"

"Oh, I'm sure he would have. He's a wonderful man, but I offered to go there first."

Translation: she hates it here, too, and couldn't wait to move as far away as possible.

"We wish you the best of luck, don't we, Sedric?" Felix said.

"Of course. Have you found a job there, yet?"

"Oh, I'm not planning on working. Dexek makes a very good living and we want to have kids as soon as possible."

As soon as possible? Give me a break. She'd known the guy for a week and they weren't even living in the same place yet. I wanted to say those things to her, but knew there was no reasoning to match the power of the lark and a dumb girl's ideas on love.

They had moved on in their conversation. Felix was asking Sedric about our week out of the office. I put my fork down.

"I'm sorry you're stuck with Honor. I know she can be quite..." he paused, searching for the most professional way of calling me a bitch, perhaps. "...well, prickly."

Not bad. I would have gone with difficult, or unruly.

"Didn't you know, Felix? I requested to shadow Honor after going through the performance records for the past year. Hers didn't make much sense, so I wanted to see what was going on. I have to say, I'm very pleased with how she handled herself with the clients."

Felix cleared his throat. "I'm glad to hear that."

He obviously wasn't.

"I understand she's not easy to work with here in the office, but she does her job well."

Alyscia giggled. At twenty-one, didn't she realize she wasn't a schoolgirl anymore? Sedric continued. "In fact, I actually think she's a rather pleasant person, once you get to know her."

Now Felix was giggling. He had to know he wasn't a schoolgirl. I found my hand gripping my fork and had to stop myself from hurling it at the wall. Or Sedric's face.

"I think she's pulling one over on you," Felix said between his laughter. "A pleasant person? Wait til you've been here longer."

I forced myself to relax my fingers and the fork dropped onto my plate. It made a sharp clink, but the three people I'd been eavesdropping on were too absorbed in their discussion of me to hear it.

"Forget about Honor," Alyscia said, once their laughter faded. "Tell us about the cupcakes – was there a note or anything with the box?"

"Um, no. Nothing like that."

"Do you know why you got your own? Usually the Fairy leaves the goodies in one of the division's lounges, and we all have to scramble to get some before they're gone. But they made sure you got one."

"I'm new – maybe the Fairy was welcoming me?"

"They've never welcomed a new person before."

I couldn't see it, but I would've sworn Sedric shrugged at that point. The pause was just right for it. "I don't know what to tell you. They were delicious, though. An infinitely better breakfast than the one I had planned."

"I'm so jealous," Alyscia whined. "But hey, maybe the Fairy will do something special for my going-away party."

"Maybe," Sedric said. Then, slower, "Who is the Fairy?"

"No one knows," Felix said. "It's our own workplace mystery."

I held my chuckles in. If anyone really wanted to figure out who it was, it wouldn't be that hard. I mean, come on, the desserts only showed up on weeks I was in the office. And I'd been doing it for nearly four years. The higher-ups like Felix had to realize it started when I started, and hadn't ended since I hadn't left. Imbeciles.

"Every office needs something like that," were Sedric's final words on the matter. He and Felix began talking about sports, so I leaned back in my chair and finished my salad.

Sedric hadn't ratted me out. He could have easily told everyone the treats were coming from me. It would have even validated his *she's pleasant once you get to know her* theory, but he didn't. Because I'd asked him not to. Because he was a good guy. A good guy who didn't deserve to be stuck with a prickly, difficult, unruly subordinate like me. I vowed to be better. Well, better to him, at least. Felix and Alyscia could suck it.

"Hey Bro, I'm sorry we didn't get a chance to connect this weekend."

Val waved at me, his smiling face on my screen another kick to my resolve. I'd be better for him, too.

"It's our fault. Handor's been having pull issues lately, so we weren't home most of the weekend."

"Issues? What kind?"

Val looked over his shoulder. "His lark has been flaring up during lessons, and his pull has been telling him to go two places at once."

"What does that mean?"

"We're not sure. I drove him around trying to figure out where it wanted him to go - that's why we were gone - but no answers. If it doesn't get better, we're going to schedule an appointment with a specialist."

"He must be confused," I said.

"He and I and Mabry; we're all confused. I've never heard of someone's pull and lark acting like this."

"It's not unheard of for a pull to be erratic – mine was."

My brother shook his head. "Yeah, but that's not what this is. His is leading him to two separate locations at the same time."

"Maybe he has two mates?" I joked. Val didn't hear me, or if he did, he ignored it. I thought it was funny, but apparently not.

"The lark burning is even more confusing than the multi-personality pull. I've never heard of larks burning like that before, have you?"

"Actually, yeah. My boss told me when he found his mate, his lark heated up – it felt like a really bad sunburn."

"That's normal. I mean, it's normal when you find your mate for it to do that," Val said.

"Oh, it is?"

"Of course, everyone knows that."

"Excuse me – no need to snap. I didn't know because it's never happened to me."

He sighed and crossed his arms over his chest. "Don't be a martyr, Honor."

"Don't be an asshole, Val."

"I'm concerned for my son. You can't understand that."

"He's my nephew. I love Handor – you know how much I love that kid."

"You don't get it."

I took a deep breath. We weren't getting anywhere bickering with each other. Valor could be as stubborn as me sometimes. He wasn't going to back down and admit he snapped, so I'd have to be the one to apologize. Gritting my teeth, I said, "You're right, Val. I don't have kids. I don't have a lifegiver's feelings. But I am worried. I wish I had known this was happening, I would have come out this weekend to help."

His expression softened. "There's nothing you could have done, but thank you. I appreciate that."

"Is he still up? Can I talk to him?"

"You know the rules about the screen."

"Okay, I'll email him – tell him to check it in the morning before his lessons."

"I will," he promised.

"And you better let me know the second you know anything. I'm sure he's fine, but I want to know either way – good news or bad."

Val nodded.

"Is Mabry there? Can I say hello?"

His eyebrows arched. "You want to speak to my mate?"

"Believe it or not, yes. I'm trying, Val."

"Give me a second to find her. I'm not sure if she's in our room or the study."

"Sure."

He walked out of view. The news about Handor was troubling. He was only fifteen. Pulls weren't strong at that age – not for most people. Usually, a strong pull at that age meant one's mate lived close by. Maybe his mate had two different homes, and that's why the pull couldn't decide where to lead him.

"Hi, Honor." Mabry sat on their brown leather couch, several feet from the screen – much further back than Val usually sat. That was about right – why would she want to get close to me? Even though we were thousands of miles apart physically, we'd always been millions apart emotionally.

"Hey Mabry, how are you?"

"I'm pretty good. How about you?"

"Just fine." Okay, enough with the pleasantries. "I wanted to speak with you tonight because..." a flicker of movement in the corner of the screen caught my attention, but it was only Valor standing in the doorway, pretending to give us privacy, "...because I know I've never been particularly nice to you and I wanted to apologize."

"Oh." She sat up a little straighter.

"Uh, yeah. So, I'm sorry. I'm sorry I never tried to get to know you before you and Val moved across the world. I'm sorry I've lied to you. I'm sorry if I've ever hurt your feelings. I wish I could say it was unintentional, but I think we both know that isn't true."

She paused. Then, "I don't understand why you hate me."

"I don't hate you. I've never really liked you, but that isn't because of anything you did. I didn't want to like you."

"Why?"

"I'm starting to think I might have abandonment and rejection issues. Valor chose you over us."

"But it's not really a choice you make."

"Logically, I know that. But in here," I tapped my chest, "that's what it felt like. I'm going to try and be nicer though. Do you think you can forgive me?"

Her gaze shifted – looking to her mate to see if this confession was real or just another trick I was playing on her. I couldn't see his response, but a moment later, she looked back into the screen and smiled. She was obviously faking it, but it was better than nothing. She said, "I'd like us to try and be friends. For Val's sake, and for Handor and Shyla. So yes, I'll forgive you."

"I'd like us to be friends, too. Whew!" I wiped my forehead and she laughed. "Does this mean no more awkward family holidays?" I asked.

"I hope not – those stories are a hit at my office."

"Did you just crack a joke, Mabry?"

"What? I can be funny. You just never took the time to listen to anything I had to say."

"Touché. Well, I'm listening now."

Chapter Ten: Puzzles

I peered around the corner into Sedric's office, and cleared my throat. *Here goes nothing.* "Good morning."

"Honor, what are you doing here so early again?" he asked, standing and coming to the front of his desk.

I stepped through the door and held out a cup of coffee. "From the café around the corner. The stuff they stock in the lounge is horrendous."

"Thanks."

"You're welcome. Anyway, I'm here early because I'm still catching up on work and we're leaving again this afternoon, so, yeah... But also, I know you didn't give up my secret yesterday when you had the chance, and I appreciate that. I haven't done much to earn your friendship, but it appears you've given it to me anyway."

"You're not as bad as you want people to think you are."

"No, I'm worse." I laughed, but he took a step closer, not even a hint of amusement on his face.

"Life is not an easy thing. Life is hard. It takes some people a long time to figure that out. It takes others no time at all."

What the hell was he talking about?

"I shouldn't try and sound philosophical, should I?"

I laughed again. "No, you really shouldn't."

"What I'm trying to say is, you've had a harder life than most, so if you want to be angry, you should be angry for a little while. A little while – not forever."

I looked down at my own coffee. "I think I'm starting to realize that."

"What are you still behind on – can I help?" he asked.

"I think paperwork on my clients is below your pay grade."

"Probably, but it's my fault you're behind. And a good leader makes it possible for his team-"

"Or hers."

"Okay, or her team, to succeed."

I considered him for a moment. Asking for help was about as easy as saying thank you. But I didn't have to ask. He was offering. "Why don't we take the paperwork to the conference room and knock it out?"

"I'll meet you there. You brought the coffee, so I'll bring breakfast."

"Deal."

Ten minutes later, I took my usual seat as far from the front of the conference room as possible, and he sat across from me, offering a blueberry muffin. I took a bite and struggled to swallow.

"What, is it not good?"

I laughed, coughing on a crumb. Reaching into my bag, I attempted to find a bottle of water to wash it down, but came up empty. Sedric rushed out of his seat over to me, patting my back furiously. "I'm okay," I sputtered. "It went down the wrong pipe."

"Paolo, you scared the crap out of me. I thought I'd killed you with a disgusting baked good."

"Don't be so dramatic."

"You didn't see your face. It instantly went blood red and you were grabbing your throat. I thought it was lodged in there."

"Um, thanks for trying to save me, I guess?"

After a pregnant pause, Sedric cracked a grin. We both started laughing. Clutching my side, tears formed in my eyes.

It wasn't even that funny, but it felt amazing to laugh. My companion looked like he needed the change of tone as much as I did.

"What's going on in here?" Felix stuck his nose through the conference room door. "Oh, Sedric, Honor, I wasn't expecting the two of you."

"We're finishing some paperwork – back on the road this evening," Sedric said through his smile. My chest grew warm – he had a really great smile.

"I never found paperwork so amusing," Felix said.

"You've never done it with me," I said, biting my lip to keep myself from losing it again.

Felix made his best *something smells really bad in here* face before leaving. Sedric tossed a pen at my forehead. "Get to work, young lady."

"Oh, yes sir! Right away, sir!" I snatched the pen from where it landed on the desk and hunched my shoulders over, miming fast and furious writing on the forms. Sedric's chuckles were more subdued, but still some of the nicest sounds I'd heard in a long time.

"You really like this job, huh?" I asked, straightening my back and selecting a real document from the stack to work on.

"I do."

"Weird."

"Maybe to you, but it suits me."

I filled in the top half of the form, glancing up briefly to catch him staring at me. We both looked away. After another moment, I paused my pen and said, "I have a feeling you'd be good at just about anything you put your mind to."

"That's funny," he said.

"Why?"

"Because I was thinking the same thing about you."

"Me? Sorry to burst your bubble, but you're wrong there." I looked down and tried to figure out where I'd left off.

"Let's see – highly skilled ballerina, gourmet chef, amazing public speaker and team-building consultant, great aunt. Should I keep listing?"

"I'm not a ballerina anymore and I'm no gourmet chef. I just bake. I can't cook worth a damn. And how do you know

I'm a good aunt? Have I even told you about my niece and nephew?"

He shook his head. "You'd still be a ballerina if it weren't for your injury, right?"

"Yes."

"It's almost as if the Gods wanted you to figure out what else you were good at."

"If that's the case, then I have a lot more to be mad at than I thought," I grumbled.

"I was trying to pay you a compliment."

"That didn't work out so great for you, did it? I guess you aren't good at everything you put your mind to."

He sighed. "We were having such a good time."

"And I ruined it?"

He shrugged his shoulders.

"Okay, yes, I did. I'm sorry." I took another bite of the cardboard-like muffin, but couldn't bring myself to chew. I wasn't *that* sorry. When I spit it into a napkin, he reached behind him and retrieved a wastebasket.

"Here."

I tossed it in.

"Is it really that bad?"

"Yeah. I'm sorry, but it really is. It's like whoever made those muffins has never heard of blending the ingredients into an actual batter. They just baked the flour."

"I've been wondering, why don't you open a bakery?"

I moved the form to the completed stack and slid a new one in front of me. "What?"

"You clearly don't like this job, and you said before you don't want to teach dance, but what's stopping you from doing something you'd actually enjoy?"

"I don't know if that *is* something I'd enjoy."

"You bake for your colleagues here all the time. Why do you do that?"

"Mostly as an apology, but it also relaxes me."

"Why wouldn't you want to make a career out of something that relaxes you?" he asked.

"Running a small business is nothing like baking random treats in my own kitchen. All the finances and marketing and hiring employees – I don't think I could manage it all."

"I think you could."

I picked up another document so I didn't have to look at him. "Sedric, you don't really know me. At least, not well. We've spent like, five, days together."

"I feel like I know you really well."

Well, you don't, I almost snapped. My mouth was open, the words tickled the back of my throat, but I stopped myself. There was no use arguing with him about it. *Be a better person,* I told myself. "Why? I haven't given you much to work with."

"I like puzzles, remember. And you are one big puzzle. I've been putting together your pieces since we met."

I laughed. "Is it just me, or did that sound a little dirty?"

Color flooded his cheeks. "I didn't mean it that way."

"I know, but come on. Say it to yourself – doesn't it sound dirty?"

He paused – thinking over the intended-harmless sentence. His lips twisted around each other, holding back his booming laugh.

"See?" I exclaimed.

"Okay, yes, a little. Get your mind out of the gutter."

"Stop sweeping me into it."

"I'd hardly call one accidental comment sweeping, but fine. Let's sit quietly and work. We won't say a word to each other; we'll finish all the paperwork and you'll have no new ammunition to tease me with for the rest of the week."

"Promise?"

He scowled playfully, motioning his index finger and thumb over his lips to zip them shut. As his hand moved, I caught another glimpse of his lark. It looked different than the last time I'd seen it. Patchy.

"What's wrong with your lark?"

His eyes clouded over, all evidence of amusement gone. His shoulders tensed and he focused too intently on the paper in front of him. Shit. Why did I say anything? I, of all people, knew how uncomfortable it was explaining lark issues to people. Concentrating on my wrist, I stroked my own lark.

"I used to think mine was beautiful. I don't anymore."

He didn't respond.

"What do you think it would have become if I found him before he died?" I held it towards him. His hand twitched, but settled back on his stack of papers. "Come on, puzzle-man. Fill in the dots. What's it supposed to be? I've always wanted to know."

"The lark usually represents the couple in some way, right?"

I nodded. That's what I'd been told. Bonnie and Caron's was a dog. They were both caring, loyal, and the best friends any human could have. Alyscia's was a tree in bloom. I could only hope that meant finding her mate was going to help her grow and blossom into a mature adult.

"Yours is the sun — how does that represent you and Zara?"

"She was the center of my world. I was the center of hers." He held up his palm — there were chunks missing from the dark brown mark, but knowing what it was, I could fill in the pieces and see the real picture emerge. Three concentric circles in the center of his palm, with flames shooting off the largest. The flames licked his fingers. How did it not scorch his skin?

"It didn't look like this when she was alive, obviously. Little by little, over time, pieces have faded away."

"Oh, Pria. Does it feel like you're losing her all over again?" I slapped my hand over my mouth. I couldn't believe I'd just said that.

"It's a daily and hourly reminder that my life is not as bright without her. Clouds are covering up the light."

I reached across the table and he offered his hand to me palm up so I could examine it. "What did it look like before you found her?"

"Similar to this, but there were more spots missing. I'm sure it will revert back to that eventually."

"Do you think it will disappear completely?"

He took his hand back and looked into his palm. "I don't know. Part of me hopes so."

"Really?"

"Then I wouldn't have to see it every day."

"But it would be blank — wouldn't that be worse?"

"I don't know. Yes. Maybe. I guess I won't know unless it happens. Has yours lost any pieces in the last couple of years, since the time you think he passed?"

"No, it's always been exactly the same. But I'm like you, I wish it would just go away already. Yours at least has happy memories attached to it, right?"

"It does. But there are a lot of unhappy memories, too."

I grinned. "Life just sucks, doesn't it?"

He laughed. "Another thing we agree on."

Chapter Eleven: Making a Bet

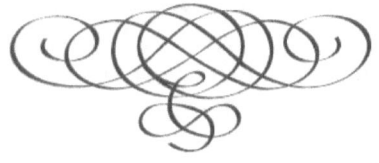

That evening we hit the road again, to Osthaven and the base of operations for Sedric's first client. Tap & Bap Industries was the leading toymaker in its region, but wanted to expand to other markets. Maling had been working with them for six months to prepare the launch, and they weren't thrilled with her promotion or the appointment of a new consultant to their case. Keeping them happy was Sedric's top priority.

I performed a team-building seminar for Maling a month after she'd started with T&B, so I'd met the CEO and his board, as well as some of the upper level managers. Sedric was hoping I'd made a good enough impression to help smooth over his introduction.

The air inside the building was only a degree or two warmer than outside. Didn't they realize winter was creeping around the corner? I actually missed the humidity of Campi. We waited a few minutes in front of the steel elevator doors, Sedric fidgeting with his tie.

"Would you cut that out?"

"Sorry, it's not sitting right." He loosened the knot for the fifth time. The doors slid open and we stepped inside.

"Hands down," I said.

"But-"

"I'm going to fix it. Put your hands down or I'll poke you in the eye."

"That doesn't seem like an appropriate punishment."

I grabbed his wrists and forced his hands to his side. "You didn't start out with a long enough tail."

"That's not a thing. It doesn't have a name."

"Hero, my lifegiver, always called it that." I completely undid the knot and readjusted the two ends before looping them over one another and forming a new knot. "Did you dress in the dark this morning?"

"I overslept, so I had to do the tie while I was walking down to the lobby."

"You overslept? That's so unlike you. There, you're done. Is that better?"

He adjusted it slightly, using the reflection from the door. "Much. Thank you."

"Why are you so jittery?"

"It's been a long time since I've done this. What if I forget everything? What if everything I have planned is irrelevant now?"

"You've been reading articles and books all week. You'll be fine. And if you're not, what's the worst that could happen?"

"They could drop their contract. I could be fired."

"There's looking on the bright side." I patted him on the back and the lift opened.

"Can you be the nice, professional version of yourself today? I'd really like things to go well," he said.

"I can't promise anything." We followed the hallway to the end and turned to the right. A set of glass doors opened into a lobby with a few metal chairs and a round reception desk.

"Welcome to Tap & Bap, how can I help you?" A woman in her mid-to-late fifties, as evidenced by deep crow's feet and graying temples, stood to greet us. She didn't bother to smile or fake excitement. I nudged Sedric with my elbow, hoping he would take her apathy as a good sign.

"We're here for a meeting with Mr. Bresline. I'm Sedric Eckland with Taylor & James Consulting."

The woman pressed a red button on her intercom. "Nayja? Sedric Eckland is here for Mr. Bresline." She held up a finger. Static crackled through the intercom until Nayja responded.

"Mr. Bresline will be with Mr. Eckland in a few minutes."

The receptionist used her already erect finger to point us to a couple of the chairs to the left of her desk. I patted Sedric's shoulder again as we sat down; his entire upper body was rigid.

"Seriously, chill. You're going to make a horrible impression on the CEO if you don't relax."

He looked around the waiting room, fidgeting some more with his tie, then gently cracking his knuckles. After a minute or two of silence between us, he asked, "Did she say 'Nayja?'"

"Um, I think that's what she called the assistant. I'm not sure."

"That's a common name, right?"

"I don't think so."

"Hmm." His hands went back to his tie. I grabbed them before he could do any damage.

"Who's Nayja?"

He shrugged, like it was no big deal, but his voice gave him away. "A friend of Zara's. Or she was. I haven't seen her in twelve years. Maybe thirteen."

"Okay – so?"

"She and Zara had a big falling out. Because of me. She didn't even come to the funeral."

"Oh."

"It's fine. No big deal." He sounded like he was trying to reassure himself, but I wasn't convinced. I desperately wanted to ask what happened between them that could have caused a fallout between Zara and Nayja. He was so mild-mannered, so polite, so willing to be friendly and helpful to everyone. Had she been a catalyst of change in him, like he was becoming in me?

The silence was unbearable. I attempted a nonchalant tone. "What happened between you two?"

"It's not important."

I didn't push – I didn't have a right to – but I was still curious as hell. Instead, I watched the clock on the wall across from us. It was one of those sculpture clocks where the hands weren't pointing to any actual numbers and didn't move in the same direction. I took turns watching the seconds and minutes tick by.

After seventeen minutes, a short, bald man in a baggy, gray suit appeared and offered his hand to Sedric. "It's nice to meet you, Mr. Eckland. I'm Bradford Bresline."

"Pleasure, sir," Sedric said, standing. He buttoned the front of his jacket and waved a hand towards me. "Do you remember Honor Sandavol?"

"I do. Welcome back, Honor." Mr. Bresline shook my hand as well and we proceeded down the hall into a large conference room with a massive, round, oak table. Six men and seven women sat in high-backed, brown leather chairs. Mr. Bresline motioned to three empty ones and I took the one closest to the door. Sedric sat to my right.

Still standing, Mr. Bresline addressed the group, "Mr. Eckland is here to pick up where Maling left off. Greer, why don't you update him on what we've been working on since Maling was last here?"

The gentleman across from me started passing out folders. Once everyone had theirs, he launched into a twenty-minute speech on marketing strategies and product distribution plans. I stopped listening after a couple of minutes and studied the faces of the seven women, trying to figure out if one of them was Nayja, and if so, which one.

Two seats to the right of Greer, a woman in her late thirties wearing a designer dress stared at her folder. Long, curly hair covered half of her face. She didn't flip through the contents to refer to each sheet as Greer discussed them. I glanced at Sedric. He was watching her, too. That was Nayja.

When the meeting ended, I started collecting the folders and handouts while Sedric walked to Mr. Bresline's office to discuss a few items there hadn't been time for. Nayja hung back as the room emptied. She gathered miscellaneous pens and pads of paper from the table. I wanted to ask her about her past with Sedric and Zara, but we hadn't said two words to each other all day, so I didn't exactly have a good way to start the conversation.

She finished tidying the room and I had everything packed in my bag and Sedric's briefcase. I took a seat to wait for Sedric and she lingered around the door, fiddling with the radiator. With a sigh, she reached for the handle, just as Sedric pushed it open.

"Nayja, you're looking well," Sedric said, extending his hand. His eyes scrunched up as if he were in pain, but his voice didn't betray him. He sounded cool as a cucumber.

She looked down at his hand with a sneer and coolly replied, "It's been a long time."

"It has. I didn't know you moved into the corporate world."

"Running your own business doesn't come with many benefits. We needed health care and dental."

"How is Brody?"

"He's fine. How's Zara?" She raised an eyebrow. I wondered if she was testing Sedric. Did she not know about Zara's death, or did she just want to make him say the painful words?

He reached up to his tie. I wanted to slap his hands away. *Just leave the damned thing alone.*

"I thought you would have heard," he started, glancing around the room and meeting my eye for the briefest of moments. "Zara passed away."

Nayja's icy exterior melted. Her cheeks relaxed in the same moment she reached for Sedric's hand. Not a test. Or, she was a very good actress. "I'm sorry to hear that. When? How?"

"Almost four years ago. Freak accident – she slipped on a patch of ice."

"I'm very, very sorry, especially since we left things so... well, you know." Her back straightened and I swear a chill fell over the room. When she spoke again, her words were clipped and seemed intended to injure Sedric as much as possible. "Then again, it's probably for the best. It's not like she was very happy when she was alive, was it?"

I wanted to punch her. I even took a couple of quick steps in their direction, but Sedric's calm response stopped me. "She was just as happy as you, I think."

"Uh, well..." Nayja's mouth hung slightly open as she tried to decide on a comeback. Apparently she couldn't come up with anything because a moment later she turned, flipped her hair, and sauntered out of the room.

Sedric's gaze moved down to the carpet and he made a soft noise, almost like a chuckle, before composing himself and facing me. "Library?"

How did he switch focus so quickly? I wanted to show him how much I appreciated his selflessness, but I didn't have access to a kitchen. "No, I'm not in the mood for research tonight. Why don't we go out and do something fun?"

"Really?"

"Yeah — my treat. Whaddya say?" Maybe if I was nice, he'd tell me what the deal with Nayja was.

"Absolutely. What do you have in mind?"

"I don't know. But it's a big city, right? I'm sure we can find something."

We stopped at the receptionist's desk on our way out and asked if she knew of any events happening in the area. With a huff and a sigh, she pulled up some tourist website and printed out a page of options for us. We thanked her and Sedric read over the sheet while we moved to the lift.

"There's a jazz club downtown and a photography exhibit at the art museum. Or a boat tour of the harbor, but it's probably too cold for that. Oh — wait. I've got it. I know what we're going to do."

"What?" I reached for the paper, but he folded and put it inside his jacket pocket.

"It's going to be a surprise, but don't worry, you'll like it."

"You can't possibly know what I'll like."

"I'll bet you dinner that you'll like it," he said.

"I already said I'd treat, so that's not much of a bet."

"You can't treat for this. Seriously, if you don't like it, I'll buy dinner all week."

"And if I do, I have to buy your dinner all week?" I asked.

"Yes."

"I could just say I didn't like it either way. You've kinda talked yourself into a corner."

"You could, but I can tell when you're lying now."

"Oh you can, can you?"

"Yes." His confidence seemed ill-placed to me, but he wore it well.

"I'd make a bet with you on that, but again, I could lie about the outcome. We'd be at a stalemate. You'd say I was lying, I'd say I wasn't. Or vice versa. An infinite loop."

The elevator doors opened and we walked through the main lobby to the exit. The sun was setting, creating a canvas of oranges, pinks, and purples across the sky. "Beautiful," Sedric murmured. Was he thinking about Zara? She was his sun. I wanted to peer into his mind – no, his heart – and see if she still lived there. The lark bonds one for life to their mate, but what happens to the bond when the mate dies? Does the bond break? Does love for them die, too?

When my lifegiver, Gizella, passed away several years earlier, Hero had been inconsolable. He wouldn't eat, he barely slept. When Valor and I tried to comfort him, he pushed us away. Then he died, too. Her death broke him. He couldn't bear to live in a world where she didn't exist anymore.

But Sedric hadn't succumbed to his grief. Did that mean he loved Zara less than my lifegivers loved each other? Did it mean he was stronger than they were?

"We need to leave here in a half-hour. Can you be ready and meet me back in the lobby by then?" Sedric asked as I got off the elevator on my floor.

"I don't know what I'm getting ready for."

"Dress nicely."

"That probably means a different thing to you than it does to me. Tell me where we're going," I said.

"Did you bring a dress?"

"Yes."

"And heels?"

"Uh huh."

"Wear those." He stepped back and let the doors close in front of him, cutting off my very witty comeback of, *You don't want to see me in a dress,* before I could get out more than the first two words.

Chapter Twelve: Pay Attention

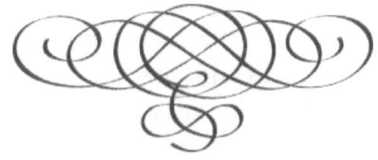

"I really hope it's not sold out." Sedric handed the key to the valet and stepped up on the curb after me. My surprise was on Main Street in downtown Osthaven, but it didn't look like your typical downtown area. There were more trees than businesses and the buildings were only a couple of stories high.

"It's a Wednesday night, not huge for going out. I'm sure we'll be fine," I said.

"You never know. I hear this show has a large fan base."

"Ah – a clue. It's a show!"

He laughed. "Sarcasm will get you nowhere."

"And you said you knew me. Sarcasm gets me everywhere."

He took my elbow and steered me down the sidewalk to a box office. The line of people was unusually long for a weeknight, so I looked to the marquee to see what the draw was.

Pria be damned.

"Honor, the line is moving." Sedric tugged my elbow, but I was frozen in place. He was both completely right and completely wrong about me enjoying this particular event.

"*Life and Death*," I mumbled. "We're seeing a ballet."

Sedric beamed as the force holding me in place disintegrated and allowed me to inch forward. "What did I tell you? I knew you'd love it."

"This is my favorite ballet." I swallowed and searched the front of the theater for posters. Was it possible another company was touring *Life and Death* at the same time as Fortune?

Not so lucky. Irina's little form and hard face graced the poster closest to the ticket window.

Sedric tried to regain my attention. "I guess you owe me dinner this week!"

I nodded slowly. It wasn't worth the conversation to tell him what was really going through my mind – that I would have gladly watched the show performed by any other company, with any other lead ballerina, and I hadn't been to a dance performance in over a year.

"I've never been to a ballet," Sedric said. We were third in line at that point. He pulled out a handful of twenty notes, and though I should have offered to pay for my own ticket, I didn't reach into my purse for my wallet and he didn't ask me to. It was unreal, standing in line to see a performance I would gladly have sacrificed my life to dance in.

"Okay, you lied. You aren't happy to be here," he said, making a motion to step out of line. I grabbed his arm and pulled him back.

"I wasn't expecting this."

"We can just go to dinner and walk around downtown. Let's forget about it."

I felt bad for disappointing him. Standing there, looking at the marquee, I knew it was time for me to get over myself. I had to admit, I was a little curious to see how Irina would handle the role. "No. This is something I should probably do."

"But I didn't win the bet."

"You didn't lose it, either."

"Then, it's a draw?"

I shrugged. "I guess."

The couple ahead of us moved out of the way and Sedric plunked his notes on the counter. "Two, please."

I pressed through the lobby, stepping on a few high-priced designer shoes along the way. Sedric's hand gently gripped my shoulder, assuring he didn't lose me in the crowd. An usher handed us programs when we finally reached the entrance to the upper level. Sedric nodded his off, but I accepted one and slid it into my purse.

Our seats were in the second row of the balcony. Not bad for a night-of-performance ticket purchase. Sedric motioned for me to slide into the row first.

"You know," I said as he sat, "when I said we should do something fun tonight, I meant something you would enjoy. You're the one who had a shitty day."

"I do appreciate your bluntness. Have I told you that?"

I grinned.

"This *will* be fun for me. I like trying new things."

"You've really never seen the ballet before?"

"Nope."

"Zara didn't like it?" I asked.

"I have no idea whether she did or not."

How could he not know something like that – something so fundamental about the woman he'd spent the majority of his life with? It took me a few seconds to realize that dancing might not be as fundamental to everyone else as it was to me.

"Anyway, I thought you'd pick something else, like going to a race track or cigar shop."

He laughed. "Boy, you sure have me figured out."

I pulled the program out of my purse and opened it to the biographies of the dancers. I tapped Irina's picture. "She's the dancer who took my place in the company."

He peered onto the page. "Is she any good?"

"She's dancing the main part tonight."

"Good for her."

Not a hint of sarcasm. How did he do that? He was genuinely happy for someone he'd never met and had absolutely no reason to care about. I closed the program. "Yeah. Good for her."

The lights went down and the chatter in the auditorium faded as the orchestra's first tones filled the space. My breath caught in my throat. I rubbed my palms together and realized they were sweating, just like they had when I prepared for a performance. It was as if no time had passed at all since I was last onstage. The curtain rose. *Life* began.

When the lights came on at intermission, I quickly stuffed the tissue I'd been dabbing my eyes with into the crack between the seat and armrest. I didn't want Sedric to know I'd teared up.

"It's amazing," he said, "the way the dancers move. Can you really spin your body around like that?"

"I used to be able to."

"Amazing."

"You're liking it, then?"

He nodded. "It's moving. I didn't know I could feel such passion emanating from people who never say a single word."

"Good choreography and acting can create whatever emotions the director wants."

"You must miss it." He knocked his fist once on the armrest, as if he too were frustrated by my plight.

Of course I missed it. Watching Irina perform the part I had coveted so long made me ache to dance. She was beautiful: graceful in her lines, poignant in every pause, light and airy in every lift. The years had given what no teacher could – love for the dance. I envied her, but I found I was also proud of her. So not like me.

"How are you feeling after today?" I asked when the pause grew uncomfortable.

"Nice change of subject."

"I do what I can."

He shifted in his seat so he was leaning towards me. "The meeting itself went well, didn't it? The team seemed open to my ideas and suggestions."

"Are you trying to be modest? They loved your presentation."

"I guess I was worried for nothing."

"And how are you feeling about the Nayja thing?" I asked.

He shifted again, this time away from me. "Fine."

I waited for him to elaborate. He didn't. "Do you want to talk about it?" I asked.

"It's a longer conversation than we have time for."

"Really? You mean I don't have to spend the next six weeks or so with you glued to my side?"

He shook his head with a smile. "Longer than we have right now during intermission."

"But I have a feeling you aren't planning on telling me even when we do have longer to chat about it."

He rubbed the stubble on his chin. It was new. He was usually clean-shaven. "I'll just say this: it was probably a good thing Nayja and Zara fought. They weren't good for each other."

"Why not?"

"Who's asking nosy questions now?"

"Okay, I get it. None of my business." I could hardly blame the guy for feeling like he couldn't trust me, but it still stung. I pulled the program back out of my purse and thumbed through the pages, not stopping on any particular one, just wanting to look busy so we wouldn't have to talk.

The curtain closed at the end of the show and Sedric offered his hand to help me up and through the row of closely packed seats. I expected to be able to feel the outline of his lark, but only felt small calluses on the tips of his fingers. His hand warmed the longer it held mine. I didn't want him to let go, and for a few seconds it seemed like I would get my wish as he led me through the balcony crowd to the stairs that would take us to the lobby. At the top of the steps, though, he dropped it.

"Dinner?" he asked.

"Yeah, I'm starving."

"Let's play restaurant roulette."

"What's that?"

"We pick a direction at random and walk. The first restaurant we come across is where we eat."

I raised an eyebrow. "Even if it's a crappy chain you've been to a million times?"

"Those are the rules. I've found a lot of amazing places this way."

"You're the boss," I said. "Which direction?"

"Hmmm..." He pulled a coin out of his pocket and flipped, catching it perfectly flat in his palm. "North." He flipped again. "West." He flipped a third time. "West it is." We reached the exit and moved out of the crowded lobby into the brisk night air. The temperature had dropped at least ten degrees during the two-and-a-half hour show. "West is this way." He pointed past the valet station and started walking.

"Remember, I'm in heels." I struggled to keep up with his long strides. Even if I'd been wearing flats, he was going too fast for me. "I know I said I was starving, but I didn't mean it literally. What's the hurry?"

"Sorry." He stopped and gestured ahead of him. "And, we're here."

"I guess restaurant roulette isn't as exciting in an urban setting," I said, looking up at the awning. "Theater Bistro. Original name. It looks pretty dark inside, think they're closed?"

"The hours say they should be open. Only one way to find out." He pulled open the door. "It's our lucky day."

I rolled my eyes as I walked past him inside and found the hostess counter. They were definitely open – there was a ten-minute wait for a table. "Or the bar is available now, if you'd prefer," the hostess said.

"Sounds good to me," Sedric replied. By which point, my stomach grumbled loudly enough for them to both hear, so I didn't protest as she grabbed two menus and led us to the bar in the back of the restaurant.

"Can I get you started with a cocktail or a glass of wine?" the bartender asked as Sedric pulled out my chair. No one had ever done that for me before, not even Val or Hero. It was a tall, backed barstool and I had to step up on the rung at the base to get to the actual seat, nearly falling in the process. Awkward. But Sedric only laughed a little.

"A gin and tonic would be great," I told the bartender.

"Merlot for me," Sedric said, taking his own seat. When the bartender turned his back, Sedric leaned towards me. "I thought ballerinas were supposed to be graceful."

"Maybe if I were still a ballerina, I would have been. Or maybe whoever invented these chairs was a tall man and purposefully made it impossible for women to sit in them so he would have something to laugh at when he went to bars."

"I like that theory."

"Why is it so dark in here? I can barely see the menu, let alone read it."

"I think," he paused to survey the room, "it's supposed to be romantic. Check it out – we're the only non-bonded people here."

I swiveled as far around in my chair as I could. He was right. Every table was a two-seater, and each was occupied by a lovey-dovey couple holding hands, looking solemnly into each others' eyes, and generally making me want to puke. "What did you say about it being our lucky day?"

"Maybe the atmosphere isn't exactly what we would have wanted, but if it's a romantic restaurant, the food is probably good."

"Can you even see what the food options are?"

"I'll do you one better," he said. The bartender turned around and set a glass in front of each of us. "What are your specials tonight?" Sedric asked.

"We have a delicious duck confit with roasted asparagus, the three-time winner of The Daily News' Best Dish in the City. Also, a grilled Portobello mushroom over lemon-sage risotto, and the Chef's new fried lamb chops with golden russet mashed potatoes – the perfect savory treat for a cool night like tonight."

"That all sounds delicious," Sedric said, rubbing his chin. "I'm leaning towards the fried lamb chops. Are they as good as they sound?"

"Better."

"Okay, put me down for that. What are you liking, Honor?"

"I'll go with the duck."

"Excellent choice," the bartender said. "I'll have a server put the order in for you. Let me know if you need your drinks refreshed." He bowed his head and slid down the counter to a new pair who had just been seated.

"This meal is going to cost as much as our hotel rooms. Think the company will accept our receipts?"

"They better." Sedric took a sip of his wine. I wished we were sitting at a table. It was too difficult to have a conversation, situated as we were. One or both of us had to twist our torsos around to face each other when speaking. Then again, a table would have been too intimate in this place. Talk about awkward.

"Did you enjoy the ballet?" I asked.

"I did, very much. It wasn't really what I expected."

"What did you expect?"

He paused, a finger to his chin. "Frilly tutus and unitards."

"There were both tutus and unitards."

"Yes, but they weren't ridiculous, and after the dance began I basically forgot about them."

I clicked my tongue. "You were buying into stereotypes."

He held up his hands. "Guilty." Then, after a thoughtful silence, "I can see you up on stage, dancing that dance."

"Except you've never seen me dance."

"There's this little thing called imagination."

Did face planting on our office's carpet indicate the level of coordination needed to perform like a prima ballerina? "And you filled in all you know about me from the very ungraceful moments we've shared together?"

He shrugged.

"You know something I just realized?" I hopped my chair around, so I could look directly at him without suffering a crick in my spine.

"What?"

"You're an avoider, just like me."

He sputtered slightly on his drink. "Is that so?"

"I suggested we go out tonight because you had a stressful day and I thought you might want to talk about it. I was trying not to be so selfish for a change. But what did you do? You chose to see the ballet because I like it. And you won't tell me what happened with Nayja. You're avoiding it."

"I don't think you're selfish."

Sometimes Sedric acted like he was trying to convince himself I was someone better than I actually was. It was really irritating. "And that proves my point. You didn't address any of the things I said about you. Please, I don't want to talk about me anymore."

He shook his head.

I continued, "I'm sure you've found this out – being alone makes you selfish. It's made me incredibly so. There are days where I feel like I'm on nobody's radar but my own – when no one else is thinking about me or caring how I am or what I'm doing. And those days suck. But do you know what's worse?"

He met my eye.

"The days when no one else is on my radar. When the only person I think about or act for is myself. I don't want to be that person. So please – please, can you help me? Let me put you on my radar for a little while."

"Honor, I…"

"What?"

"I don't know." He dropped his hands to his lap.

"I don't know either. I don't know you."

"Yes, you do."

"I don't. I've never really been able to get to know men. It's missing from my DNA or something."

"Maybe you just don't pay attention." He patted my arm and my brain focused on his touch – the calluses on his fingers. He liked to work with his hands. At Bonnie and Caron's he mentioned he had a shop and worked on cars. But was it just cars? No, he always smelled faintly of sawdust and something else woodsy. Maybe he carved wood or built furniture.

Conversations with him came back to me like a slideshow of vacation photos. He was a foodie – he loved trying new foods and liked to find new, fun places to eat wherever he was. I looked him over. He was tall, a big man, but not overweight. With all the eating he did I'd expect him to be at least a little chunky, but he was muscular, lean even. So, he must do some sort of workout or exercise regime.

I thought about all the times he mentioned puzzles and challenges. He liked to study and fix things. He probably selected me as his guide through the company because he could tell I needed a lot of fixing.

His hand was still on my arm. I gently took it in my own and flipped it over to see his lark. He was hurt, scarred, and even broken. Just like I was.

When I looked up, his eyes were waiting. No one had ever looked at me that eagerly. What did he want from me? To admit that I did know him, or at the very least, that I was getting to know him? Or was it something more that he wanted? Something the Gods hadn't predestined for us – something that could never be.

I dropped his hand. For a moment, it felt like it had burned me. He turned away and faced the wall behind the bar, staring at the different colored bottles of vodka, gin, rum, and tequila.

It was too much. He was supposed to be helping me discover who my mate was, but in that moment all that mattered was learning more about Sedric. The backs of my knees were sweating and caused a little squeak when I shifted in my seat.

Sedric cleared his throat, but didn't look at me. "You want me to talk about myself. Is there anything in particular you want to know?"

I shook my head, but he still wasn't looking at me. "No," I whispered. Now that he'd agreed, though, there were so many things I wanted to know. What was his family like? Why had he gone into business consulting? Why didn't he and Zara have children? He chose the one topic I would never have had the courage to ask about.

"It was winter, the first big snow. Zara wanted to watch the neighborhood children throwing snowballs at each other and making snowmen and angels. She insisted, even though she didn't particularly like our neighbors or kids, and I didn't really see any merit in watching anyone else have fun out in the cold.

"She wrapped a scarf around my neck before putting on her heavy coat and gloves. I told her I would make us some hot chocolate and meet her outside.

"I took my time. I didn't really want to go out. We had a fire in the living room and it just seemed pointless. I added whipped cream and cinnamon to the top of each drink and headed for the front door. I couldn't see her through the glass, it wasn't until I opened it and stepped onto the porch that I saw her." His voice faltered and he took a second to thumb his palm.

"She slipped on the first step, I think. It was covered in ice and I guess she hadn't bothered with the railing. I don't know if she screamed or cried out for help. When I came outside, she was lying on the path leading up to our steps..." he choked up again, but seemed determined to get through it, "...a pool of blood around her head."

I knew it was coming, but I couldn't stop the gasp that escaped my lips.

"I dropped the mugs, they shattered. I ran to her, lifted her up, but her pulse was gone. I yelled and yelled for help. I don't know how long I yelled. Finally, a neighbor came running over. He shouted to his mate to call for an ambulance. There was nothing the paramedics could do for her when they got there. She was gone."

"Oh, Sedric."

He laid his hand, palm up, on the bar, looking into it as if he could see her there, lying in the snow, surrounded by blood. "I could not have been prepared, even if I'd known it was going to happen. Nothing prepares you for the pain you feel when you lose your mate. Not just the emotional pain, it's physical, too. My body didn't know what to do with itself. My pull kept trying to find her, like it refused to believe she was gone. It would lead me all over the city, to her favorite spots.

"There were days I wanted to die. I wanted to give up everything and follow her to the grave. I think it could have happened if I let it. If I had just given up and stopped living, my heart would have stopped beating and I would have been with her again."

"Why didn't you?" I asked.

"I don't know. I guess I had more willpower than I thought. I knew my lifegivers would be devastated, and my brother and his family. And Zara's lifegivers – they lost their daughter, I thought I owed it to them to live on."

"For what it's worth, I'm glad you did."

"There have been times, little moments every day since the initial shock wore off, where I've felt that pull to just die. But, since I've met you, they haven't been as frequent. What do you think that means?"

I gulped and finally picked up my drink. The glass left a ring of water on the bar in its place. I swirled the contents and took a sip. "I'm not Zara, Sedric. I can't be her."

"You're nothing like her and I wouldn't want you to be. But we're friends, right? I think I really need a friend."

Hesitating, I took another sip. He watched me set the glass back on the counter. I met his eye. My chest tightened. "Yeah, we're friends."

Chapter Thirteen: Baking is Complicated

I didn't suggest another outing the following night, Thursday. We headed to the local library and continued research into the likely reasons my lifemate would have moved from region to region so quickly. I didn't ask Sedric to share any more of himself and he didn't try to steer the conversation toward me. We didn't say much at all except to compare notes on new theories.

I told him I'd understand if he didn't want to continue researching with me – if it was too painful to be reminded of his own mate so constantly – but he said it helped keep his mind off her. I tried to believe him.

On our way to the airport Friday night, Sedric broke our quiet-in-the-car rule. "I did something a little stupid."

"Just one thing?"

"Recently."

"What did you do?" I asked.

"I told my brother and his mate how delicious your cakes are."

"I thought you said stupid. That sounds like a pretty genius move to me."

"You're not going to think so in a minute. My lifegivers' anniversary is this weekend and when I talked up your baking skills with my brother, he assigned cake duty to me for their party." He looked over his shoulder to check his blind spot before switching lanes.

"Do you know how to bake?"

"Not at all. I was hoping-"

"You want me to bake a cake for your lifegivers?" I turned the radio down and crossed my arms. Why had I told him the truth about the Dessert Fairy?

"Or teach me how to make one."

I groaned. "You're right. You did something really stupid."

He laughed. "Can you help me?"

"I'd say no, but then I'd be a colossal bitch, wouldn't I?"

"You mean, because I've been helping you without asking for anything in return?"

"Here comes the return."

He switched lanes again, using his blinker like a good little boy. "If it's too much trouble…"

"It's not. Not *too* much. When's the party?"

"Sunday."

"I guess I'm coming over tomorrow."

Sedric's house, much like him, was unassuming and simple. Just your basic, two-story, brick house. I noticed a wooden shed in the backyard when I drove around the corner to park, and the garage was larger than average.

The path to the front porch felt ominous. I thought I saw a patch of grass growing darker than the rest of the lawn at the base of the steps, but it was probably my eyes playing tricks on me. I gripped the rail tightly as I climbed the steps, then reached for the doorbell.

"Hey!" Sedric threw the door open, inviting me in with arms spread and a wide grin.

"You're chipper today."

"It's cake baking day."

I laughed. "Did you get all the ingredients on the list I gave you?"

"In the kitchen. This way." He led me through the narrow parlour off the front door, down a hallway, and past a larger, open living room. Several cardboard boxes were stacked against the walls in the latter. The kitchen looked like it had never been used – it was both spotless and empty. No dishes in the sink, no magnets on the fridge.

It dawned on me: this wasn't the home Sedric shared with Zara. He had just moved in. He must have relocated for the job. What was that like, leaving behind the home and all the memories he'd shared with his mate?

I guessed it was better than living with daily reminders.

"Do you have bowls, beaters, that kind of thing?" I asked.

"Somewhere." He brushed past me and started opening cabinets. "Junie helped me unload the kitchen stuff. I'm not sure where she put everything."

"Who's Junie?"

"One of my lifegivers."

"Ah. If she's anything like me, her kitchen organization is all about practicality. We're going to use the island here to prep our baking, so the bowls and mixer should be in the cabinets beneath it." I opened them and found exactly what I needed. "Junie and I think alike."

"You actually do remind me of her a little."

"I hope that's a compliment."

"It is."

"What else do we have in common?" I busied myself about the kitchen, pulling out everything we'd need to make the cake. His fridge was completely empty except the ingredients I'd instructed him to buy.

"She doesn't back down easily, either. Neither of you let a lot of people in."

"That doesn't sound like a compliment."

"I didn't mean it as one. How's this, you both have lifelong friends you are incredibly loyal to?"

"What you know about me and Bonnie doesn't exactly point to loyalty on my part."

He rolled his eyes, but looked thoughtful when he continued, "Maybe your situation reminds me of hers."

My situation? Which situation was he referring to? Mateless, or stuck in a thankless job, or denied my true calling due to really bad luck? I didn't even want to know. "Here, crack two eggs into this bowl and then add the milk and butter."

I mixed the dry ingredients in a separate bowl while he followed my instructions, referring to the recipe I laid on the counter for measurements. I didn't ask any more questions about Junie. Once the batter was smooth and the oven pre-heated, I slid the pan in and set the timer.

"We've got about thirty minutes, but it still has to cool before we can ice it."

"So, time to kill?"

"Basically."

"Wine?" he asked.

"I'd love some."

He uncorked a bottle and pulled two wine glasses out of a cabinet above the fridge.

"You know where those are."

"The most used items in my house," he said.

"Mine, too."

He handed me a half-full glass. "Music?"

"Sure."

We walked into the living room and he motioned for me to take a seat while he fiddled with the control panel on his screen for a few seconds, ultimately landing on a classical station. "Is this okay?"

"It's pretty." Strings blended with wind instruments and took me out of the room – onto a stage. Lights down, curtain up, and hundreds of blank audience faces, waiting for me to take the first step, leap, and turn. "I've danced to this piece before," I said to myself, forgetting Sedric was there.

"When?"

His voice pulled me back to the present. "Years ago. In school. We did *Spring in Bloom* as our final graduation performance."

"Do you remember the moves?"

"The moves? Man, you really know nothing about ballet, do you? It's called choreography. The individual steps are broken up into eight counts."

"Excuse me. Do you remember the choreography?"

"I think so."

"Can you show me?"

"Here? There's not enough room." I thought that would be the end of it. I didn't want to show him. I hadn't danced in years. Even though I was sure I'd remember it the second I started moving – dancing was like riding a bike to me, once learned never forgotten – what if I wasn't as good as I once was?

We'd just seen the best company in the world perform the best ballet ever written with the best choreography ever designed. I did not want him to think it was a good thing I'd been injured and forced to stop.

"I have a basement. It's an open floor plan. Would that work?"

Hopefully not. "Depends on how wide the room is and how tall the ceilings are."

"Let's go have a look. I'd love to see you dance."

Why couldn't I just tell him I didn't want to do it? I looked at the grandfather clock standing against the wall in front of me. 5:17. That couldn't be; I'd arrived around one. "Your clock isn't right."

"It's been broken for a while."

"Why don't you get it fixed?"

"I, um… it's not that easy." He took a sip of his wine and played some more with the menus on the screen.

"There are a lot of repair shops downtown."

"I'm sure I could find someone to repair it. Hell, I could do it. I don't want to get it fixed, I guess."

I turned to look at it again. The second hand was twitching as if it wanted to move forward, but just didn't have the stamina or momentum to do so. "It's a beautiful clock. It seems a shame to let it perish without trying to help it."

"I replaced the glass, that's the best I can do."

"What happened to it?" I stepped towards it and let my fingers glide over the mahogany – over the carved suns, moons, and stars around the face.

"I punched it."

"What?" Sweet, mild-mannered, nothing-fazes-him Sedric punched the glass out of a clock? What could have set him off?

"I made it for our fifth anniversary. She hated it."

"How could she hate this – it's gorgeous! You really made it?"

"She didn't like the noise. It ticked very loudly. I tried changing the mechanisms, but it must be the acoustics of the piece itself, because I could never lower the volume of the ticking."

"The suns – those are for her?"

"Yeah."

The pad of my finger circled around one of the spheres. It was about the same size as Sedric's lark. "I can't believe she didn't like it."

"I stopped liking it after a while."

"And that's why you punched it?"

"No. We fought about it constantly, but I didn't break it until after-"

"Oh. The reminders."

"Sort of. After her funeral, I was just so angry and confused by my pull, and everyone was giving me advice and it was too much. The first thing I saw when I walked into the house was that damn clock. I remembered how much she hated it and the hurt and pain built up until I needed an outlet."

"At least it doesn't tick loudly anymore."

He laughed. "That's another reason I did it."

I sighed. How could I deny dancing for him after that? "The basement?"

"This way."

A string hung from the top of the doorframe, and when Sedric tugged on it, a shaky light bulb sputtered to life. The stairs down were wooden, poorly stained, with nails sticking out in random spots.

"Watch your step."

"Yeah, I got that on my own, funny enough. Sedric, if I didn't trust you, I'd think you were leading me down to your chamber of torture. This is super creepy."

He chuckled. "What makes you think you can trust me?"

I gripped the railing tighter and took a step backward towards the door.

"I'm kidding! I know it's a little scary right now, but I haven't had time to remodel yet. It's on my five-year plan."

"You have a five-year plan?" I asked.

"You don't?"

"Do I seem like the type of person who has a five-year plan?"

"Don't I seem like the type of person who does?"

I moved back down so we were on the same step. I wanted to look into his face and the wise lines around his eyes. "You do, but why would you want to be that way? I tried to plan my life and look where it got me. Alone, trapped in a horrible job while everyone I love moves on with their lives."

"If I don't, I'll go crazy. It's one thing to take risks and try new things; it's another to not know where your life is going."

We reached the bottom of the steps and he found another string. More shaky, yellow light. It lit the room, but just barely. The space was open – wide enough to turn and stride through the choreography, and high enough to leap and jump without hitting my head.

"This'll do," I said. "I don't know that you'll be able to see much, though."

"There's a big lamp down here somewhere." He strode across the floor to the far north corner of the room. *Click.* More light. Enough for what we were doing.

The room was almost completely empty. The lamp he turned on and a bare bookshelf near the entrance were the only pieces of furniture. A few more boxes provided storage beside the shelves.

I walked the length of the room, then the width, my brain taking cues from my body to alter the blocking of the dance to account for the space. Sedric kept quiet.

"I can't hear the music," I said.

"I think I can turn it up loud enough to hear down here. Don't start until I get back, okay?"

"Sure."

He sprang up the first couple of steps and out of my sight. I stretched my arms over my head, trying to reach the ceiling, then bent at the waist for my toes. I wasn't as limber as I once was and the effort ached. Backing up against a wall, I lifted my right leg until my foot was over my head.

"Damn!" Every muscle screamed that I'd pushed too hard. I stretched the left leg the same way. It wasn't the best warm up, but I didn't have a bar, or a coach yelling out positions.

Strains of the piece from earlier floated down the stairs and through the vents. It gradually grew louder until I could plainly hear the tempo and lovely nuances of each instrument. I practiced a turn. My feet responded with dull pain.

"Hey," Sedric complained, "you were supposed to wait for me!"

"I'm not starting, just warming up."

"Oh. Okay. Sorry."

"It's not going to look as good as the ballet we saw. I'm out of shape and I don't have my pointe shoes. Don't expect greatness, got it?"

"I'm not."

I took a deep breath and positioned my feet in first. "Get as far into the corner as possible."

He shuffled backwards and sat atop one of the banished boxes. I took another breath and raised my arms above my head in a halo. In a whisper, I counted off, "five, six, seven, eight," and began.

The steps came effortlessly, as if they'd been waiting a long time for me to visit again. The soreness in my muscles disappeared and my arms became wings, helping me soar above the room. My unhappiness and bitterness worked their way through my toes, knees, thighs, and up my torso until I released them into the air through my fingertips. My shoulders were a million times lighter as I spotted my turns using Sedric's eyes as a guidepost. His intensity matched my own. I attacked the dance, like a mother bear protecting her cub.

In the final notes of the song, I leapt, landing perfectly on my tiptoes and bowing into the end. A five second pause between songs enabled me to remain in trance, but when it transitioned into an angry cello piece, I snapped my head up. Sedric was wiping his eyes.

"That bad?"

"Pria, no! It was beautiful. Absolutely amazing. I didn't expect it to be more graceful than *Life and Death*."

"There's no way it was better than the one we watched together."

"You lit up the room. It's like you were the dance; like it was coming straight out of your heart."

I could feel the heat on my cheeks, and it wasn't from the exercise. "That's sweet of you to say, but..."

"I'm not trying to flatter you, or lying to make you feel good about yourself or anything. I mean it. I've never seen a performance like that." He stood and took a few steps toward me as I moved for the stairs.

"But you don't watch dance anyway."

"If you're determined not to take the praise, fine. But you are amazing. I can't believe you just stopped."

"The timer is going to go off any minute now. We don't want to over bake the cake. No one wants a dry cake." My feet hurt again, but I let them carry me quickly up the steps, feeling every splinter and knot in the wood through my flats. My body groaned under the strain of walking. Practicing that dance without any kind of preamble was stupid. I would feel the effects even worse the next day.

Perfect timing – the buzzer started dinging as I entered the kitchen. "Where are your potholders?" Sedric opened a few drawers beside the stove and produced a pair of bright orange ones. "I'm guessing you picked these out," I said.

"Huh?"

"No woman would choose bright orange potholders that clearly do not match anything else."

"Excuse me, they match these." He swung a set of measuring spoons with orange handles from his index finger.

"My mistake." I opened the oven door and slid the cake out.

"Is it ready?"

"Stick a toothpick in and we'll find out."

He rummaged around several more drawers before finding a small pack of wooden toothpicks. It rattled as he approached the cake. "Anywhere?"

"The middle is best. Edges cook faster, so they aren't a good judge."

He jabbed the pick into the center and turned to me eagerly. "Now what?"

I laughed. "Pull it out. If it comes out clean, the cake is done."

He gingerly removed the stick and held it up for me to inspect. A few miniscule crumbs clung to it. "Not bad. It's not quite done, but if we leave it here on the stove, the internal heat will continue cooking it and it will be perfect."

"How long does it need to cool before we can ice it?"

"We'll give it about ten minutes before we take it out of the pan, but it will need to cool down to room temperature before we frost it. Probably another ten minutes. Maybe fifteen. It varies. We can make the icing after we flip it out of the pan."

"Not now?"

"No, it will start to harden if we let it sit too long."

"Baking is complicated."

I threw the toothpick away. "Not really. You just haven't done much of it."

"You like pointing out when I don't know a lot about a topic."

"Not just you, everyone. It makes me feel superior."

"I guessed as much," he said.

"Ten minutes to kill, then."

"Do you want a tour of the house?"

"I've already seen the basement – is the rest of the house as exciting?" I asked.

"Even more so."

"Can't resist that, can I?"

He looked around, trying to figure out where to start. "Okay – this is the kitchen."

"Yes, I think we've covered that."

"Follow me, fair lady."

"That's unnecessary," I said.

He laughed. "This is the living room."

"Yep, we've been here already, too." I patted the side of the grandfather clock.

"Up we go, then." He bounded towards the main staircase. I'd never seen him so exuberant. Weird, considering he hadn't lived there long. How attached to the house could he be?

The staircase leading to the upper level contrasted sharply with the one leading down. It was beautiful, with natural, smoothly polished wood and a handrail curled into a spiral detail at the footer. Along the wall hung several framed photos, because isn't that where everyone memorialized their loved ones? The first showed him as a teenager with another young man, two men in their early-to-mid forties, and a woman, probably in her late thirties. One of the men was very short, with a full head of graying hair and ridiculously thick sideburns. The other was very tall; at least six inches taller than the short man, and a head taller than Sedric himself. He was going bald, but kept a neatly trimmed beard. The men stood side by side, the tall man's arms around the short man's shoulders.

"My family," Sedric said.

"Junie?" I pointed to the woman. She was seated in the center of the portrait, with all of the men in a semi-circle around her.

"That's her."

"You have her wise eyes."

He raised an eyebrow. "You think I have wise eyes?"

"Has no one ever told you that before? You have wisdom just oozing out of them."

His hand came up to the side of his neck – was I embarrassing him? I turned back to the photographs. "Your brother, I'm guessing," pointing at the other teenager.

"Mateo."

"And these gentlemen?"

"Reuben and Hal. My lifegivers."

"But Junie..."

"Also my lifegiver. We have a very unique family," he said.

"So it would seem."

"Come on, don't you want to see the rest of the house?" He ascended quickly, leaving me no choice but to follow and forego examination of the other pictures.

"My home office." He opened the door on a very basic room: desk, chair, bookshelves, and small leather couch.

"Nice."

Crossing the hall, he peered into another room. "This will be a guest room when I have the time to get furniture made, there's not really anything in here yet."

"Okay."

"And my bedroom." The last room on the hall took up most of the second floor. It reminded me of the fancy hotel suites we'd been staying in – open, large furniture, but no real life. Where were the condensation rings on the nightstand, or laundry hamper overflowing with clothes? It was sterile. Even the bed looked like a maid had just completed turndown service.

"Check out the closet," he said, pushing aside a sliding, mirrored door. I stepped in and gawked at the square footage devoted to Sedric's wardrobe, which didn't even fill half the space. A wall of shelves for shoes only held six pairs. It was a fashionista's dream.

"This is really lost on you, isn't it?"

"Not after seventeen years living with Zara. If she were here, my clothes would be in the guest room, or the office."

"Are you going to fill it up?"

"Nah. I'll remodel this level after the basement. Probably condense this room, add another, and expand the bathroom so it can be shared."

"But it's just you."

"I know," he said, wistfully. I hadn't meant to burst his bubble, but who was he making plans for? Why did he need a third bedroom? And who did he need to share the bathroom with?

"Oh, the cake!" I checked my watch. "It's time to flip it out of the pan. This will really show your lifegivers what a pro-baker you are – that you aren't serving it in the same pan you baked it in."

"I'm aiming to impress them as much as possible."

"Go down and assemble one of the boxes I brought. Do you mind if I use your bathroom?"

"Not at all. See you in a second."

I used the bathroom quickly, washed my hands, and took a moment to look inside the medicine cabinet behind the mirror. Nothing out of the ordinary – aspirin, razors, and shaving cream. I picked up a green bottle and popped the top to inhale the scent. Mmmm... Sandalwood with a hint of pine. I wanted to dab some on my clothes so I could take the scent home with me, but instead, I recapped it and placed it on the second shelf before closing the mirror and walking away.

What I really wanted to see, and the real reason I stayed behind, was at the top of the stairs. A picture of Sedric and Zara in a sleek, black frame. She had long, dark hair, wide eyes, and a crooked smile. Sedric was standing behind her, his arms engulfing her body, one around her waist, the other crossing over her collarbone. He was laughing as he looked down at her. Biting my lip, I looked away. Whatever this friendship between Sedric and I was, he would never look at me like that. Never hold me like that. No one would. Why was I torturing myself?

In the kitchen, Sedric had successfully extracted the cake from the pan and set it on a cooling rack. The ingredients for the icing were on the island, in a neat little row, arranged according to the list I'd given him.

"You okay, Honor?"

"Of course, why?"

"Your eyes are red."

"I sneezed. My eyes must have watered up."

"Check it out." He pointed at his triumphant cake. I clapped my hands together a few times. "Thank you, thank you," he said.

We made the icing and frosted the cake – Sedric didn't have much luck spreading smoothly. He kept getting crumbs from the top of the cake mixed in with the icing. "How do you make it so pretty?" he groaned.

"It's not your fault, it's mine. We didn't let it cool long enough. Don't worry, it'll still taste good."

"I wanted it to look nice for them."

"It will. We're going to add words, too. Here, let me." I took the piping bag and used a gentle hand to spell out, *Happy Anniversary*. "Do you want names, too?"

"Yeah. Reuben and Hal."

"What's the story there?"

"Hal and Reuben are mated. They wanted kids; enter Junie."

"What's Junie's story?"

"It's a lot like yours and mine. That didn't come out right. Your story. My story. Our two separate stories, not our story."

So that was the situation. "I got what you meant. Her lifemate died?"

He nodded. "Hey, would you like to come to the party tomorrow? It's mostly family, but we'd be happy to have you. And we can leave straight for the airport."

I looked from him to the cake. Celebrating a happy pairing would have sounded like a death sentence to me a few days ago, but in that moment, it just sounded nice. "I don't want to be a bother, or in the way."

"Not at all."

"Okay then. Yes. I'll go."

Chapter Fourteen: Playing House

The cake balanced on my lap, in a white box with one of my Dessert Fairy stickers keeping it sealed, all the way to Sedric's lifegivers' house. The drive took about an hour Sunday afternoon and we were heading straight to the airport afterwards for another week of client workshops.

"Welcome, welcome, my darling!" Junie opened the door and engulfed Sedric in a hug. Her face was bright, warm, and just as inviting as her greeting. "This is your friend?" She reached a hand out to me.

"Yes, this is Honor. We work together."

"And isn't my darling a wonderful man to work with?" she asked me.

"He's okay." I smiled and she gripped my right hand, laughing, while I balanced the cake with my left.

"He told me about you, said you were quite the jokester. I like you already, Ms. Honor."

"Well, that's different. I like you already, too."

"Come in, come in, you two. Don't stand in the doorway. Sedric, my darling, introduce your friend to everyone."

"I was planning on it, Junie." Sedric grinned at me with a careless roll of his eyes. If Junie had been out of earshot, he would have said something like, "lifegivers, never letting you grow up." At least, that's what I would have said.

When we passed through the entrance and found ourselves alone, I poked him in the ribs. "I thought you said it took a while to get to know her. I already feel like I do."

"You've only seen the surface."

"Who doesn't love such a wonderful, shiny, happy surface?"

"I'm surprised. I thought you'd immediately dislike her for exactly those things."

"I dislike happiness when it's ignorant or vapid. Or, if I'm being completely honest, when it reminds me of what I can't have. Junie is none of those things."

An eyebrow arched, but he didn't say anything as he opened the patio door and led me to a walled-in, screen-covered porch. A hole in the ceiling let out smoke from a fire pit. It only needed night to fall to be completely charming and over-the-top.

When we crossed the threshold, Sedric waved to two gentlemen sitting on a squishy couch across from the door. They looked like the men from his family photograph, but older of course. Standing, they came towards us. Each hugged Sedric and turned to me with tight, closed mouths. The shorter one looked at me like I was wearing an 'I kill puppies for fun' sign on my forehead.

"This is my friend, Honor," Sedric said.

"Welcome to our home." The taller man held out a hand for me to shake. His expression was friendlier than his mate's, but not by much. Maybe instead of killing the puppies, he thought I only tortured them.

"Happy Anniversary." I handed him the cake box.

"How... sweet," he said. "We'll be sure to put this out after dinner."

"Sedric made it."

"I don't believe that," the shorter one said, lightly jabbing Sedric's shoulder, who feigned a pained expression. His being playful with Sedric seemed like a step in the right direction, but when he looked back to me, it was like the joking gesture never happened.

"He did, I promise. I gave him directions, but that's all." I tried to smile, but the two gentlemen were looking me up and down, and exchanging furtive glances with each other. My face stiffened and I squared my shoulders, determined not to let them see how much their reaction was bothering me.

"I didn't tell you who was who, did I, Honor?" Sedric asked. I shook my head. "This is Reuben." He gestured to the shorter man. "And this scoundrel is Hal." Another teasing punch, but from Sedric to his lifegiver that time.

Hal responded with a quick head nod and a, "Make yourself comfortable," before the pair walked into the house.

"Why do I get the feeling they don't want me here?"

Sedric's gaze followed after them, a confused expression scrunching up his eyebrows. "I don't know. That was really weird. Oh, look," he pointed behind me, "that's my brother. Let me introduce you."

"Because the last introduction went so well."

He steered me past a couple of family friends and put me in the care of Mateo, his brother, and Mateo's lifemate, Senner. "I'm just going to touch base with Hal and Reuben and see what's up with them." Sedric went inside and I put on a fake smile.

"Do you enjoy chaos, Honor?" Mateo asked. He practically had to shout over the raucous conversations and games going on around us. One group of people was tossing marshmallows at each other, trying to catch them in their mouths. A couple making out in the corner created slurping noises loud enough to invoke images of water slides. Gross.

"I suppose so, as much as anyone else."

"This is chaos central, so beware."

"I can see that. I thought Sedric said it would be mostly family."

"Yeah, that's right. A few friends here and there," Mateo pointed at the slurping couple, "but mostly just the Eckland and Rogerstan clans."

"No outsiders welcomed in to the chaos?"

"Not usually." He grinned. "Can I get you something to drink? It's not normal to see anyone around here without a glass in their hand."

"You don't have to do that. I think I passed through the kitchen on the way out here. I can get something for myself."

"Are you sure? I don't mind."

"Yeah, you look comfortable. It would be a shame to make you leave the chaos." I stepped over an ottoman and went back inside, thankful to get away from the noise and regretting that I came. After a few twists and turns, I found myself at the end of a hallway, a door on each side. The left hand opened into a bathroom. I put my hand on the knob of the right door, when I heard voices. One was definitely Sedric's; the other was male, so I guessed either Hal or Reuben. I didn't remember coming through that particular hallway when we arrived, so I figured I made a wrong turn somewhere, and was about to move on when the unidentified male voice said my name.

I wanted to walk away, but the sound of my name was too enticing and my feet remained planted firmly in the carpet. I twisted the knob slowly and eased the door open.

"I don't understand what you're doing."

"I'm not doing anything," Sedric said.

"You've brought her here, to a family function. She knows your situation. You lost a wonderful, sweet, woman. You can't just replace Zara with this girl. You're going to give her the wrong impression."

Sedric's voice was strained. "What exactly do you think the wrong impression would be?"

"That you're available to her."

"That's uncalled for. I can't believe you, of all people, are lecturing me on this. You and Hal and Junie created one of the most untraditional families I've ever seen, and it's always been wonderful and loving."

"You want to have a family with this woman?"

"That's not what I said." There was a pause. When Sedric spoke again, his voice was lower. "I lost Zara, but does that mean I should never have a family?"

I closed the door. I didn't even try and keep it quiet. I didn't deserve to be talked about like that and didn't want to hear their argument. Winding my way through the house, I finally located the kitchen and searched through the drink selection, deciding on a sweet white wine to take the edge off.

"Oh, it's my darling's lovely friend. Hello, Ms. Honor." Junie came toward me, arms open and smile wide. She looked like her son. I took a gulp of wine.

"What is troubling you?" she asked.

"Did Sedric tell you about me? About my lark and my mate?"

Her smile drooped. "Ah, yes." She took my left hand and covered it, pressing gently. "I know and I understand. Look at this." Releasing me, she bent slightly and lifted the hem of her floor-length skirt to reveal her right ankle. A black blob covered the bone. "You see, my dear, my lark never filled in either. My mate left this world before I had the good fortune to find her."

I took another sip of wine. My head spun, but not from the alcohol. I'd never met anyone else like me before.

"Come, my dear, let's chat for a few minutes." She took my arm, looping it through hers, and pulled me after her. We landed in a large sitting room with several cushy armchairs and a massive stone fireplace. A few tiny logs emitted smoke and flame, the remnants of what must have been a roaring fire hours earlier. Junie directed me to a dark blue chair and she took a green one facing me.

"My darling says we have a lot in common."

"He told me the same thing."

"You know sadness, don't you, my dear?"

It took all my strength to nod.

"And my darling, he knows pain. Poor child, to lose the person he loved so dearly."

Deep breath.

"I believe my darling said your mate passed a few years ago?"

I cleared my throat. "Yes, five, I think."

"I am sorry for you, my dear. How old were you?"

"Twenty-five."

She nodded her head vigorously a few times.

"How old were you?" I asked.

"Too young. Nineteen."

"I'm sorry," I croaked. I kind of wanted to cry. Junie seemed like the type of person who would hold and rock me until I felt better. I hadn't had that in a really long time. Not since I was a kid and Gizella and I actually got along.

"Some things are not meant to be," she said. "Even the things that were. If I had met my mate, I would not have my darlings. It all worked out." She stared into the flames as she spoke. I wondered if she was trying to convince herself that things had worked out.

"Aren't you lonely?"

"Ah, yes, sometimes I am. Other times I am not. Reuben and Hal are family." She seemed just as sincere and kind as Sedric, yet she had to know the harsh reality.

"But you don't mean as much to them as they mean to each other."

Her eyes met mine. "I suppose that's true, but it's an awfully sad way to look at it."

"I can't look at it any other way."

She shrugged her shoulders. "I wanted children; I always knew I was meant to give life. What other option did I have?"

I didn't answer. She was brave. I wouldn't deny that and didn't want to take it away from her; I just couldn't imagine her life for myself. Never being first with anyone. Always the third wheel. It would drive me insane.

"Do you want children, my dear?" she asked.

"It doesn't seem to matter one way or another what I want."

"Of course it does. We control our own destinies."

"Do we? Because I wanted to be a professional dancer, and I broke my ankle. I wanted to love and be loved, and my mate died. I want children, but who am I going to have them with? Two mated men who need a womb? No offense, but that doesn't sound like a destiny I would want, even if I could have it."

"My darling wanted children, his mate did not. Does that mean he'll never have the chance?"

"Zara's dead, he could ask another woman to carry his child if he wanted children so badly."

She smiled. "He could indeed."

"Not me. That's not what I meant." I drank the rest of the wine in my glass and set the empty vessel on a coffee table.

"Why not you? He wants children, you want children."

"I want a family. A man who loves me and a partner in life. Sedric already had his love and I'll never have mine."

"You believe you will never love or be loved?" she asked.

"What else can I believe? He's gone. My mate is dead. I can't change that. I can't go back in time and find him now."

"My dear, you are bitter. You are angry. You are scared."

"I'm not scared."

"You are. You don't know what the future holds for you. You don't have a path neatly laid out like your friends do. It is okay to be scared. Do not let that fear prevent you from living." She pushed herself up and got to her feet. "My darling thinks highly of you. Show me why." And then she left me alone.

"Was this some kind of sick joke?" I asked Sedric when he found me, still alone, an hour later.

"What?"

"Bringing me here to meet your family. Reuben is warning you to not let me get ideas in my head about you and Junie wants me to have your children. I only came here to be part of a happy occasion where I didn't feel envy or guilt, but I walked into an ambush."

"You heard Reuben talking?"

"Just a small portion of your conversation. He doesn't like me, which is fine, but what could he have against me already? We've only just met."

"He doesn't have anything against you. He's more concerned about me, really. From his viewpoint I've moved to a new city, taken a new job, bought a new house, and he thought you might be trying to be my new mate."

"That's ridiculous. It doesn't work like that." Part of me wished it could, but I knew better. The Gods picked ideal matches. It's the only thing I knew with any certainty. Bonnie and Caron. Hero and Gizella. Perfect pairs.

"He's trying to protect me; I told him he had it wrong."

"Did you tell Junie, too?" I stood and walked through the room, looking for a way to exit.

Sedric followed. "What exactly did she say to you?"

"That we both wanted children and should have some together."

"Really?"

"She actually said the 'both-want-children' part. The other part she implied."

"You misunderstood her. Or she meant we could make an arrangement like she did with Hal and Reuben." He motioned left and led me to the front door.

"I think the arrangement is exactly what she meant."

He paused and his knuckles whitened as he gripped the doorknob. "We could, you know."

"Now you're joking." I reached for the knob, too, but he refused to let me grab it.

"Look how great it worked out for my lifegivers."

"Did it, though? Junie says she's happy, but is she, really? How do you imagine we'd arrange things? We'd go down to the fertility doctor, you'd give a sample, and then boom, nine months later, I'd be moving into the spare room with a baby on my hip?"

He shrugged, but let go of the door and let me open it.

"We can't play house. I can't pretend you're my mate and I'm yours. That's not reality." There was a reason the Gods didn't give us matching larks. They knew we weren't right for each other. No matter how much I liked his smile or his laugh, or the way he kept his cool in every situation.

"I know that."

I glanced sideways and he nodded.

"Really, I know it's not an option. I'm sorry," he said.

We walked down the path to the driveway and Sedric's car. I gave a quick jab to his shoulder. "Just making sure," I said. He feigned a laugh. Hopefully that was enough to drop the subject for good.

Chapter Fifteen: Potentials

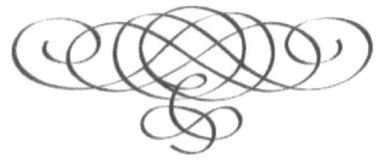

The airplane touched down and my heart fluttered. I could almost sense my pull again. That was crazy, of course, but wasn't the entire journey? I hadn't come to Eribank since my pull abruptly stopped; at the time, I thought it was a sign to stay away. I'd avoided all clients here, but Sedric had one, so it couldn't be avoided any longer.

"You're looking under the weather. Did the flight upset your stomach?" he asked as we exited the airport. I grimaced and shook my head. "Well, what is it then?"

"Nothing." Back to lying. My default mode.

It took what seemed like forever to hail a cab. Eribank was the largest city in the region and traffic was notoriously bad, so we decided not to rent a car. Finally, a bright blue sedan pulled up to the curb. Sedric tossed our bags into the trunk and opened the door for me. We didn't speak at all on the ride to our hotel.

When we parted in the lobby to go to our separate rooms, he turned back and touched my elbow. "Can we be okay? Can we forget the weirdness of visiting my lifegivers?"

"Already forgotten." Another lie, but he looked relieved enough to let me enter my room and close the door on him. I'm not sure how he expected me to forget. I'd been feeling closer and more tenderly towards him – ways I should not have been feeling. His lifegivers were a much-needed wakeup call. I needed to be careful. He was a nice guy; that was all. I couldn't keep confusing him with my long-dead mate.

I powered up the screen and called Val. No one answered. I left a message with the code for my hotel and room number.

It was stifling in the room. I wanted a glass of wine, but that would only make me warmer, so I exercised the little self-control I had and opened a window instead. The breeze that blew in was cool – much better than the sticky heat of the room. I could have changed the thermostat, but I liked the natural air.

I lay on the bed and considered calling Bonnie, but decided against it. I was still angry with her and she hadn't reached out to apologize. I'd also had enough baby talk the last twenty-four hours. I didn't need more. My mind drifted over dozens of topics as I tried to sleep, but settled on Sedric. I wondered what he was doing in his room.

Stop it, stop it, stop it. Stop thinking about him.

I did the only thing I could do to get my mind off Sedric – powered up my laptop and began looking through obituaries.

Melvin Engane, 77

Drenda Malgrove, 81

Fousta Wyndom, 94

Gregory Pulte, 27 – there was a possibility. I clicked the link on his name and a picture of a young man and his dog appeared above a short paragraph.

Gregory collapsed while running a marathon, and passed away in the ambulance on the way to the hospital. He is survived by his mate, Tana, and their beagle, Lucky, as well as his lifegivers Len and Mari Pulte.

I clicked the back button. Gregory had a mate, he wasn't my guy. I continued scrolling through the pages of obituaries from the ninth month of 2008. Hansen Hart, 26, died of an infection following surgery for a ruptured spleen. Alonso Forte, 28, was the victim of a freak accident. A ceiling fan in his living room flew out of its bearings and hit him in the head.

They were all survived by their mates.

Frustrated, I slammed the laptop closed and turned off the lights.

The air around me glowed a purple haze and my body hovered weightlessly above the ground. I wanted to go higher, so I stretched my neck and spread my wings. Zooming upwards, I sped through dewy clouds and didn't stop until I could feel the sun warming my feathers. In this new world, the air was orange and tasted like citrus.

I heard my name — someone below called repeatedly for me to come down. But there was nothing down there. Nothing left for me. Then I heard his voice.

It was deep and warm, flowing out of the bright orb in front of and above me. "Keep flying, Honor," he said. "Keep coming to me."

I wanted to touch him, though I knew touching him would burn my wings and I would fall. It seemed worth it, just to feel his heat that closely. My wings stretched forward; suddenly it was my fingers aching to grasp the sun's rays. Only an inch or two more, the heat was so intense, my face felt like it was melting, but still I went for it. Almost. So close. Just one more second...

I woke in a sweat, though the open window sent cold gusts of air over the bed. A bird flying too high, too close to the sun. Wasn't that an old story?

Every time I closed my eyes, the bright light of the sun scorched my pupils and refused to let me rest.

"You're alert today," Sedric teased, finding me curled into an armchair in the lobby of our hotel, eyes half-closed.

"Don't start. I didn't sleep well." The roughness of my voice would have warned even the dimmest of men to back off, but Sedric only smiled.

"I guess we'll have to get some caffeine in you, then."

"Ugh." I stood, my legs shaking and my head spinning, and followed him outside. The streets were crowded and cabs weren't stopping, so I begrudgingly agreed to walk to our client's building, ten blocks away.

We stopped at a coffee shop, and I vaguely heard Sedric ordering two large coffees. He closed my fingers around a cup a moment later and instructed me to drink. "Why'd you have such a rough night?" he asked once we'd rejoined the horde of pedestrians on the sidewalk.

"Bad dreams."

"That's the worst."

I groaned. The coffee stung the back of my throat. "It's bitter."

"You wouldn't wake up to tell me how you like it."

"You mean you don't know?"

"No need to get nasty."

I forced myself to take another sip. "Now that I think about it, the dream wasn't that bad. Nice, actually. Just the kind I shouldn't be having."

"Why not? You can't help what you dream about."

"Can't you?"

We arrived at his client's office and I swallowed the rest of the coffee. "I don't know if I'm going to be able to workshop today." I was supposed to lead a segment on team building with new employees before Sedric discussed marketing with the managers.

"You'll be fine."

I clutched the empty cup, my fingers curling into it and leaving dents until it was crumpled trash in my hands. "I'm not fine."

He paused, turning to face me in front of the glass doors. City life buzzed around us. People hurrying to work. Car horns honking. Messengers whizzing by on bicycles. "What's going on?" Sedric asked.

"This is the place. This is where my pull was leading when it suddenly disappeared."

"This building?"

"No, this region. This city."

He let out his breath and relaxed his shoulders. "That's right. I didn't realize. Well, that's good."

"Good?"

"Yeah, we'll be able to find more clues."

"I looked through a ton of obituaries online last night, but couldn't find any men who were mateless."

"You were looking at obituaries from papers here?" he asked.

"Yeah."

"I thought your theory was he moved around a lot."

I nodded. "It was. It is."

"Then his obituary wouldn't be in the papers here, would it? It would be in the papers of his hometown."

I hadn't thought of that, but it made sense. Sedric patted my shoulder, but I was focused on the mashed paper cup in my hands. My entire life felt like that cup. Once useful, now nothing but a piece of trash. When he opened the door to let me through, I stopped and placed my hand on his arm. "If his obituary isn't here, how am I going to find him?"

He glanced down at my hand, then met my eye and smiled. "I'm going to help."

The day passed in a blur. My fatigue made enthusiasm difficult, but Sedric pulled through and perked me up whenever he saw me fading. I don't think the group even noticed. At four o'clock the receptionist gave us directions to the closest local library. Sedric patted my shoulder as we headed down the street on foot. "Ready for another night pouring over old newspapers?"

I shrugged, but my insides churned for the duration of the five-block walk. *Tonight might be the night I find out how my mate died. Tonight might be the night I find out who he is.*

The library was a ten-story building, situated on the corner of a busy intersection. A plaque embedded on the side boasted its status as the largest library in the world. A bus dropped off a group of teenagers as Sedric and I approached. "I have a feeling we're not going to get the archives to ourselves tonight," I said.

Entering the front door, we came upon a spacious lobby with plush armchairs and racks of magazines to our right, and a busy cafe with two-seat tables and a harried barista to our left. Sedric strolled ahead, eyes open for a map or signage to point us in the right direction. A massive yellow staircase loomed toward the back of the floor, but the open layout enabled everyone in the library to see it, no matter where they were.

"Sixth floor," Sedric said, suddenly by my side again. "Elevators are behind the magazine racks, or we can take-"

"-the stairs." I was already walking toward them. From the bottom step, I looked up and could see all the way to the top of the building. The vastness and brightness of the place helped me finally appreciate Val's love of libraries. We trudged upwards. I was out of breath by the third floor, and the steep incline got to Sedric as we hit the fourth.

"The elevator would have been a lot easier," he panted.

"The stairs just seemed like the way to go. It's kinda ridiculous, isn't it? We're both in pretty good shape, but we can't walk up five flights of stairs."

"These aren't regular stairs. These are evil stairs."

"Then we've overcome." My foot hit level six and I backed against a wall to wait for Sedric to point the way to the archives. More teenagers passed us while he tried to get his bearings. They didn't seem fazed by the climb at all.

"You know what that means, right?" I pointed them out.

"What?"

"We're *old*."

He laughed heartily, clutching his side for a moment. "I'd rather be old than a snot-nosed, punk kid."

"Really? I think you'd make an excellent snot-nosed, punk kid."

"Come on, I think we need to go this way." He turned left and we followed rows of books to the back of the floor, where a cranky-looking woman sat at a very modern and probably very uncomfortable desk.

"Excuse me, ma'am." Sedric leaned forward, both forearms against the desk. "We're looking for the news archives."

"You've found them," she said, pointing to her right and a row of computers connected to reel projectors. "What time period are you interested in?"

"2008. The ninth month, specifically," I said.

She stood and unlocked a door behind the row of computers. A moment later she returned with what looked like a wooden shoebox. She dropped it in front of Sedric. "Do you know how to work the reels?"

We shook our heads. She sighed painfully and shuffled to the first empty computer. Sedric picked up the box and we followed.

"Put the slide here. Flip this switch. The clip will appear on your screen. Use the knob to scroll through. Flip switch again. Remove slide. Repeat. Got it?"

"Yes, ma'am," Sedic said.

"Don't get those out of order."

"We won't." Sedric offered the seat to me then took the computer beside mine. Crankypants walked away. Sedric got straight to work. "We're looking for any accidents where a young man died, or any listings of death records." He handed me the first slide in the box. "Are you okay to do this?"

Our eyes met. I'm sure mine told him the truth – that I was scared. Scared I wasn't doing the right thing. Scared I was chasing a ghost who didn't want to be found. Scared I wouldn't like what I did find. But all I said was, "Yes."

I read through each headline in every section of the issue on my first slide. Nothing. I did the same for the second. No dice. By the third, I just looked through Section A. Deaths weren't likely to be reported in Arts and Leisure.

"I've got a possibility," Sedric said after twenty minutes of silence. I pushed my chair back so quickly it tipped over and landed me a stern look and "shhhh" from our crotchety instructor. But who cared? I leaned over Sedric's shoulder and read the headline:

Prominent Businessman Leaps to His Death

"Oh, Pria, suicide?" I muttered, reading through the short article to learn more. Brownston Ackles, 29, jumped from an eighteen-story downtown banking institution after being fired for embezzlement. No mate, no children, but a lifegiver was listed as his only survivor.

Sedric's hand landed on my arm. "It's probably not him."

"It fits, though. Right age. No mate. And a businessman – it doesn't say what business, but he may have traveled. We have to consider him. Can you print that?"

Sedric fiddled with the available commands and finally found the print option. When I approached the librarian, she stood and gave me a reproachful glance.

"The chair was an accident," I said.

"Hmph."

"Where can we find the printer attached to these computers?"

"Right here. Every piece of paper is one coin."

I reached in my pocket and pulled out a handful of change. I slid a coin to her and she gave me the page. "We may be printing more."

"Hmph."

I took that as my dismissal and headed back to the computers. "That old bitch could give even me a run for my money."

Sedric laughed. "Want me to do some research on the businessman?"

"No, keep going through the slides. We can do more research on each individual later. Let's not waste our limited time here."

He nodded and put his next slide in. I took a deep breath. The first potential our search produced had committed suicide. Why? Because he hadn't found his mate? Did he even care that he was leaving someone behind? What made him embezzle from his company? I hoped it wasn't him. I wanted answers, but I didn't want those.

Sedric had a lot more luck than me. He found a second possible mate two slides later. Harrison Lionel, 26, had an accident at the firing range he often went to on the weekends. His friends said it helped him relieve stress. He was on his way to a booth to shoot targets when he tripped, dropped the gun, and it went off – hitting him in the heart. He'd forgotten to engage the safety. Again, no mate, only lifegivers listed as survivors.

"I wonder why I didn't find his obituary," I said after Sedric printed the article. "It sounds like he lived in the area. That puts him behind Brownston Ackles on the probability scale."

Thirty minutes later, I found my first prospect. Zachary Blake, 28, a musician touring with his band, stepped into a crosswalk and was hit when a driver ran a red light. After three days in a coma, his lifegivers chose to remove him from life support and he passed away peacefully.

"A touring musician," Sedric said.

"I know. But, a three-day coma. My pull stopped immediately. Seems like it would have kept going, maybe fading, if my mate had been in serious condition. Or it might have gotten even more intense, trying to get me to him before it was too late. Nothing like that happened."

We spent another two hours going through slide after slide, examining all major headlines, and came up with two other potential dead lifemate candidates. I paid the librarian for our pages and thumbed through them, hoping someone's photo would strike a chord, offer me some sort of recognition. But I felt nothing.

"We're taking the lift down, right?" Sedric asked.

"Sure thing."

Chapter Sixteen: Trying to Catch the Sun

Back at the hotel, I spread the articles on my bed and re-read each one. I wished for a spark, for a remnant of my pull to be awakened and tell me if I was on the right path, but again, nothing happened. Sedric sat at the desk beside the window, typing away on search engines, trying to find evidence that the potentials had been to cities listed on my timeline. If he did, or if he couldn't find anything at all, he looked for the last known addresses and contact information for their lifegivers. I reminded him to hunt for pictures, too. If we could find a photo of each of their larks, we'd be able to narrow it down to the one who matched my own.

Garson Kirkey, 27, suffered a rare and incurable disease. The paper examined the treatments he'd gone through, and interviewed the physician at Eribank City Hospital who performed one last surgery in hopes of a miracle. The doctor made a breakthrough, but had been unable to save Garson's life.

Malichi Saunders, 30, a street performer, was found dead, facedown in a puddle, in an alley near a homeless shelter. The coroner hadn't ruled a specific cause of death, but drug abuse was suspected. He'd traveled through many cities along the east coast, leaving a trail of hospital bills and arrest warrants in his wake.

Malichi's story scared me even more than Brownston Ackles's suicide. A drug addict and vagrant wasn't the kind of person I wanted to be associated with. Not knowing kept me free from the stigma, but the second I knew, and other people found out, I would be permanently bonded with him in society's eyes. It wouldn't matter that I hadn't known him in life.

I almost told Sedric to stop looking – that it wasn't worth it. But the pictures of the other three men encouraged me to go on. Didn't they deserve someone who wanted to be bonded to them? Didn't their lifegivers deserve knowing their son would have been loved and cared for? I wanted to be able to meet them and tell them I'd been looking for him, that I hadn't abandoned him or my lark. It might mean something to them.

Sedric packed up his laptop and left the room just before midnight. I lay awake for another hour before my brain finally shut itself down and let me go to sleep.

Heat, glorious heat filled me. My wings carried me higher. I could see the sun. It was so close. My wings pumped harder, desperate to get closer. When it was within reach and I could taste the spicy, tangy rays, my fingers reached forward. I braced myself for the burn.

Beep beep. Beep beep. Beep beep. Ugh. I pounded the snooze button to shut up the alarm clock. I didn't try to get a few more minutes of sleep, though. I didn't want to fly close to the sun. I didn't want to burn anymore.

Birds chirped outside my window. Mocking me. No, that's stupid. They're just birds; they have no hidden motivations. I hadn't done anything to them, why would they do something to me?

I threw the covers off and ambled to the window. The morning was cool and grey – no sun in the sky. I slammed the window shut.

Sedric and I spent another evening in the library, scrolling through slides. Sedric proved himself a much better researcher than I by discovering the Death Records section in the back of the city's largest circulation paper. I'd skipped right over it. The problem with the records, though, was they only gave us a name and age, so every time we came across a male-sounding or gender-neutral name in their mid-to-late twenties or early thirties, we still had to figure out if they were mated.

Luckily, though, there weren't many young men on the lists. After three and a half hours, we had nineteen names that required further research.

"There's only a handful of slides left. We may actually get through them all tonight," Sedric said, feeding one through his projector.

"Good thing. I don't know if I can take another night of the librarian glaring at me. Seriously, what's her problem?"

Sedric glanced behind me to the desk. "She's watching us now."

"She needs to get a life."

He shrugged. "She's just protective of the equipment, I guess."

"Do we look like hooligans who are going to destroy her precious slides, computers, and projectors?"

"You more so than me." He grinned, turning back to his monitor to scan the next list.

I slapped his shoulder. "I can't help it that I'm not a charming, tall, responsible-looking man."

"Charming, huh?"

"She perceives you as charming. That was my point."

"Ah. I guess it's lucky one of us is," he said.

"I don't want to be anyway."

"Big shocker there."

I rolled my eyes. "Okay, okay. I know, I'm a hard ass, I'm a bitch. Can we move on?"

"I don't think you are either of those things. You're just not sunshine and rainbows."

Funny he mentioned sunshine, since I couldn't stop dreaming about it. I couldn't obtain it sleeping or awake, apparently. "What am I then?"

"You're a realist. You don't sugarcoat things."

"Very true. But neither do you."

"I throw a little sugar on." He smiled. "Reality goes down easier that way."

"Reality always tastes fairly bitter to me."

"Hence the sugar."

I focused on my monitor and thought that over. Would life be easier if I just added a little sugar? If I tried to focus on the positive instead of the negative? Probably.

"Do you think we're actually going to find him?" I asked.

"If you really want to find him, we will."

"What's that supposed to mean? If I really want to find him?"

He pushed his chair back from the desk, putting some distance between us. "Do you?"

"Why else would we be here, doing this?"

"You mean this isn't your idea of a fun Tuesday night?"

"I feel empty. Do you understand that?"

He nodded slowly. "What's to say finding him is going to fill you up?"

"Nothing else has."

Sedric wrapped his hand around my wrist; his thumb gently rubbed my lark. I tried to pull away, but he held on. Not forcefully, but reassuringly. "I'm happy to continue helping you look. I'll search every engine, scroll through every one of these slides, pretty much anything short of committing a felony; but I have to tell you, I don't think you're ever going to be satisfied. Finding out who he was can't make up for the fact that he isn't here now."

"It's easy for you to say that."

He sighed and let go. "I suppose it is."

We finished looking through the slides in silence. I didn't invite him to my room for more elimination research, and he didn't offer. I wanted to tell him I would stop looking in a different world — one where we could choose our own fate. But that wasn't an option, so I went to bed early and dreamed about trying to catch the sun.

Chapter Seventeen: Going Through a Phase

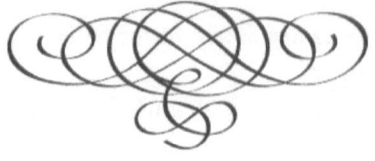

aggage claim was a mess. I cursed silently for checking a bag; I'd always prided myself on my packing abilities. I really should have managed with just a carry-on. One after another, the other passengers from my flight collected their luggage and left the carousel behind. Finally, my grey suitcase tumbled onto the belt. I hauled it down and headed for the exit.

Standing just outside the doors, wearing a chauffeur's cap and holding a white sheet of paper reading "Welcome, Honor," was my beautiful, nine-year old niece. Snow-capped mountains loomed in the distance, creating quite the picturesque scene for my arrival.

"Shyla! Hey, kiddo!" I scooped her into a hug and squeezed.

"Hey, don't break a rib now. I need those."

I laughed and stepped back so I could look at her. "You've gotten so tall. Have you been sneaking growth hormones or something?"

"No, Val says I take after Hero."

"You do look a little like him. Where is your lifegiver, anyway?"

"Circling around. The security guards wouldn't let him stay parked in the loading zone."

"He left you here alone?"

"Oh no, Handor's with me."

I glanced around the sidewalk and into the glass doors leading back to baggage claim. "Um…"

"He *was* here with me. He said he was going to find a bathroom, but I don't really believe him. He didn't want to babysit me. Don't tell Val he left, though. He'll get so mad, and he and Handor have been fighting a lot lately."

"About what?"

She groaned. "Ev-er-y-thing. Handor's been a real jerkface."

"But you don't want him to get in trouble?"

"I don't want him mad at me, too."

"Gotcha. Well, I can't say I'm happy he left you alone, but you're okay, so I won't say anything to Val."

She hugged me again. "You're so awesome, Honor. I wish Val and Mabry were as cool as you."

"No one is."

Shyla laughed. "Look, there's Val coming around the corner."

"And no Handor."

"He'll come back in a minute. We timed how long it took for Val to do a loop."

"You kids are a lot smarter than we were at your age."

She beamed at me as her lifegiver's car pulled along the curb and stopped next to us. The passenger window rolled down and he stuck his head forward to peer at me. "Hey, hey, little sis."

"Hey, hey, big bro."

Val got out of the car and jogged around the front end to hug me. "Man, it's good to see you in person. You look tired, but really good."

"Gee, Val, should I say you look chubby, but it suits you?"

"Let's set a good example for the kids, now." But he smiled. Then he realized only one kid was there to hear our bad influence. "Where's your brother?"

"Bathroom," I said, so Shyla wouldn't have to lie.

"Nope, right here." A finger tapped my shoulder and I spun around to see a tall young man, much too mature-looking to be my precious nephew.

"Great, all accounted for. Let's go, I'm exhausted." I put my arm around Handor and steered him to the car. "Good to see you, buddy." Lowering my voice so Val couldn't hear me as he loaded my bags in the trunk, I added, "Don't ever leave your little sister alone like that again."

Handor didn't respond, but I could feel the dramatic roll of his eyes. I remembered that time, when every adult was the enemy, and every small act of rebellion felt like a victory over oppression. It probably lasted longer for me than most.

Once everyone was situated in the car with seat belts fastened and Val had merged onto the highway, he glanced over his shoulder and asked, "Did Shyla give you the good news?"

I nudged my niece, who was sitting beside me. "No, do tell."

"I got the lead in my dance studio's production of *The Little Doe*." Her smile stretched from ear to ear.

"That's amazing – congratulations!" I reached over and gave her a high five. The road made a sharp turn and began a steep, winding descent into the valley. Rock formations whizzed by on either side of the car. I always thought Esterland was one of the loveliest cities in the world and had been completely jealous when Val moved there.

"You know Honor had that same part when she was your age," Val said.

"Really?" She looked at me with the type of admiration reserved for heroes and role models. *Is that how she sees me?* I nodded and tried to rein in my freakishly wide grin.

I was actually two years younger when I danced the doe, but no need to mention that. Performances of *The Little Doe* were popular all over the world for mid-level classes who weren't old enough for pointe yet. In the dance world, it was considered a starter ballet – it only lasted about an hour and had a lot of roles to give large groups chances to cast every student. Still, no prima ballerina had ever risen to the top without dancing the lead role in her youth. Even at nine, Shyla was considered young for it. She must have beaten out a lot of older girls with more training and experience.

"When are the performances?" I asked.

"That's the best part," Shyla said, bouncing in her seat. "They're while you're here. Priamus night and the next."

"Rock on. I can't believe you didn't tell me sooner, Val."

"We wanted to surprise you," Shyla said.

"I'm very happily surprised. I can't wait to watch you again. You're a natural."

"Just like her aunt," Val said. I'd never heard such pride in his voice before, at least not when he talked about me. I reached a hand forward and squeezed his arm.

"You're awfully quiet up there, Handor." I leaned into the space between the front seats and rested my chin on his shoulder. He shrugged it off.

"Ballet doesn't exactly excite me."

"He takes after his aunt, too, in different ways," Val said.

"Oh, you mean he's grumpy and completely impossible?" I asked.

"Pretty much."

"I'm right here, you know," Handor grunted.

"It wasn't a compliment for me, either, but I'm laughing," I said. I could see him rolling his eyes through the rearview mirror.

I didn't want to push him so I turned back to Shyla and asked about her costume for the dance. She spent the rest of the drive to their house filling me in on every detail of the production, from her tutus to the lighting cues and the horrible, prissy eleven-year old who'd been torturing her ever since she'd beat her for the part.

Oh, the drama of a ballet company. I missed it.

Val's house was one of my favorite places in the world. I don't tend to see beauty in a lot of inanimate things, but his house really can't be described any other way. It's enormous for one thing – three stories, all brick, with a chimney sticking out of the roof like a cherry on top of a sundae. It had an antique, wise aura about it – like it had seen so many people come and go since it was built over a hundred years before and wanted to tell every newcomer its stories. Walking inside was like being greeted by a long-lost friend. Every time.

Mabry was in the kitchen washing dishes when we arrived. I heard the clatter and clanking and running of water, and decided the best way to uphold my promise to try harder would be to offer my assistance.

"You just got here, Honor. No need to get to work immediately. I'll need plenty of help once we start preparing for Priamus dinner, trust me. Thank you, though, for offering," she added sweetly at the end. Her smile seemed more genuine than mine ever had. How had I gone so long treating her so badly?

"Anything you need for Priamus, I'm all yours."

"I already have a list." She pointed to a magnetized notepad on the fridge.

"Great." I scanned it and saw my name next to several desserts. "Perfect, you know to play to my strengths."

"Valor made them last year." She lowered her voice, "It was a disaster."

"I'll bet. If you really don't need help right now, I'm going to get in touch with Bonnie – let her know I made it here. Then maybe I'll see if I can convince Handor to go on a coffee run with me. Do you want anything?"

"That would be great – large chai latte."

"Coming up."

Val was in the main family room, checking the screen for messages. I bumped into his shoulder and he dropped the clicker. "Starting already?" he asked.

"You know you miss my antics when I'm not around."

"Uh huh, sure."

"Do you mind if I use the screen for a few minutes? I haven't talked to Bonnie in a while and she'll want to know I made it here safely."

He handed me the remote. "I'll be in my office if you need anything. But you never do, do you?"

I shook my head and watched him move down the hall. Since when was independence a bad thing? I guess since it meant I hadn't spoken to my best friend in two weeks. I entered her code and waited while the screen attempted to connect. It wasn't entirely my fault; she hadn't reached out to me, either.

Keep telling yourself that.

After a minute with no response, a prompt to record a message appeared. "Hey, Bon. I'm in Esterland with Val. Made it here safely. Only a couple of jackasses on the plane. Call me when you get this. You have the code, right? Anyway, I'll talk to you later." I hit 'accept' to send the video and the screen went blank. There was nothing left to do except hope she called back soon.

I climbed two flights of stairs and knocked on my nephew's door, worried he wouldn't hear me over the insane bass booming from inside the room, but he answered after a few seconds.

"Want to get out of here for a little bit?" I asked. He smiled, but almost immediately realized he wasn't supposed to appear happy about anything and let it fall.

"Whatever."

"Great. Get your jacket and meet me downstairs."

He shut his door and I heard the bass fade out as I walked back down the stairs. I ducked my head in Val's office on the second floor.

"I'm going to take Handor out for coffee. Can I borrow your car?"

"What will you do if I say 'no'?"

"Get Handor to borrow it?"

He pulled keys out of his pocket and tossed them to me. "See if you can get him to talk to you. He's been surly and impossible for weeks now."

"That was kinda my idea. Any news on the lark front?"

Val shook his head. "He won't talk about it anymore, so I don't know what's going on with it. If he's feeling his pull, he's ignoring it."

"It could have dulled on its own. It's not normal for the pull to be so strong at his age."

"Maybe. Either way, I'd like to know what's going on. We've never fought like this."

"Have you considered that maybe he's being impossible now because he's a teenager?"

He frowned. "Of course I have."

"Some people go through difficult phases. Look how long mine is lasting."

"Lasted," he corrected.

"Aw, shucks."

"Ready, Honor?" Handor slumped into the room, his hands stuffed in the pockets of his black, hooded sweatshirt, and his head down.

"Yep. You want me to bring you back any coffee, Val? I'm getting something for Mabry."

"No, thanks." He slipped a twenty note in my hand. I tried to push it back, but he refused to take it.

"I don't need your money," I said.

"Use it for Handor's and Mabry's, then."

"Don't worry, I can handle it."

"Seriously." He pressed the note into my palm and I stopped arguing. I'd just find time to put it back in his wallet later on.

"Let's go, kiddo." I headed to the first floor, trusting my nephew to follow me. When I heard the front door shut behind us, I dangled the car keys on the edge of my index finger. "Want to show me your driving skills?" I swiveled to face him, offering the key ring. His almost-smile popped up for a moment, and he grabbed the keys without a word.

After ordering our drinks, we found a table in a corner by a window, away from other patrons. Handor unzipped his hoodie and slung it on the back of his chair. "I know what you're doing," he said.

"Existing in my general state of awesomeness?"

He rolled his eyes. "Val asked you to talk to me."

"Not exactly, but he thought it was a good idea that we talk. He's worried about you."

"No, he's not, he's frustrated with my lark."

"I'm sure he seems frustrated, but that's because he cares about you. It's not easy for him to feel out of control, and your lark is leaving him helpless. Especially now that you won't talk to him about it."

"He wouldn't understand."

"Maybe I will." I held up my wrist, pointing the unfinished lark at him. He eyed it for a second, then looked at the table. At the counter, a barista called our names. He jumped up and collected our drinks. I wanted to point out, *there's the Handor we all know and love*, but bit my tongue and just thanked him when he set my drink in front of me.

"You're lucky," he finally said, after the silence between us became so palpable, I was sure everyone else in the shop could feel it.

"How so?"

"No pull, no mate. You don't have to deal with any of that crap."

I pursed my lips, but didn't respond.

He continued, "I mean, it's gotta be nice only having to worry about yourself, right?"

"I suppose some people would see it that way."

"You don't?"

"No. I think it would be really nice to have someone to worry and care about. You don't want to be like me, Han. I'm a grumpy, lonely, selfish person."

"I've never thought of you as any of those things."

"Of course not, I've always been your super cool, fun, amazing aunt. But other people don't like me very much."

He took a swig of his coffee. "What would you do if you had to choose?"

"What do you mean – choose what?"

He looked around the restaurant to make sure no one was watching him, then lifted the side of his shirt. On his ribs was a dark brown pattern. I leaned closer. "Wait – Handor, I thought your lark was on the back of your neck."

He turned around in his chair and pointed to the black splotch there.

"Whoa. You have two larks?"

He settled back into his original position and adjusted his shirt. "I've always had the neck one, but the one on my side has been developing over the last couple of weeks. I didn't tell my lifegivers. It's weird, right? I'm some sort of freak."

"No, you're not! I've never heard of that happening, but that doesn't mean you're the only one it's ever happened to. Look at me, I thought I was the only person to never meet their mate, but I've been finding all kinds of evidence to the contrary."

He sighed. "I don't know what to do."

"The dual pull you were feeling – that started when the second lark appeared?"

He nodded.

"Where is each leading you right now?"

"Right this minute, one pull wants me to go to Kataloo, and the other wants me at Juneville, but I don't know which is which. If I did, that might make it easier. I'd go with the one I've had longer."

"Those are both cities in this region."

"Yep."

I tapped the table with a fingernail. "Has the pull always been telling you such close places?"

"Pretty much, always within this region."

"That's crazy."

"I know. You see what I mean about choosing?"

I nodded. "What if those people only have one – you're their one shot, and you choose, and the one who isn't chosen ends up mateless?"

He put his head in his hands. "It's too much pressure. I don't even want to find out who they are."

I put my hand on top of his head and stroked his hair like I had when he was a toddler. "I'm really sorry, Han. This sucks. Really sucks. I can't even give you advice, because I have no idea what I'd do in your situation.

"I just don't understand why," he said.

"Because life's not fair?" I offered.

He smiled and didn't try to stop himself. "Your mate is a real prick for not finding you."

"Damn right." We finished our drinks, ordered Mabry's, and headed back to the house. In the car he made me promise not to tell his lifegivers. He wanted to talk to them about it in his own time, after he'd decided how he wanted to proceed.

Chapter Eighteen: Happy Priamus

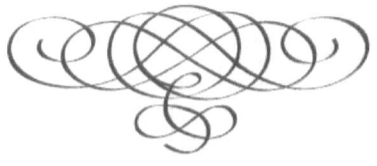

Priamus is the holiday dedicated to the Goddess Pria. It's a day to gather around family and friends and thank Her for the blessings She has given. When I was a child, Priamus was my favorite holiday. In addition to the week off from lessons, our extended families would descend on whomever's home had won the war to host that year.

The kids would drink hot chocolate and make marshmallow Prias with candy eyes, mouths, arms, and legs. Sometimes hair, if the adults remembered to buy licorice. Our lifegivers, aunts, uncles, and grandgivers would spend all day cooking the best food on the planet: macaroni and cheese, roast duck, peach cobbler, loaded potato soup, and broiled asparagus with parmesan. Every year Hero would invent a new game for us to play to remind us to be grateful. My favorite was a scavenger hunt with clues hidden throughout the house and yard. Each clue led to a member of the family who would give us a challenge to complete. One challenge was bringing in logs for the fire. Another was helping unload the groceries. We didn't realize at the time they were just getting us to do chores.

By the time Gizella and Hero passed away, though, our family had stopped coming together to give thanks. We were spread far and wide, and so many of my favorite aunts and uncles had grown too old to travel. Valor and I made the trek to see our lifegivers each year until they died, and then it was down to just us. I wanted Handor and Shyla to have the same experiences Val and I had growing up, but they saw right through my attempts to recreate Hero's games, so I stopped trying and helped Mabry. Luckily, I was much better at making pastries than planning games.

"Do you have everything you need?" Mabry asked, handing me an apron. I looked over the list of desserts and scanned the kitchen counter. Val and Shyla had gone grocery shopping while Handor and I made our coffee run the day before, and brought back flour, sugar, graham crackers, cream cheese, vanilla extract, apples, peaches, a pineapple, chocolate bars and syrup, whipped cream, eggs, and dozens of other items Mabry needed for the actual dinner.

"I think I'm all set, but we can always send Val out if we're missing something."

She laughed. "That's the one thing he's good for."

I started with the chocolate cheesecake – it would need time in the fridge to set. While Mabry peeled potatoes at the sink, I blended the cream cheese with chocolate and a little extra sugar. Folding the mixture into itself was soothing, as usual. Mix. Swirl. Beat.

I set the cream cheese bowl to the side and picked up the box of graham crackers. I hurled it onto the floor. *Slam!*

"What the..." Mabry spun around, potato in one hand, peeler in the other.

"Gotta crush the crackers for the cheesecake crust."

"And you have to throw grenades to do it?"

"Only if I want to have some fun." Speaking of which. "Hey, where's Shyla? I bet she'd have a blast helping with this." I retrieved the box from the floor, setting it on the counter, and went to the second level of the house in search of my niece.

The door to her bedroom stood open and strains of Framini's Fifth Concerto floated into the hallway. I peered into the room and saw Shyla at her balance bar, feet in first position, practicing arm motions. She reminded me of myself at that age. A performance only hours away, but instead of letting jitters shake her spirit, she returned to the basics. Her face in the mirror showed calm contentment. Focus. She was centered. I remembered feeling that way, a long time ago.

The desire for everything in my life to be good and right again, even for just a moment, was overwhelming. Unconsciously, I clutched the doorframe, my hip bumping into the door and sending it banging against her wall. Shyla jumped and spun around.

"Hey, kiddo, sorry to interrupt."

She turned off the music. "S'kay."

"I thought you might want to help me with some of the desserts. You get to throw a box of graham crackers all over your lifegiver's kitchen."

"Awesome!" She bounded through the door past me, taking the steps two at a time. She already had the box in her hands by the time I made it to the kitchen. "What do I do?" she asked.

"Throw it as hard as you can on the floor."

"Don't make a mess," Mabry warned, but Shyla wasn't listening. She had the box lifted over her head and wasted no time flinging it to the floor. The crunching of the crackers was wonderfully satisfying for me, but Mabry winced at the noise.

"Can I do it again?" Shyla asked.

"Let's check the structural integrity of the box – we don't want it busting open and spilling crumbs all over the place. There won't be enough for the cheesecake if that happens."

"And you'll have to clean it up," Mabry added.

Shyla picked the box up off the floor and handed it to me, gently, with two fingers on each top corner, as if afraid her grip would split it open. I tried not to laugh. The box didn't look much worse for the wear; a few dents, but no holes, and the top didn't show signs of straining.

"Give it another go." I tossed it to her and she immediately chucked it down. She did it a few more times before I held out a hand to stop her. "You're really good at that," I said, "but let's dump the crumbs in a bowl and crush the rest by hand."

"Cool," she said, picking up the box with the same care as her previous retrieval. She placed it on the counter and I slid my finger under the top, peeling it open. Peering inside, I was glad we stopped throwing it. The bag the crackers were in had busted, and crumbs were leaking into the box. I used scissors to cut the top off the plastic bag and dumped the crumbs into a white mixing bowl. There were still several larger chunks needing to be broken down.

I handed Shyla the meat mallet I'd cleaned earlier and told her to beat the crackers until they were fine as dust. She went to town.

"My kitchen has never been this noisy," Mabry said. She was trying to keep the irritation out of her voice, but didn't fully succeed.

Things like that, I remembered, that's why we hadn't always gotten along. I bit down my retort about her kitchen never being this much fun and put a stick of butter into a bowl. "Is the microwave free?"

"All yours," she said, watching Shyla with a pained expression on her face.

I knew Mabry was good with her children, but moments like that made me hate her a little. Shyla was only nine. How many more years would she even agree to help in the kitchen without threat of punishment? How many more years til she stopped finding joy in little amusements like throwing a box of crackers on the ground? It couldn't be many. Mabry was wasting them with her sighs and nagging looks.

The family gathered around the table that evening with a feast spread before us. I felt a little out of place in the extra chair Val had found in the attic for me, but was still glad to be part of the celebration.

"Should we say what we're thankful for?" Val asked, putting a hand out to stop Handor from filling his plate. Mabry agreed immediately, but the kids and I groaned. Sure, technically that's what the holiday was about, but wasn't it enough that we were spending it together?

"I'll start," my brother said. He took a long look at each of his kids and his mate and beamed. "I'm so proud of our family. Shyla, you are an amazing young lady. I'm thankful every day for your spirit, your wit and intelligence. I am very blessed to have you for a daughter."

"Thanks, Val-ey," she said. I hadn't heard her call him that little endearment in years, not since before she went to school. It was sweet, not heartbreaking, so why did I want to cry?

"Handor, son, I know you're at a rough age and I don't always make things easier. I appreciate your intelligence, your determination. You always do the right thing in the end. I hope that as we both grow older, our minds will grow more alike. But, even if they don't, I wouldn't trade you for anyone or anything else. I'm blessed to have you for a son."

Handor leaned back in his chair and looked to me for a second. I nodded, hopefully encouragingly.

"Mabry," Val continued, "there aren't enough words to express how thankful I am to have found you. You are my light and dark, my north and south. You have given me so much happiness in our life together and in our children. Thank you, my love."

Okay, I had to pull it together. Mabry was responding to Val, but I couldn't hear her – it was like there was water in my ears. My eyes were swimming in tears, but I refused to let them fall. What would be the point? I was supposed to be past trying to make everyone else feel my pain, right?

"Honor," Val said. I blinked rapidly a few times and met his eye. I hadn't been expecting him to give me a little speech, but I guess it would have been mighty awkward if he'd left me out, since there was no one else there. "Honor, having a sister like you has been an experience. I've loved every minute of it. There are days I find myself asking, 'What would Honor do?' when I'm faced with a tough decision. For better or worse, we're a team. I've got your back; you've got mine. Thank you."

I gulped. My tears were gone, but the knot in my throat grew larger by the second. Thankfully, no one waited for me to respond.

"Shyla, why don't you go next, sweetie," Mabry said, squeezing her daughter's arm. The child cleared her throat.

"I'm thankful for my family and friends and that I get to dance tonight."

Mabry took it upon herself to go next, and while she didn't wax poetic about us each individually, she spent what felt like fifteen minutes going over, in painstaking detail, how thankful she was for her family and every aspect of her life. There wasn't one thing she'd change. I wanted to smack her. My resolve for playing nice evaporating quickly, I took a long sip of the wine in front of me. When she finally finished, I almost puked at the sight of Val's happy, love-struck grin. Seriously, if they weren't mated, he wouldn't have been able to stand how melodramatic she could be.

Handor was next in the circle. For a moment, I didn't think he was going to say anything at all – he looked so embarrassed. Eventually, though, he slid his chair back and stood. "Val, Mabry, Shyla, I know I haven't been easy to deal with the last couple of months. Something happened I wasn't prepared for, and I didn't know how to handle it. Talking to Honor yesterday sorta helped me see that I should have been talking to you guys about it all along, so..." he lifted his shirt and pointed at the lark.

"What is that, honey?" Mabry cried, jumping from her seat and clutching his side.

Val's face looked ashen. He cleared his throat a few times before croaking out, "Is that what I think it is? A second lark?"

Mabry gasped and Shyla's mouth fell into an "o" shape. Handor nodded.

"How is that possible?" Mabry asked, touching the mark and then pulling her hand back like she'd been burned.

Handor shook his head. "No idea. That's why my pull's been so weird, I think. I don't know which lark to follow."

"We need to take you to the doctor. This is unheard of." Val's shoulders slumped back. I thought he was being a tad dramatic. Maybe he'd picked it up from Mabry.

"It's unusual, yes, but there isn't anything wrong with him," I said. The entire family looked at me as if they'd forgotten I was there.

"I don't want to talk about it any more tonight." Handor put his shirt down and sat. "I thought I should tell you, but let's not make a big thing out of it, okay? We still have dinner and Shy's dance thing."

"Handor, we have to work this out," Val said.

"We will. Tomorrow."

"But..."

"So, Honor, what are you thankful for?" Handor asked, his eyes pleading with me to be on his side. But I already was.

"It's been a tough couple of months for me," I started and paused. No, Honor. Think positively. "I am thankful for my family. Seriously, the best niece and nephew a girl could ask for. How do you guys kick such major ass?"

"Honor!" Mabry exclaimed.

Shyla giggled. "We take after you."

"Remind me to buy you a present before I leave."

"Okay!"

"Bro – you rock. Really. I'm so thankful to be your sister, and I'm especially thankful that you haven't stopped taking my calls over the years when I've been at my bitchiest."

"Language, Honor, please," Mabry said.

"And Mabry, I am thankful for how happy you make my brother. He's a…" I looked to Val and summoned the best lie I had, "lucky man."

Mabry smiled, but I don't think I quite made up for my propensity to swear in front of her children.

"As ever, I'm thankful for such good friends as Bonnie and Caron and sweet little Lang. And I have a new friend to add this year. Someone who's been helping me, without asking for anything in return. The kind of friend I hope to be, someday."

"Who's that?" Val asked.

"No one you know. Can we eat now?"

"Please!" Shyla said.

"I'm starving." Handor rubbed his stomach and eyed the platters in the center of the table.

"Oh, alright." Val grabbed the platter of duck and served a few slices to each of the kids, then Mabry and myself. He filled his own plate last, before passing the side dishes. Everything smelled heavenly. Once my plate was full and I stuffed the first bite into my mouth, I was ready to forgive Mabry every annoying thing she'd ever done. She was the best cook I'd ever known.

"You've outdone yourself, sweetie." Val's plate was already half-empty.

"Amazing," I agreed.

"Don't let me eat too much," Shyla said in between bites. "I have to dance in two hours."

"What you have on your plate is enough," Mabry said. "But there will be leftovers if you want any more after the performance."

It reminded me of the many conversations Gizella and I had about food when I was in training. Actually, they were arguments. I always wanted to eat less, she always wanted me to eat more. We'd get in screaming matches and drive Val and Hero bonkers. Finally, Hero stepped in. He convinced Gizella that I was eating, had never starved myself, and wasn't trying to. He warned me if they ever got the impression that I was, I'd be yanked out of my dance classes so fast there'd be skid marks in my wake.

I never starved myself, but that threat always loomed over me. There was - is - nothing I love more in life than ballet. I would have eaten lard at every meal if they'd told me I had to in order to keep dancing. In another year or two, I'd have to tell Mabry about that compromise, to make sure Shyla didn't let her dreams take over her good sense.

"What are you smiling at?" Val asked.

"Just remembering Gizella and Hero. I think they'd be shocked to know I voluntarily made the desserts."

He laughed. "Yeah, I think they would. Although, they always seemed to see right through us, even when we thought we were being sneaky."

"I was better at being sneaky than you."

"Got any tips?" Handor asked.

"Hey," Val said, giving his son a stern look.

"I'll tell you later." I nudged Handor with my elbow and gave him a little wink. He smiled and dove back into his plate.

Chapter Nineteen: The Little Doe

Walking into the concert hall was like walking into my childhood. Two or three times a year, I went backstage to the dressing rooms, hung my costume on the rack, and sat patiently while Gizella brushed my hair and pinned it into a dancer's bun. She let me wear blush and lipstick, but only for performances, so she could see my face from the audience. The other girls would look enviously on while she applied the bright red makeup to my lips, then prance around me in circles begging for a kiss so they would have some, too. I kissed Bonnie once and her lifegivers were so angry. They said she looked like a clown and too mature for her age. It never made sense to me how those two things went together in their minds. Gizella tried to explain to them that she only let me wear the makeup for the performances, but they wouldn't listen. They thought I was a bad influence.

Luckily, Bonnie knew I wasn't. I don't know how she did it, but she finally convinced them to let us spend time together outside of dance class. And then she dropped out of ballet.

Mabry came down the steps from the stage, looking through the crowd. Val waved, and when she spotted us, she huffed over. "Honor, Shyla wants your help."

"For what?"

"Her hair. She says I don't get it tight enough."

"Oh, sure thing." I tried not to smile too brightly as I stepped around the guys; Mabry did not look thrilled at being supplanted, and I wanted to be gracious about it.

The side door leading to the dressing rooms was unlocked, but a tall man with a clipboard stood just inside it and blocked my path. "Only dancers and lifegivers beyond this point," he said.

"I'm Shyla's aunt. You know, she's the lead? Her lifegivers sent me back here to fix her hair."

He raised an eyebrow and consulted his clipboard. "Your name?"

"Honor Sandavol."

"You're not on the list of lifegivers."

I spoke slowly, to ensure his pea-sized brain understood this time, "Because I am not a lifegiver. I am her aunt. Do I need to bring one of her lifegivers back here to give permission, or can I go see my niece?"

He frowned and pulled a walkie-talkie out of his pocket, turning away as he spoke into it too quietly for me to hear. After a minute, he stepped aside and let me through. It was kind of ridiculous – having a guard for the dressing rooms. Who did the kids need protection from?

Shyla was sitting in front of a mirror in the main dressing room, just a step away from the stage, her hair hanging past her shoulders. She swiveled in her chair when I approached. "Thank Pria you're here, Honor. Mabry has no idea what she's doing."

"Happy to help." I put my hands on the back of her chair, turning her around and looking into her reflection. She had looked older at the airport, but with the lights shining on her, and her fellow dancers jabbering away while she sat soberly concerned about her hair, she looked mature.

I ran my fingers through her dark brown locks. "You want a classic bun, or something a little special?"

"Doesn't it have to be a bun?"

"You're not in the chorus tonight."

She smiled and tilted her chin up. "I guess I'm not."

"Special it is, then. Hand me your brush and get the bobby pins ready." I combed her hair, taking my time to clear any snags and make sure it was silky smooth. "Gizella used to do this for me. She would have loved seeing you dance."

"I wish I could have known her better. I think Val really misses her."

"They were close."

"Were you?"

I shrugged my shoulders. "When I was little, I guess. We didn't get along when I started getting older."

"Like Handor and Val."

"Sorta, but I think they're going to be fine now. Gizella didn't really understand me, and I didn't understand her. She loved watching me perform when I was your age, but when I wanted to make a career out of it, not so much."

"Do you think that's going to happen with me and Mabry?"

I stopped pinning pieces of hair and squeezed her shoulder. "No, I don't. I don't think you'll let it."

"But I want to be a ballerina, too."

"I know, but you are much sweeter and kinder than me, and Mabry is not Gizella. She wants you to be happy."

"Gizella wanted you to be happy, too, didn't she?"

I separated three thin sections of hair and began braiding them. "She did, in a way. She thought I'd be the most happy if I found my lifemate and had children. She thought touring and classes and auditions were keeping me from my real destiny. It's kinda ironic, I guess. I hurt myself and never found my mate, so now I have neither."

"Val says you were a beautiful dancer."

"He has to say that because he's my brother." I started another braid and winked at Shyla in the mirror. Her lips twitched. "You're not nervous, are you?"

"Maybe a little."

"No need, you're going to be great. And you know, even if you aren't, it doesn't matter, because it's all about having fun and doing something you love. You do love it, kiddo, don't you?"

"Yeah. I love it more than anything else in the world."

"I thought so. So, don't worry about the audience, or your teachers or classmates. Go out there and dance as if you're the only one in the room and you're doing it just for you. Got it?"

She nodded. I started another braid.

"Can we dance together sometime?" She caught my eye in the mirror.

"Absolutely." I tucked in one last bobby pin to secure her updo and examined all sides to make sure there were no errant strands. "Hairspray," I commanded. She handed it to me and squeezed her eyes shut as I assaulted her head with the aerosol. "Perfect. Take a look."

She spun her chair around, her fingers clutching a handheld mirror. "Wow!" Dozens of tiny braids wove around each other to create her bun, culminating in a perfectly spiraled center. "I've never seen a ballerina with a bun like this."

"You'll see a ton of styles when you get to the companies, but for your first lead, I think this is elegant and understated."

"I love it! Thank you."

"You're welcome. One more thing before I head to my seat." I opened my purse and dug to the bottom. "Ah ha – I knew it was in here." Pulling out a black tube, I held it out to Shyla.

"Lipstick?"

"You're the star of the show, kiddo. Let's make sure people know it." I popped the cap off and she parted her lips so I could smooth the color on. When she looked in the mirror next, her smile was a lovely, bright rose red.

"Knock 'em dead." I hugged her and kissed the top of her head.

"You're the best, Honor."

"I know." I winked one more time and left to find my seat before the curtain.

"How's she doing?" Val asked as I sat beside him.

"Good. I think she was a little nervous, but we talked and I gave her a confidence boost."

"What did you say?"

"The same stuff Gizella used to tell me."

The lights in the auditorium began to flicker and butterflies in my stomach began to flutter. I think I was more nervous for Shyla than I'd ever been for myself during a performance.

Anxious lifegivers scrambled to find empty seats as the orchestra struck their first notes.

The curtain lifted and a spotlight sought out the stage. It landed on a ballerina kneeling in the center, her back to the audience. Shyla. She rose in perfect harmony with the music and moved into a graceful pirouette.

"Red lips!" Mabry hissed at Val. "Did your sister give her lipstick?"

"It would appear so," Val said. I could hear the curl of his lips – the expression he made when he was amused. He shifted in his seat so his face was closer to mine than his mate's. He whispered so Mabry couldn't hear him, "I like it. It reminds me of going to see you when you were her age."

I bumped his shoulder with mine and focused on the stage. The ballet told the story of a young doe separated from her herd, trying to find her way back. She comes across a loveable group of woodland creatures who want to help her: a fiery fox who jumps and leaps with excitement at the prospect of a new friend, but knows nothing to help her find her family; a shy-but-kind bear, who provides shelter in her cave when night falls; a squirrel, who offers nuts when the doe gets hungry. The band of happy creatures runs into a coyote – a half-starved, desperate creature. The gang flees and the curtain closes for the end of Act One.

"Wow," Val breathed out slowly, "she's remarkable."

"Yeah," I choked out.

Mabry leaned over her mate and touched my arm. "Why the makeup?"

"It's just lipstick. To give her confidence. Gizella used to do it for me before every performance. I stood out from the other kids. It's silly, I know, but it made a difference. The audience saw me as something special; my classmates did too, and eventually the teachers did. Then I did. It was powerful."

"She's a little girl, and she's already the lead. She doesn't need to be made special."

I shrugged. Mabry had never been anything special in her life, not until she met Val, and he made her the center of his world. I understood where she was coming from as a lifegiver, but she needed to realize I knew what to do in the ballet department.

Her hand squeezed my arm. "Her hair looks very pretty, though."

I smiled. Maybe Mabry realized I wasn't the only one causing friction in our relationship.

"What's the second act about?" Val asked.

"Running from the coyote, eventually finding the doe's herd."

Handor sat up in his seat on the other side of Mabry, and turned to face the rest of us. "I don't get it, couldn't the bear scare off the coyote?"

"Theoretically, I guess, but this is a very timid bear."

"So timid she invites a fox and doe she just met into her cave late at night?"

"Don't spoil the magic, Han," I teased. When he was little, I used to read him fairy tales when I visited. He analyzed them to the point where all thrill and beauty were lost. He was never a believer. I wondered if that's why he ended up with two larks. The Gods wanted to show him that not everything in life was black and white. It was best to leave some things unexplained.

Oh crap. Did that mean I needed to stop searching for my mate? Maybe I wasn't actually meant to know him. Were the Gods teasing me, too? I had an urge to speak with Sedric. He'd been supportive all along, but he didn't really believe finding my mate would help me. He didn't think it would bring me closure. Was there something else he thought would?

My family was still debating the premise of the ballet and the likelihood that the doe and her new friends could take on the hunger-weakened coyote. Other members of the audience were moving about: going to the restroom and concessions, saying hello to other lifegivers they knew from years of taking their children to the same dance studios. I sat in my seat, perfectly alone.

I was always alone – with my family, with Bonnie and Caron, in the office. Just me. Honor, the team of one. Except... no. Well, maybe. Except when I was with Sedric. I didn't feel so alone when he was laughing at my sarcasm, showing me a new restaurant, or taking me to the ballet. He did things for me my mate should have been doing.

The lights flickered again and a calm settled over the crowd. I wanted to dash out before the curtain rose, find a screen, and call Sedric. I wanted to ask him why he was so nice to me, and why at this moment, my friendship with him was the only thing keeping me from going absolutely crazy.

But I stayed in my seat and watched the rest of the ballet. Shyla's technique still needed age and experience, but her showmanship was unbelievable. She was not only dancing from her heart, she was acting from it. Every facial expression conveyed the proper emotion for the scene, something most ballerinas have a hard time incorporating until their teen years, when studios bring in acting coaches. Shyla was years ahead of the other dancers on stage. She grabbed the audience, forced us to watch every step – we couldn't tear our eyes away – but if she noticed her captive fans, she didn't show it. She wasn't dancing for us. She was dancing for herself.

Damn, I was so proud.

When the curtain closed after the happy reunion of the little doe with her herd, the audience rose as one to its feet, thunder reverberating off the walls of the auditorium. The youngest class, who made up the majority of the chorus, came out for their curtain call first, and a few lifegivers whistled or yelled out their child's name. Next came the middle class and the rest of the chorus. Then, the students who danced the parts of the doe's herd. When the woodland creatures and coyote appeared, the applause grew louder.

Finally, Shyla sashayed onto the stage. The applause was so deafening around me, I wanted to plug my ears to prevent the drums from rupturing. I whistled and called out along with Val, Mabry, and the rest of the audience. Even Handor was on his feet, cheering for his little sister. She looked like a deer in headlights. Funny, since she'd just been playing one for the past hour. I loved that she seemed so shocked by her reception – she hadn't noticed the crowd at all during the performance.

Her cheeks were turning pink as she made a graceful, low bow and stepped into line with the rest of the cast. The entire group bowed together, and then the curtain closed for the final time.

"You were saying something about being powerful, Honor?" Mabry asked when the cheers and clapping died down, and we could actually hear each other again.

"Right now your daughter is the most powerful dancer in her school, and she doesn't even realize it. This won't be the last time she gets the principal role in a performance. I wouldn't be surprised if her teachers advance her ahead of schedule after seeing that."

"Really?"

I nodded. "Go on backstage and congratulate her. She did an amazing job, but I bet she won't believe it until she hears it from you."

Val pressed my hand, and Mabry smiled warmly at me. "Come on, Handor," Val said.

"I'll wait with Honor."

"You sure?"

"I'll congratulate her in the car. Don't want to be around all those teeny boppers."

I laughed as Val frowned, but he took Mabry's hand and they joined the throngs of lifegivers attempting to get backstage. Handor moved down the aisle so he could take the seat next to me.

"That was pretty cool, the way she danced."

"Yeah, it was. She's a natural."

"You used to do that?"

I nodded and put both hands on the seat in front of me, looking to the stage. The longing in my chest was more powerful than the desire to find my mate had ever been. "I was that good. But it was fleeting. I guess it wasn't meant for me."

"Maybe it's not meant for Shyla."

"Don't say that."

"But that's what you're thinking."

I stared at him. "No, I wasn't."

"That's what I'd be thinking if I were in your shoes."

"No, you wouldn't."

He looked down at his hands. "Why is life so unfair?"

"Ah, now that's the question for the ages, isn't it? Sometimes I really, really hate the Gods. Like, wish I could murder them, hate them. But in the end, are my problems worse than anyone else's? Probably not. Life is hard, but it's hard for everyone."

"I don't know if that's true."

"Look at our family. You've got me – bitter and depressed because an injury ended my true calling just as my career was about to begin. Plus, on top of that, I'm doomed to grow old alone because my stupid lifemate got himself killed somehow or another before I found him."

"Heavy stuff," he said.

"Yeah, but is it any heavier than what you're dealing with? Two larks, one appearing out of nowhere, each leading you to a different place and a different person. Forcing you, at a very young age, to decide to follow one of them, or follow neither. Knowing no matter which choice you make, at least one of the people with your match is going to be left alone. And you don't want to do that, because you've seen how depressed and un-fun it's made your favorite aunt."

His mouth opened slightly, before clamping shut. Oh, teenagers. Always thinking they are so misunderstood.

"It's really sweet you're thinking like that," I said, "but I'm fine. I'm getting better, anyway. More used to the idea, I guess. I haven't found my mate, but does that mean I can't live a fulfilling life?" As I said the words, only started out of a need to comfort my nephew, I realized they were true. Even though I'd glossed things over for Bonnie in the past, I'd never really considered my life as having much validity.

Because in this world, if you weren't mated, who were you? What was your purpose? I was Honor Sandavol, damn it. I was an intelligent woman who loved her niece and nephew, her brother, and her friends. I made one hell of a pastry. And I saw beauty in movement, found peace in music and rhythm. I didn't need another person to love me in order to live a worthwhile life.

"I've been thinking I should find them both and explain," Handor said.

"That you're going to break one of their hearts?"

He shrugged. "It seems like the right thing to do."

I put my arm around his shoulders and squeezed. "You're going to be just fine, you know?"

He snorted. "Sure."

"Really. You've got a much better head on your shoulders at fifteen than I have at thirty."

"Your head looks fine to me."

"Well, thanks. If you find both and explain the situation, then what? Do you imagine the three of you living happily-ever-after, or is some other scenario playing in your head?"

"I don't know. I don't have anything specific in mind. But wouldn't you want to know?"

I squeezed his shoulders again. "Yes."

Chapter Twenty: Worth the Pain

The auditorium had mostly cleared out, but Handor and I were still waiting for Shyla, Val, and Mabry to reappear, so we played a game of dots on the back of my program. He was kicking my ass, mostly because I wasn't paying attention to the entire board – I was focusing too much on the cluster I'd started in the corner, while he strategized agonizingly over every move. He beat me fifty to fourteen. Yeah, I basically sucked.

We were still waiting when he grabbed my arm. "What?" I asked.

"My pull," he said in a whisper.

"It's leading you somewhere?"

He turned his head, focusing on the door behind us opening to the lobby. "I'm supposed to go outside."

"Right now? We need to wait for your family."

He was standing, his face flushed, wiping his palms on his jeans. "I think one of my mates is across the street, having a late dinner with his lifegivers at the little café."

That was specific. His pull told him all that? Mine had never revealed those kind of details, but Sedric's had – it led him to his university and a little bookstore. It was also the first time I'd ever heard Handor refer to a gender when talking about his mate. Which, now that I thought about it, was weird in itself.

Handor was a few feet up the aisle, looking at me, pained. "I have to go, it almost hurts." His lips were pressed tightly together, his fists clenched. He took another step up the aisle.

"Let's go get Val and Mabry, so we don't lose them. We'll all go together."

"Hurry!"

"Okay, take a few deep breaths. Don't leave without us." I stumbled through the row to get to the aisle and bounded up the stairs leading to the stage's side door. He remained standing in the aisle, now holding onto one of the seats to keep himself from moving forward.

I threw open the door and charged into Shyla's dressing room. Luckily, there was no guard to stop me this time. Apparently, security after the show was not deemed important.

"Honor!" Shyla squealed, disengaging from a group of her classmates and their lifegivers and throwing herself at me. I hugged her hastily and put her at arm's length.

"Where are your lifegivers? We have to go now."

"What, why? We're having fun."

"I'm sorry, kiddo. It's your brother. We really have to go." I moved towards the door and called out, "Val? Mabry?"

"They're talking with my teacher. This way." A bummed Shyla grabbed her bag off the floor and waved goodbye to her group of admirers. They groaned that she was leaving too soon, but she didn't wait to apologize. I wanted to kiss her forehead and thank her for being such a selfless, wonderful human being, but that would have to wait. Every second wasted pushed Handor further out the door, and I couldn't bear the thought of him meeting one of his mates without his family there for support. It didn't have to be so urgent, but it was.

Val and Mabry were standing a few yards down the hallway from Shyla's dressing room, engaged in quiet discussion with a woman who must have been a few years younger than me. Not good enough for a company, I had to assume, but good enough, or at least dedicated enough, to teach.

"Val, Mabry, we have to go. It's Handor," I said, interrupting their conversation. Mabry appeared irritated for a split second until she looked into my eyes. She said a hasty goodbye to the teacher and grabbed Shyla's hand.

"Let's go."

"What's going on?" Val asked as we fled to the stage door.

"His pull. He's feeling it very strongly. His mate is across the street."

"Oh, Paolo. Both?"

"No, I think just one." I flung open the door and sped down the steps, the others following at my heel. Handor was at the last row now, just a foot away from the exit.

"We have to get there now, or it will be too late," he said, darting through the door without waiting for us to reach him.

"They should really be meeting him halfway," I grumbled, running to catch up.

Handor soared through the lobby and pushed the main doors open so hard, I almost expected them to fly off the hinges.

"It's not life or death," Val shouted.

"Isn't it?" Handor yelled back, but he stopped suddenly in the middle of the street, face-to-face with a tall young man. The new boy was skinny, with floppy black hair and a long nose.

"Hey," Handor said, panting.

"Hello," the boy said.

"Ow!" Handor's hand reached for the lark on the back of his neck.

"Mine burns, too." The boy grinned, rubbing his own neck.

Val and Mabry took a step forward. "Are your lifegivers in the restaurant?"

The boy nodded.

"Why don't we all go in and have a little talk?" Val motioned with his arm and the boys started to move. I touched Mabry's elbow.

"Maybe I should take Shyla home while you and Val take care of things with Handor."

"Good idea." Suddenly, my brother's mate had her arms around me. "Thank you for everything, Honor." I didn't know what to say, so I just nodded and took Shyla's hand. Mabry followed after her guys.

"You don't need to hold my hand." Shyla yanked it away and started walking towards the parking lot.

"Sorry. Hey, you know I don't have a car here, kiddo. We'll have to get a cab. Let's go back into the theater and get someone to help."

She turned and entered the doors Handor had nearly taken off. Quietly, so I almost missed it, she muttered, "This is so typical."

"Hey, I know this isn't fair to you. But it's not like he could help it."

She sighed. "I wanted to go out and celebrate with my friends, but instead…"

I put my arm around her shoulder. "Instead, how about we go back on the stage and dance together? If the theater will let us."

Her smile lit up her face and all glumness disappeared instantly. "Really? Yes! I bet the theater managers won't care – they love me. They're probably backstage, still. Come on!" She grabbed my arm and dragged me through the auditorium and up the stairs to go backstage. It was empty, but she followed a hallway to a row of offices, and we heard voices behind the second door. She pushed it open.

"Hey, Mr. Keye. Can my aunt and I use the stage for like a half-hour or so? My lifegivers had a sort of emergency, and we don't have a way home."

A gentleman behind a desk looked at his watch. "That should be okay, Miss Sandavol. Do you need a ride? I'll be heading out in about an hour." Another man sitting opposite him closed a folder and excused himself, passing by us through the narrow door.

"That's nice of you, but we'll call a cab," I said.

"No need for that, I've driven Shyla and some of the others home before. I already know where it is."

"His mate is one of my teachers," Shyla explained.

I didn't like the idea of taking a favor from a man I didn't know, but it was better than paying an astronomical fee for a taxi. My pocketbook got the better of me. "Okay, sure. We'll be on the stage until you're ready to go."

As we walked away, Shyla burst forth, "This is awesome, Honor! My teachers are really nice, but they aren't as good as you."

I laughed. "You've never even seen me."

"Well..." She tried to look timid, but didn't quite pull it off. "Not in person, but Val has some videos."

"What? He never told me that. I don't even have videos of myself dancing."

"Hero gave them to him, right before he passed away."

"Why would he give them to Val and not me?"

Shyla shrugged. "Come on, race you to the stage!" She sprinted off and I cantered after her, my brain reeling. It didn't make sense. Hero hadn't left me anything of sentimental value.

I approached the stage with bated breath. Shyla was already in the center, practicing her pliés. There was a design painted on the floor at my feet. The Premiere Ballet Company's logo. I went to the next wing. Logo of Passé Company. In the next, Cherry Blossom Company. They must have performed on this stage at some point or another, or donated to it, or something like that. In the last wing, an olive branch and pointe shoes made up the logo for Fortune. I gulped.

"Have you seen these?" I asked Shyla, finally gathering the nerve to step onto the stage.

"Oh yeah. They're all over the place. Not just ballet companies, either. There are drama groups, choirs, and orchestras. But come on, you're going to show me a Poisson. My teachers can never really get it right."

"It's been a long time. I probably won't get it right, either. I'm out of shape, so don't expect much."

She grinned, disbelieving, but said, "Okay."

I replaced her in the center of the floor and put my feet into fifth position. "The position of your feet is so important. I'm sure your teachers have told you that time and again, but never underestimate it. Poor turnout can wreck any movement." I leapt, arching my back and making sure to keep my legs in fifth, then landed lightly on my feet. "Of course, you usually do Poisson with a partner, so you don't need to master that yet."

"That. Was. Perfect," Shyla said.

"What else do you want to see?"

"Do that again!"

I laughed, but obliged her.

"How do you get your back to arch like that? It's a perfect semi-circle."

Let me see yours."

She leapt and tilted her head back, but didn't attempt the arch.

"You can't be scared to go for it. Your body is flexible. You only used your neck that time. Practice arching back over my arm." I got on my knees behind her and held a rigid arm level with the small of her back. "Go ahead."

She moved into fifth position and raised her hands over her head. After a moment's hesitation, her spine relaxed and her body curled backwards.

"Good!" I said as she came up.

"I don't know if I can do that in the air."

"You'll be able to. Wait til you have a partner – it's going to be so ridiculously easy because they support you while you're doing it."

"Isn't it weird dancing with a partner? The lifts look... uncomfortable." She blushed and performed some basic rond de jambes to regain control of her embarrassment.

Trying not to laugh, I joined her, circling my pointed foot on the floor. "At first, I guess it is. But you forget about that when you realize you are flying through the air. Plus, the guys you'll be partnering with are just dancers like you. They aren't trying to take advantage of you or anything."

She stopped circling her foot, her mind darting to a new topic. "I can't wait to go en Pointe."

"Two more years, kiddo."

"A year and a half," she corrected.

"It's a lot of hard work."

"I don't mind."

"I know you don't, but prepare yourself. Your feet and toes are going to be sore. Bloody, bruised. You'll have calluses and in-grown toenails. Basically, your feet will look disgusting, like someone put them through a meat grinder. Forget about flip flops for the rest of your life."

"But it's worth the pain?"

I smiled, memories of perfecting all three transitions vivid in my mind. "Totally." The euphoria of physically accomplishing something the human body wasn't intended to do was up there with an orgasm, if not more so. Of course, I couldn't say that to a nine-year old.

"Let's do triple runs!" Shyla exclaimed, beginning a large circle around the stage. I fell in line behind her and hummed a tune as we went. Big step, little, little. Big step, little, little.

"Watch your arms," I called out. Her left elbow was bending too much. She adjusted and carried on. One of the things that made Shyla such a great dancer was her ability to take criticism and apply it immediately. She never got angry or doubted herself because of it. Making herself better - the best - was all that mattered.

"Pas de chat," I called out. Immediately, she switched gears and jumped sideways, bringing her knees up and apart. "Feet," I said. She did it again, pointing her toes sharply. "Much better!"

She kept going until I yelled out, "Pas de cheval," and she immediately switched to the step of the horse. We kept going – her in the lead, performing whatever command I barked out and me giving suggestions. We went through the pas de poisson and pas de valse, petit saut, jeté, and grand jeté. Time stood still while we practiced, like it knew I didn't have opportunities like this frequently, and it wanted me to make the most of it.

Mr. Keye appeared stage left and watched us for a few minutes; Shyla hadn't noticed him and I didn't want to stop, so I said nothing. After a round of grueling pirouettes, he cleared his throat. "Ready, ladies?"

Shyla collapsed into my arms, laughing. "That was so much fun! You need to move here so we can do this all the time." She skipped over to the wings and collected her gym bag, slipping it over her shoulder as she made her way to the edge of the stage. "Thanks, Mr. Keye."

"You're welcome. Ready to go?"

I nodded and followed them to the car park. Shyla snagged the front seat, but I didn't care. Her chattering with Mr. Keye prevented me from having to. I let my brain replay the hour on stage, unwilling to give up time that had been so precious. My body had responded exactly as it used to, without any warm up. It knew precisely what to do.

I thought of Sedric's praise when he watched me. Was it ridiculous for me to think about starting to train again? I knew it would be difficult and painful, but hadn't I just told Shyla the pain was worth it?

"What do you think, Honor?" Shyla turned around in her seat, staring at me.

"About what?"

"Coming here to teach. Mr. Keye says Mrs. Keye has been looking for a new teacher. You could do it. You're great."

"Oh." How silly of me to consider trying to perform again. No matter how good I'd been, or even still was, I was thirty. Well past the prime for a new company member. No one would take me. Sure, teaching was an option, but it wasn't the same. "I'll think about it, kiddo. I don't know if teaching's the right fit for me, though."

"Actually," Mr. Keye said, "I think you're a natural. You had great command over Shyla, but you weren't harsh or condescending. And, most importantly, you know ballet."

"I'm sure I *could* teach. I mean, be capable, I just don't know if I want to."

"Aw, come on!" Shyla pleaded. Her puppy-dog eyes did their best to crack me, and it almost worked.

"Like I said, I'll think about it."

Mr. Keye pulled into the driveway and we thanked him while getting out. "No sweat," he said. "I'll have Dani give you a call, Ms. Sandavol. How long are you here?"

"Two more days."

"Got it. Bye, Shyla," he said.

We headed up the path to the front of the house as he drove away. "You could live here, if you wanted," Shyla said, getting out her key to unlock the door.

"Mabry would love that," I said, sarcasm dripping.

"I would."

I brushed a strand of hair away from her face. "Oh, kiddo, you're the best, you know?"

"Yep, I do!"

Shortly after we got back I sent Shyla to bed and tried calling Bonnie again, but she didn't answer. I changed into my pjs and searched through the drawers in the family room entertainment system to find the videos of my dancing. No luck. I checked Val's office on the second floor next. There were no dvds or cds laying around that fit the bill, so I booted up the computer and checked the files. Still nothing. Damn it. I should have asked Shyla where they were before she went to bed.

The guest room I stayed in anytime I visited was on the third floor, down the hall from Handor. I couldn't decide between going up and attempting sleep, or going down and waiting for the rest of the family to get home. I knew I wouldn't sleep if I went up; my mind was too full to shut itself down and allow rest. I went to the stairs.

Handor was fifteen and had found his mate. Okay, it wasn't ideal. To put it mildly, it was complicated. But, still. Fifteen! It was early by anyone's standards. I tried to believe what I'd told him earlier – that my problems were no worse than anyone else's, but it really didn't feel that way. I didn't know if I could see him and act happy and interested. It was Bonnie and Caron's pregnancy all over again. On top of all that, I had Mr. Keye and Shyla's proposal to consider. I'd never wanted to teach. How could I watch young, promising dancers prepare for the career I'd been denied? But being up on stage with Shyla just hours before, I'd felt alive. Released.

Sedric asked why I didn't teach. It had been his first instinct after I told him about my injury. Perhaps that was why I'd always avoided it. I didn't want to do what everyone expected. That had never been me, and I still didn't want to be that person, but could teaching bring a new kind of happiness to my life? Would it fulfill me rather than depress me further?

If I did decide to teach, did I want to come here to do it? I'd love being close to Val, Handor, and Shyla, but could I keep playing nice with Mabry if I had to see her on a regular basis? And Handor would be heading out on his own in a few years. Sooner, actually, depending on what he decided to do about his mates. There was no way to predict where he'd be going for school or work or to start his family.

Then, there was Bonnie. I had moved to Linhill to be closer to her, and I couldn't imagine not being around to see Lang grow up or become a part of the new baby's life. I worried if I moved away from her that we'd rarely talk. If I did decide to teach, I didn't have to do it at Shyla's studio.

I reached the bottom step and looked at the clock on the wall. Eleven twenty-three. The seconds ticked by. I'd never noticed how loud their family room's clock was. Suddenly, I thought of Sedric. What would become of us if I moved?

Us? There was no us. There was a Sedric, and a me. We were nothing to each other, and I needed to stop thinking like we were. I couldn't change the way the world worked. Sedric and I had both been dealt shitty hands by the Gods. We could bluff and go all in, but in the end, we would lose. No one got to choose whom to love. It was decided before we were even born. Sedric and I couldn't be together, even if we both wanted to. Who was I kidding? He wouldn't want to be with me anyway. All this speculating led to that one, simple fact. Sedric had known and loved a kind, sweet woman. He wouldn't move on to a bitchy, bitter one.

I turned the screen on and tried Bonnie one more time. It was dinnertime in Linhill, so I didn't really expect her to answer. I didn't bother to leave a message when the prompt appeared.

Mabry always kept a selection of gourmet coffees in her pantry and had said when I arrived to help myself. No better time than a night alone in their house. While milk heated on the stovetop, I chose a white mint hot chocolate from her stash. The kitchen filled with the scent of peppermint as I added the powder to the milk and stirred. The liquid looked like it was about to boil, so I turned down the heat and took the saucepan off the stove.

Back in the family room, a steaming mug warming my hands, I fumbled through menus to find a show or movie worth watching while waiting for everyone to come home. Nothing looked interesting and I was about to give up when I noticed an option for "Family Videos." I selected it and scrolled through titles like "Bringing Handor Home," "H's first b-day," "Shyla's First Recital," "bathtime," "Priamus 2009" –

then finally, at the end of the list, "Honor." Just one word, but it let me know everything I needed.

I pressed play and the screen went dark, but after a moment, shaky camerawork showed a stage similar to the one Shyla had performed on that evening, lights lining the front floor and spotlights hitting the curtain. Gizella stepped in front of the camera. Hero's voice asked, "Is she ready? Is she nervous?"

"Cool as a cucumber. Plus, I gave her an extra boost of confidence."

"How?"

"You'll see."

Val's teenage voice came from off camera, "How long is this thing going to last? I'm supposed to meet up with my friends."

"Program says about an hour for the show, and there's a fifteen-minute intermission, but you might as well forget about hanging out with your buddies. We're taking your sister out after this to celebrate."

"What if she sucks?"

Gizella's arm went across the screen and Val let out a small "ow." She'd probably jabbed him in the shoulder. I'd forgotten she used to do that.

"She isn't going to suck. They wouldn't give the lead to a dancer who couldn't handle it."

"Shh, you two. I think it's starting," Hero's voice said. I wish I could have seen him on camera, too. I missed him.

A few minutes into the show, after Hero was able to figure out the zoom and focus features of the camera, his voice whispered, "Red lipstick again. I thought you said her teachers told you no."

"They did," Gizella whispered back.

I laughed. Laughter turned to tears. They poured down my cheeks and a few splashed into my mug. I set it on the coffee table and grabbed some tissues. She'd never told me they asked her to stop. She kept breaking the rules because she knew I needed it. I paused the video and stumbled across the room. At the entryway, I slipped my purse off its hook and fumbled around inside until I found my tube of red lipstick. I applied it with shaky hands, checking a small hand mirror to make sure it hadn't gone outside the lines of my mouth or onto my teeth. Nope. It looked fine, even though my wet cheeks and eyes made the rest of my face a glistening, puffy mess. I lay back on the couch and started the video again. I didn't care about seeing myself dancing anymore. I just wanted to hear their voices, so I closed my eyes.

"Honor, wake up." Val shook my shoulder and I struggled to comprehend where I was. His voice sounded distant to my ears, but I could sense his presence close by. "Hon – are you okay?"

I rubbed my eyes and sat up. The room was dark; the screen had shut itself off automatically after a long period of inactivity. Mine did the same thing.

"Wouldn't you be more comfortable upstairs?" Val asked, offering his hand to help me up.

"I can't believe I fell asleep down here." I arched my back and stretched my arms over my head. "Man, that is one horribly uncomfortable couch. I think I messed up my neck." A sharp pain was running up the left side of it.

"Now you know why I'm so nice to my mate. Slept on it once, vowed never to do it again."

I let out a sleepy giggle, mostly just air puffing out of my nose faster than normal. "How'd things go with Handor and his mate?"

"You're half-asleep. I'll fill you in tomorrow morning." He steered me to the staircase, right past the loudly ticking clock.

"It's already tomorrow morning," I joked.

"Go get some sleep."

"I'm up now, you might as well tell me what happened." My foot was on the bottom step, but I leaned against the rail instead of going up. I accidentally closed my eyes.

"You're not up. You're falling asleep standing."

"I'm fine."

"Night, little sis."

It wasn't worth arguing anymore. I stepped up, turning my back to him, and waved my hand behind my head. Through a yawn I said, "Night, big bro."

Chapter Twenty-One: Past Grievances

Val and I didn't talk the following morning. Mabry's relatives were in town, and she had enlisted our help for a second Priamus feast. "Honor, can you do desserts, again?"

I acquiesced and got to work. Luckily, her family wasn't big on sweets, so she only asked for two – raspberry-filled vanilla cupcakes and a peach cobbler. When I finished, I strolled into the family room and attempted another call to Bonnie.

No answer.

"Damn it, Bonnie, I'm getting worried. Please call me back. Is everything okay?" She never traveled for Priamus – she and Caron chose to live in Linhill because it was almost exactly equidistant for both of their families to travel to them for holidays. Bonnie was an only child, and Caron's older brother and his family usually alternated years with her and his mate's lifegivers. Why weren't they answering?

I still had the remote in my hand, and no one else needed to use the screen, so I flipped to the "Place a Call" option. I didn't know the number, so I clicked on the "Locate" button in the bottom right corner and typed in *Sedric Eckland*. It searched for a few seconds before coming back with two results. The first was in Nouthridge, several hours away from where we lived. But the second... I hit "Call" before I lost my nerve.

He's not going to pick up, I thought. *His family is close by. He's with them.* I moved the cursor over to end the call, but before I could hit it, Sedric's living room came into view.

"Who's there?" He squinted into his screen, so I adjusted the light in the family room. "Honor! Hey, I wasn't expecting to hear from you until the end of the week."

"Yeah, I wasn't really planning on talking to you before then, but I can't get Bonnie to answer."

"And that's strange?"

"Yeah. I mean, I wasn't super nice the last time we saw each other, well, you were there, but she always returns my calls. I'm worried."

"Do you want me to go over there and check on them?"

I looked down at the remote in my hand. It wasn't the reason I'd contacted him, but what a lovely excuse. "If it's not too much trouble. No, that's asking too much, isn't it?"

"No trouble at all. I have to run a few errands today anyway. I'd be happy to."

"Thanks. See if you can get her to call me back."

"I will."

"Great."

"Is that it?" he asked.

No. But what else to say – *it's good to see you? Can we just talk about nothing for a few minutes? I actually kind of miss you. Okay, not kind of, I really do miss you.* "Yep, that's it. Did you have a good Priamus with your family?"

"Yeah, I ate too much, though." He patted his stomach, though if he was trying to imply it was still full, he wasn't fooling me. It looked as lean as ever. "How was yours?"

"Eventful." I raised my eyebrows a couple of times in quick succession.

"I'm intrigued – what happened?"

"Well..." I took a few steps back and inclined my head in the direction of the kitchen to make sure none of the family would walk in on me. Sounds of dishes being moved about and spoons beating against bowls indicated all was safe for the time being. "...for starters..." I sat on the couch and relayed the past two days. He laughed, expressed shock in the right moments. All-in-all, a perfect audience. I found myself smiling more and more as I told the story. When I got to the part about the video of my recital, he stopped me.

"Wait – those are on Val's screen? You can send them to yourself, you know."

"Really? How? I've never done that."

"Move the box with me to the corner and pull up the menu where you found the video."

I followed his instructions. "Okay, now what?"

"Hover your cursor over the link, but don't click on it. An options box should pop up."

"Got it!"

"Now select 'Send to a friend' and enter your code."

I bit my bottom lip, concentrating on typing the number correctly. "How do I know if it worked?"

"As long as you hit send, it should be waiting for you when you get home." He paused. "But, if you want to make sure you did it right, you can send it to me and I'll tell you when it comes through."

Wow. Was he aiming for co-worker of the year, or something? "Are you going to watch it?"

"Not if you don't want me to."

Not good enough, buddy. "Do you want to watch it? It's just a silly ballet recital. I was only seven."

"I wouldn't mind watching it. Were you as good at seven as you are at thirty?"

"As a dancer, you mean?"

"Sure."

Wait – what was he doing? What was I doing? This was so stupid. "Tell me your code, I had to look it up in 'Locate.'"

He stated it clearly as I typed it in the box. After about fifteen seconds, his face lit up. "I got it."

"Great, so it works. Um, I should probably get going. Mabry's family is coming in today and I want to make myself scarce."

"Oh. Okay. It was good to see you."

"Yeah." I ended the call and watched his face fade away. *Damn it, Honor. You're an idiot.*

I left the house as Mabry's family started arriving, around noon. I didn't want to be part of the happy reunion of a bunch of people I neither knew nor liked. Mabry seemed relieved I was taking myself out of the equation.

The majority of my day was spent wandering about the city, checking out the numerous pastry shops the area was famous for. When I got back to the house, Mabry's extended family was in the living room, playing board games. I waved a brief hello and headed for the kitchen to see if there were any leftovers from dinner. Val was sitting on a barstool at the counter, covering his ears and hovering over a mini, hand-held screen.

"Whatcha watching?" I bumped his shoulder.

"Football game."

"All alone?" I asked, mocking innocence.

"Her relatives sorta took over the rest of the house. I wanted to shut myself in the office, but would never have heard the end of it from Mabry."

"You wanna sneak out? Take a drive?"

"You've been gone all day and you want to leave again?"

"I thought I stayed long enough for everyone to be gone."

"Ah. I could have told you the flaw in that plan. They are never leaving." He groaned, so I patted his head. "They're going to the recital tonight," he added.

"Don't worry, little Val, I'll take you away from here. Let me fix a plate first, though." Plundering through the fridge, I selected the best of the leftovers and zapped them in the microwave. Yanking a paper towel from the roll and sticking a bottle of water under my arm, I was ready.

"Let's do this."

Val laughed. "Out the back. We'll arouse less suspicion that way. Hell, Mabry might not even notice we're gone. We just need to make sure we're back in time for Shyla's performance."

Val drove us to a drive-in movie theater a couple of miles from his house. "Remember these?"

"Um, yeah. It's been forever. Are there any good movies playing now?"

"Who cares? We never watched the movies."

"Touché."

Val bought a ticket for the car and found a spot in the back row. I unwrapped my plate of leftovers and started picking at the fried chicken.

"How did it go with Shyla last night? Was she okay that we had to leave her?" he asked.

"She wasn't thrilled about it, but we asked the theater manager to let us use the stage, and she got over it quickly once we were dancing."

He reached over and squeezed my knee. "Thank you for that. We planned to take her out for ice cream, you know, like we used to after your recitals. I felt so bad that we couldn't do that. She deserved our time last night, but I guess we can still do it tonight."

"You couldn't help it. She understood. She's a resilient kid."

"You'd make a really good lifegiver, Honor. I don't think I've ever told you that."

I dropped the chicken bone onto my plate and swallowed the lump in my throat. "What happened with Handor's mate?"

"His name is Nevin. We met his lifegivers, Glory and Cucumo."

"Glory! Is she our long-lost sister?"

He laughed. "And I thought Cucumo was the name you'd exclaim at."

"Well, yeah, what kind of crazy person names their child Cucumo? That goes without saying. But Glory? Hero would have thoroughly approved."

"Moving on. They were nice people. A little strange…"

"Clearly, with names like Nevin and Cucumo."

"But nice, overall. We let the boys talk for a little while, getting to know each other stuff, and then we dropped the bomb."

"How did they take it?"

The large screen at the front of the parking lot came to life, flashing the radio station to tune into to hear the movie's audio. We ignored it.

"Not well. We were sitting in the middle of the café, and I thought management was going to ask us to leave. Nevin, particularly, got very loud. He was enraged – said it wasn't fair, and he was the original mate, so Handor better not even go looking for the other one. The lifegivers were slightly calmer, but they thought we were trying to pull one over on them. They forced Handor to show them the lark and then they tried to wipe it off, just to make sure we hadn't drawn it on or something."

"Why would anyone do that?"

He shrugged and held up his hands.

"Damn, how did Handor handle it?"

"He kept pretty silent. Tried to defend himself at first, but then kind of shut down."

"Man, I could kill them for treating him like that," I said.

"They were confused. Shocked. They thought they were meeting their son's lifemate, and then we dumped this disturbing information on them."

"Still, they didn't have to be asses about it."

"I'm sure you would have been roses and kittens in the same situation."

I probably would have been a lot worse. He was right, they needed to process the information, and then, once they realized Handor didn't plan or intend to leave Nevin out in the cold, they'd come around.

"What now?" I asked.

"Well, the boys want to continue getting to know each other. We all agreed they are too young to move in together and complete the bond now, so Handor has a couple of years before he has to make any lasting decisions."

"Where do Nevin and his lifegivers live?"

"Kataloo, about an hour and a half away."

"Did they follow his pull here last night?"

Val nodded. "I'm worried about Handor. It's a lot of pressure on him and he's still so young."

"He's almost sixteen. It's not an ideal age to find his mate, but be thankful he's not younger. Remember that girl from our school who found hers when she was thirteen?"

"Who?"

"You know – she was a few years younger than you and her mate ended up being a twenty-year old teacher. Talk about awkward."

"Oh yeah! How long did her lifegivers make her wait to bond with him?"

"I don't know the details, I just remember at the time Gizella thanking Pria it wasn't me. Although, she changed her tune later on."

"Cut her some slack, Hon. Can't you put past grievances behind you?"

"I'm working on it." I paused, taking a sip of water and peeking at the screen to see a cartoon monkey chasing a live-action human. Weird. "Speaking of Gizella and the past, Shyla told me Hero left you some videos of me dancing when I was younger."

"He did." Val turned to face the screen, too, and his hands moved to grip the steering wheel. "But they aren't mine permanently. I'm supposed to give them to you when you're ready."

"When I'm ready? For what – the zombie apocalypse?"

"No, to watch them without sinking into depression again."

"I'm sorry, what?"

"Hero wanted you to have them. He knew at some point they'd bring you joy, but after your accident, you couldn't bear to hear anyone even mention the word 'ballet.' He didn't think it would be a good idea to remind you of all your promising talent."

"You should have given them to me anyway."

"I was worried about you, too, Honor. Still am, most of the time. That accident changed you. You say it just ruined your career, but it did more than that. You stopped being you for a while. You never answered my calls, and when Bonnie forced you to talk to me, you never said more than a few words at a time. You stopped eating for a little while, then ate everything in sight. You screamed at anyone who tried to suggest a next step, career-wise. Then you got obsessed with your lark and that's all you could talk about."

He put his hand on my shoulder, but I shrugged it off. My face felt like it was on fire. I stared out the windshield at the movie screen without my eyes processing what they were seeing. Val was wrong. I hadn't been that bad. I couldn't have been. He was still talking.

"Shyla and Handor were the only people you were normal with. And don't even get me started on how you treated Mabry. Hero and Gizella tried to help you, but you wouldn't listen. You refused therapy. It took them dying to finally shake some sense in you. Can you imagine how Hero felt when Gizella passed, knowing you had that weight on you, too, and wouldn't talk to anyone about it? I wish they could have lived to see you starting to return to normal."

Normal? What was normal? Who was he to judge it? "And when exactly was that?" I snapped.

"I'd say a few weeks ago."

"Go to hell, Val." I shoved my door open and hopped out, sprinting towards the concession stand. Val didn't follow. I got in line for a hot dog, even though I wasn't hungry, and ordered one even though I had no intention of eating it. That's why I didn't want to live near Val. After all that time, finding out he'd been conspiring with our lifegivers even beyond their deaths – it was too much. And it wasn't fair.

I didn't need his protection, and I sure as hell didn't want it. Gizella and Hero knew I wanted to take care of myself, and yet they pulled shit like that. I wanted to scream. To belt out a growl that would frighten the children in the dozens of minivans who had come to see the movie, and possibly, just maybe, make myself feel in control of my own life for a few seconds.

The hotdog was ready. I let the teenager behind the counter hand it to me and grimaced at the sympathetic look she gave my lark when I reached for it.

I didn't need anyone.

"Honor, Bonnie called for you while you were out," Mabry informed me as we entered the house a couple of hours later. Mabry's extended family was in chaos, donning coats and galoshes, preparing to head out the door to Shyla's second performance of *The Little Doe*.

"Okay," I said. I went upstairs to my room and began packing my suitcase. I was leaving the next day, and it couldn't come soon enough.

Chapter Twenty-Two: Almost

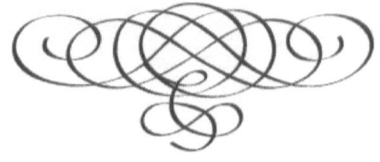

B ombs were going off inside Bonnie and Caron's house. At least, that's what it sounded like when I approached the front door. I rang the bell, but didn't have much hope they'd hear it, so I pulled out my key and let myself in.

Lang came around the corner, squealing at the top of her lungs, and ran straight to the door. "Honor!" she shouted and threw herself behind me, grabbing my legs and stuffing her face into the crook at the back of my knees.

"What the..."

Sedric appeared, fingers curled into claws, shoulders hunched over, growling. "Oh!" He straightened up and dropped the monster act. "Honor. Hey."

"He-ey. What's going on?"

"Um, I came to check on them the other day, like you asked, and they were having trouble with their dishwasher, so I fixed it. They invited me over for dinner tonight, sorta like a thank you."

"He's going to get me, Honor! Don't let him," Lang cried, her voice muffled, but still audible.

"Don't worry, kiddo." I patted her head, which took some impressive upper body flexibility to reach. "Where are Bonnie and Caron?"

"Caron had a doctor's appointment."

"So, you're the babysitter?"

"If you want to put a label on it," he said.

"Okay. Well..."

"Did they know you were coming?"

"No."

"Well, you're welcome to wait for them. They shouldn't be much longer."

"I'm welcome to wait? Are you freaking kidding me? Lang, go to your room for a few minutes, please."

"But we're playing," she said.

I gritted my teeth and tried to keep my frustration at Sedric out of my voice when I answered her. "I know, sweetie, but I need to talk to Sedric about some adult things. Can you give us just a few minutes?"

"I don't wanna go to my room!"

"How about we play hide and seek, Lang?" Sedric said, crouching down and peering around my legs. "Honor and I will hide and you come find us. Your room will be home base. Go in there and count to a hundred."

"Okay!" She released my legs and scampered to her room.

I wanted to hit Sedric in the mouth. I hadn't talked to Bonnie in weeks, but Sedric was having dinner with her? She wouldn't call me back, but she'd let a virtual stranger watch her child? It was almost worse than Val hiding the video from me. Bonnie was supposed to be my ally. The person who loved me most.

"Who do you think you are?" I seethed. "Bonnie and Caron are not your friends. Lang is not your Goddaughter. What the hell are you trying to do?"

He put his hands up. "I was trying to help out. To be *your* friend."

"Ugh, you're just so perfect, aren't you? So helpful, so polite, so goddamn calm all the time."

He took a step towards me. "What's wrong with you?"

"What is wrong with *you*?" My finger pointed angrily at him, jabbing with every syllable. "Why are you trying so hard to inject yourself in my life?"

"You are the most egotistical woman I've ever known."

My mouth opened to scream a response, but what could I say to that? He was right. Everyone was right about me. "I need to sit down." I walked slowly to the living room and sank into the couch.

"Why are you acting so crazy?" Sedric asked, sitting on the edge of the loveseat across the room.

"Because I am crazy."

"I already knew that." He grinned.

I wanted to both smack him and kiss him. Everything he'd done over the last couple of weeks gave me conflicting desires. Did I want him as a colleague, a friend, or something more? What would the something more be? "If I'm crazy, you are certifiable for wanting to spend time with me."

"I'm not sure I want to after that," he said.

"You do, or you wouldn't be smiling."

"Seriously, what happened?"

I shook my head. "I don't know. It was kind of like a weird, protective instinct came over me."

"Protective or possessive?"

"A little of both?"

He leaned forward, elbows on his knees. "I guess I get that, but something else is going on to make you blow up like that."

Lang popped into the room. "I found you!"

"Great job! Let's play again. Go count," Sedric said.

"Okay!" She ran off. He motioned for me to talk. What to say? That everything seemed so screwed up I could barely breathe? That I was worried Bonnie only kept being my friend out of obligation, rather than genuine affection? That I had no idea what to do about the tug in my heart whenever he matched me, snarky comment for snarky comment?

"I told you about Handor and his lark situation."

Sedric nodded.

"And Mabry is a pain in the ass. I tried really hard to be friendly, and the kind of sister-by-bond Val has always wanted me to be, but she's so damn annoying."

He stifled a laugh.

"And I couldn't reach Bon the entire time I was gone — you know that — but I'm worried that means something, like she doesn't want to talk to me. Like I've finally ruined everything with her."

"You haven't," he said.

"Did she say something?"

"She thought it was really sweet you sent me to check on her. I watched while she tried to call you. She felt horrible for missing your calls."

"Oh." Relief washed over me. "I fought with my brother, too, because apparently now I yell at everyone who cares about me."

He smiled and bent his head down, looking at the floor. After a moment, he looked up and met my eye. "What did you and Val fight about?"

"Our lifegivers and the video they gave him. They didn't think I could handle watching it. Like I'm some fragile, little girl or something."

"But you're not?"

I nodded. "Damn right, I'm not."

"You do seem to break easily."

"Don't you dare get me started."

"I just mean you're very quick to lash out and react emotionally. Did they think the video would make you angry?"

"Depressed."

"And how did you feel when you watched it?"

Incredible. Joyous. Somehow, hearing Gizella and Hero's voices was more soothing than dancing. "Happy."

"So, they were wrong. Why get angry now? They're gone, aren't they? It takes an awful lot of energy to stay mad at someone who doesn't exist anymore."

I started — his voice wavered on those last few words. I took in a few deep breaths and tried to sound calm. "Were you angry with Zara?"

"Yes."

"Why?"

"Because she left," he said matter-of-factly.

"She didn't want to. It wasn't her fault."

"Your lifegivers didn't want to hurt you, they wanted to protect you. They didn't know how you'd react. They made a guess for what they thought was best."

I shook my head. "They didn't know what was best for me."

"But that didn't stop them from loving you."

"How'd you get over it?"

"My anger at her?" He wrung his hands together. "Time. Reflection. Making the conscious choice to not be angry anymore."

"It's not that easy."

He sighed. "Things worth doing rarely are."

"What are you, a philosopher now? I thought we agreed you wouldn't do that."

He laughed and looked like he had something to add, but was cut off by my four-year old Goddaughter. "Hey!" Lang stormed in, her little fists clenched on her hips. "You were supposed to hide!"

"We did, but you're so good, you found us!" Sedric said.

"Don't patronize her." I turned to Lang. "I'm sorry. We'll go hide right now, I promise."

She raised her eyebrows and unclenched her hands. "Okay."

"Count here." I picked her up and put her on the couch beside me.

She pushed her face into a pillow and began, "One... two... three..."

Sedric grabbed my hand and led me across the house to a guest room. We went in and closed the door quietly, backing up until we were on the other side of a dresser, along the same wall as the door.

His hand was warm and his fingers engulfed mine. They felt impossibly long. Lang's footsteps came close to the door, but she didn't open it. Sedric drew closer to me; our arms were touching.

"Where'd you guys go?" Lang shouted.

Sedric shifted so we were facing each other, my nose hitting his chin. "What are you doing?" I whispered.

"I don't know." He let go of my hand and moved his up to brush the bangs off my forehead. I tilted my chin up so I could look into his eyes. The intensity between us actually created heat; Sedric's hairline boasted a few beads of perspiration.

"Are we going to..."

"Do you want to?" His mouth was descending, coming so close to mine.

How could he ask me that? It wasn't a simple matter of yes, I wanted him to kiss me, or no, I didn't. Sedric wasn't like the other men I'd kissed in my life. He wasn't a faceless one-night stand, or a kid from ninth year I'd asked to show me what his tongue felt like. I'd remember Sedric's name in five, ten, fifteen years. I'd remember how brown his eyes were looking into mine. And how his lips parted ever-so-slightly as he leaned toward me. I'd never forget the way he smelled like he'd been outside, chopping down trees all day.

I'd remember it all, but I didn't know if I would regret it. My eyes closed and I sighed, waiting.

"Are you in here?" Lang burst through the door and Sedric jumped back a foot.

"Wow – you are really good at this game," he said. My hand clutched my shirt above my heart, trying to muffle the pulsing. I didn't want him to hear it beating.

"Bonnie and Caron are back," Lang said. "They brought pizza. Come on, Honor!" She grabbed my arm and started dragging me toward the door. My gaze searched for Sedric's, but he was staring at the ground, stuffing his hands in his pockets.

"Honor!" Bonnie came forward to greet me, her arms outspread. I rushed into them, holding onto her tightly, afraid she'd vanish if I let go.

"I'm so sorry, for everything. For getting mad at you the last time I was here, and for always thinking only of myself, and for never being one hundred percent supportive of you. And, for apparently being a zombie after my ballet accident."

"What are you talking about?" She tried to push away, but I held on tighter.

"Val said after I hurt my ankle I went into this depression, and he and our lifegivers were worried about me, and if they were, I know you were, too. So, I'm sorry I did that to you."

She smoothed my hair. "It's fine. It's completely okay."

"You don't hate me?"

"Never. I could never hate you. Even when I'm pissed off at you, I love you. You know that, right?"

"I was worried maybe I finally went too far."

"If you ever do, I'll tell you. We'll talk about it. I promise."

"Okay." I reluctantly released her, suddenly aware Sedric was standing behind me.

"I'm sorry you had to send Sedric over to check on us. We were swamped with Priamus, and Caron's been having complications with the pregnancy."

"What? Why didn't you tell me? Is she okay? What complications?"

"Breathe, Honor. She's fine. The baby's fine. We didn't tell anyone because we didn't want anyone to worry. We didn't even tell our lifegivers. If anything needs to be communicated, you'll be one of the first to know, I promise. You're family."

I hugged her again, but a little less like a creepy stalker.

"Guys, pizza!" Lang sang from the kitchen.

Bonnie put her arm around my waist as we moved towards the sound of her daughter's voice. "I don't know if I like this soft Honor. I miss my hard-ass best friend."

Sedric laughed.

"What?" I said, trying to glare at him, but failing. I couldn't forget our almost-moment and didn't know if I wanted to.

"Oh, nothing. I think there are merits to both versions." We locked eyes and I knew he wanted to get me alone again, to finish what we started. I wanted to yank him outside and plant my mouth on his, but I remembered what Bonnie and I had discussed. It wasn't healthy for either of us. He'd eventually realize I couldn't make him as happy as Zara had, and that would break my heart. So, I looked away.

Chapter Twenty-Three: Nothing's Changed

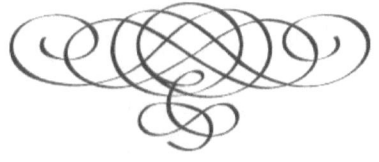

I ignored Sedric the rest of the week, hiding in my house and baking every recipe in my repertoire, but Sunday came and forced us together with an airport and two tickets to Highby. Security kept him pretty occupied when we first arrived, but by the time we reached the gate, there was nothing to distract him.

"Honor, can we talk about what happened at Bonnie and Caron's?"

"It's unnecessary. We're both lonely; it was a weak moment. That's it. We don't have to make a big deal out of it."

"But we could. Can't we discuss the possibility of-"

"We don't have matching larks, Sedric."

He put his hand on my arm. "Who cares?"

I shook his fingers off. Even if somehow we did manage to make something work, it wouldn't be accepted by anyone else. Non-mated couples never survived the backlash. "The universe. Why put ourselves through the pain?"

"What if-"

"No. No what-ifs. Not with you. Other than Bonnie, you're one of the best friends I've ever had, and I've only known you, what, a month? Let's not mess it up." I flipped open a magazine and tried to engross myself in an article about cuticle care, but could feel Sedric watching me. I refused to turn my eyes to check. When we'd been silent so long it was inevitable one of us was about to speak, I decided it would be best if it were me.

"Do any of the potentials have family where we're headed?"

"You still want to find out who he was?"

"Of course. Why wouldn't I? Nothing's changed." Except everything.

He squared his shoulders and brought his left leg up, resting the ankle on his knee. Then he started fidgeting with his tie. "Right. Nothing's changed. One of them. We can go as soon as we land, if you want."

"It's okay. We have an entire week."

"Why wait? You want to know who he was, better to find out earlier than later. Gives you all that extra time to get to know him." It wasn't like Sedric to be sarcastic in a mean way, but I would have been worse in his place, so I didn't bite back, even though I really wanted to.

"First thing's fine with me," I said.

"Good."

"Great."

He turned away from me and opened his own magazine.

"This is it," Sedric said as he pulled the rental car to the curb and parked in front of a small house. The grass was dead, leaving patches of sand and dirt, and the walkway leading to the front door was littered with old newspapers and soda bottles. "How are you feeling?"

I gulped. "Great. Good. This is good."

"You sure you want to know if this is the place your mate lived? Possibly grew up?"

I looked out the window at the overflowing trashcan beside the mailbox and the rusted chain-link fence around the yard. It certainly didn't scream, *cozy*. "I... uh, yep. Totally sure. Do you want to come in or wait in the car?"

He hesitated, keeping one hand on the wheel and the other on the gearshift.

"Don't worry about it. Just tell me the name again."

"I can come if you need me to."

"Don't bother. Name?"

"Malichi Saunders. The possible drug overdose."

"Alright, then." I closed the door behind me as I got out and faced the house. If I didn't walk forward, Sedric would know I was having doubts, but my legs wouldn't move. The engine shut off and I heard his door open and shut. He leaned against the car beside me. I was tempted to reach for his hand and gain the confidence I needed from the strong grasp of his freakishly long fingers. Instead, I forced myself forward. Knowing he had my back would have to be enough.

I didn't see a doorbell, so I knocked a few times and waited. A car sat parked in the gravel driveway; I hoped someone was home, but after a few minutes there was still no answer.

"Try again," Sedric said. He was at my shoulder. I thought again about reaching around and squeezing his hand, but didn't.

I rapped three more times. The door creaked open, and an older man wearing a white undershirt and loose jeans squinted through the screen at me. A cigarette dangled from his mouth. "Whattya want?" he barked.

"I'm sorry to bother you, sir, but did you have a son named Malichi Saunders?"

He took the cigarette from his mouth and tucked it behind his ear. "Did he owe you money or something?"

"No, sir."

"Hmph. Then I don't know why you'd be coming to ask about 'im. He wasn't good for nothing."

"I'm looking for my lifemate-"

"Why you here, then? Malichi's dead."

I cleared my throat. "I know. He died in the city my pull was leading to when it stopped. So, I, uh..."

"Look here, lady, if Mali was your mate, you're better off without 'im."

A scratchy voice yelled from further inside the house. "Who's at the door, Morty?"

"Some lady asking about Mali," he shouted back.

I held out my wrist, worried I was losing his attention. "This is my lark, where was Malichi's?"

He didn't look at it. His head was turned into the house, and a robust woman with wild, frizzy hair came stomping into the front room, her finger wagging at the door. No, not at the door. At me.

"What're you comin' round here askin' about Malichi for? He's dead, ain't he? We don't want you comin' round here no more. Whatever your problem with our son was, it died with him." She had her face pressed nearly into the screen, her index finger poking at the net. I took a few steps back, but Sedric's hand on the small of my back stopped me. "Get the 'ell outta here!" the woman screamed.

"I just want to know-"

"Out!"

Sedric took my elbow and tried to turn me around, but I couldn't leave yet. I didn't know. They hadn't given me any answers. "Please, where was his lark – just tell me that!"

The woman slammed the door; Sedric tried to pull me away, but I rushed forward and banged on the frame. "I need to know! Please, please..."

"I'm calling the police if you don't get the 'ell off my porch," the woman bellowed. I banged my fist on the wood one last time, scraping the side on a rusty nail sticking out where a peephole should have been.

"Damn it," I cried, bringing my hand closer to my face for inspection.

"What did you do?" Sedric asked. I showed him the scratch. "We should get that cleaned. You don't want to get tetanus." I allowed him to lead me to the car and numbly got into the passenger side.

"It wasn't him. He wasn't the one," Sedric said, buckling his seatbelt.

"We don't know that. They wouldn't even look at my lark."

"There was a picture on the wall across from us. The man who opened the door and a younger man. It was him, I'm ninety-nine percent positive from the photos I found online. Malichi had his shirt off and on his chest, clear as day, a lark."

"Are you sure? Maybe it was just a tattoo."

"If so, he was drunk when he got it. It was a jumble of brown spots."

"He wasn't the one?"

"Nope."

I breathed a sigh of relief and relaxed into my seat. "He wasn't the one. Thank Pria." Anxiety rolled off my shoulders, but a new fear was beginning to plague me. "Are they all going to react like that?"

"I doubt it. I think most lifegivers would be grateful that someone is looking for their child. That someone cares enough to go door to door."

"But it's only going to be the right house one time. How are all those lifegivers who turn out to be no's going to feel? Am I going to be reopening their wounds, only to pour salt in them?"

The light ahead of us turned red and Sedric eased to a stop. "I don't know. Honestly, I wish they would all welcome you with open arms as the daughter they should have had, but that's unrealistic. Actually, I hope the next one is the correct one, so you don't have to keep going through this time after time, but what's the likelihood of that happening?" Green light. Pedal to the floor. "Do you want to keep going?" he asked.

I looked out my side window, watching shabby houses evolve into pristine ones. Dead lawns made way for thriving ones. Even the sky seemed bluer the farther we went from the Saunders' house. A few days before, I'd let my head be clouded and angered by my brother's idea that I didn't know what was best for me. Now, I couldn't have stated emphatically what was best for me if someone held a gun to my head. If I kept going, I ran the risk of another family like the Saunders – more people hurt by my quest than helped by it. If I stopped, I feared I'd slowly go insane with all the what-if's still torturing my mind. Finding out meant answers. Not all the answers, but answers nonetheless.

"Yes."

Chapter Twenty-Four: Make Up Your Mind

The next week brought a new city, new company, and new potentials to visit and rule out. Sedric stopped trying to talk me out of finding my mate and instead, pretty much stopped talking to me altogether. About anything of substance, at least. He said good morning and made polite conversation over lunch, but there was no laughter or teasing.

I missed him, the way he was before that stupid game of hide and seek. The calm demeanor had turned cold and I didn't know how to warm it.

Okay, maybe I did. But I wasn't going there. Setting myself up for disappointment with the men who might have been my mate was one thing, but with Sedric, it was something different. Something painful. We weren't mated, so it didn't matter how we felt, and I couldn't bear the thought of someday, inevitably, hurting him when things fell apart. He'd been hurt enough.

He continued to drive me around. I offered to get a separate rental car, but he said there was no need. I was glad he wasn't so upset that he stopped being there. His presence helped, even when his actions and words did not.

The second house we visited painted a drastically different portrait than the first. We were so far south it felt like spring, and a flower garden bloomed in the front yard: roses, lilies, tulips, gardenia. A woman in her early sixties tended it in a wide-brimmed, straw hat. She shielded her eyes with a dirty-gloved hand as I approached. "Good morning," I said.

"Morning. How can I help you?"

"I'm looking for Garson Kirkey's lifegivers."

She lowered her hand and squinted at me for a moment before attempting to rise to her feet. I gave her my hand to help.

"Thank you." She breathed quickly; standing or my question had knocked the wind out of her. "Garson was my son. Did you know him?"

"Not exactly. I'm looking for my mate. My pull stopped abruptly five years ago, around the time your son passed away."

"And you think Garson was him?"

"My pull was leading me to Eribank when it disappeared."

She let out a low whistle. "Why don't you come inside? Would you like some lemonade?"

"That would be nice." As I followed her to the house, she brushed dirt, grass, and flower petals from her clothes.

"Since he passed, gardening's been the one thing that helps me forget."

"I'm so sorry for your loss."

She opened the door and motioned for me to go ahead of her. "I'm sorry for yours, too."

It caught me off guard. No one had ever said that to me about my mate before. I tried to smile my gratitude, but didn't know what else to do or say. I'd been mourning for myself, never for the person I'd lost.

"Have a seat." She gestured to a couch in a sitting room off the front door and disappeared. I looked at my watch and thought about Sedric in the car, but he was just going to have to wait.

There were framed photos all over the walls of the sitting room, and instead of settling on the couch I studied them, wondering what his family was like. In one, the gardener had her arm around a young man standing in front of a green and khaki jeep. An elephant roamed in the background. In another, the teenager sat at a desk while an older man looked over his shoulder.

Each picture told a different story. In one, the boy I assumed was Garson proudly showed off a missing tooth. In another, he wore a dark green cap and gown and stood between his lifegivers, posing with a diploma. It looked like they traveled all over the world. In addition to the Safari photo, there were snow-capped mountains, rushing rapids, and green forests. He had adventures.

I would have loved experiencing those places and things. With him. If he was my mate. I couldn't find a photograph among the gallery that showed a clear view of his wrists, though. I wondered if he kept going on adventures after he got sick, or if he went because he was sick.

His family looked so happy, too. What would it have been like, joining them? Would there be more photos on the wall – ones that included me?

Mrs. Kirkey approached, holding out a tall glass filled with ice and lemonade. "Here you go. What's your name? I'm sorry I didn't ask before – you took me by surprise."

"It's Honor. And thank you." I took a sip and gestured to the photographs. "Is this him?"

"Yes, that's my Garson. He was a sweet boy. Worked hard in school. Life wasn't kind to him."

"I'm sorry, it can't have been easy on you." I took another sip of the drink, unsure what other platitude to give. She reached a finger out and touched my wrist.

"Your lark?"

I nodded.

"I'm afraid he can't be your mate." She walked to the other side of the room and took a picture off the wall. She handed the frame to me – a child jumping into a swimming pool, a black cluster on his right shoulder blade. I hadn't noticed it because I wasn't looking for a lark there.

"Oh." I gave it back to her. "Thank you for humoring me. And for the lemonade." I gave her the glass as well. "I'll get out of your hair now." I didn't try and hide my disappointment. I didn't know much about Garson or his family, but they seemed like good people. I would have liked being part of their family.

She set the frame and glass on a side table. "I think it's nice that you're looking for him. Part of me wishes it had been

Garson. It would have been like having a part of him back again."

I squeezed her hand, comforting her as well as myself. "Maybe they'll come and find you one day."

"Maybe. Good luck, Honor. I hope you get what you're looking for."

Sedric folded the newspaper he was reading in half and tucked it between his leg and the driver's door as I got in the car. "How'd it go?"

"Not him. She was kind, though." No need to go into more details.

"You want to try the next place now or later?"

"Might as well go for now."

He put the car in gear and directed it to the highway. I fiddled with the radio while he drove, surfing the stations, listening to a song for a few seconds then turning it, hoping for something better. After about fifteen minutes of that, Sedric's hand covered the controls. "Make up your mind, Honor."

I left the radio alone after that, even though it ended up on a horrible talk-radio program about ice fishing. Sedric stared straight ahead at the road, refusing to turn his head even when he needed to check his blind spots.

I went back to looking out my side window. It seemed to be my new default for car rides with Sedric. An amusement park passed along one stretch; shouts of glee pinpointed the location of the rollercoaster, but after a few seconds, it was behind us. A strip mall. Billboards. We left the city limits and headed into the rural portion of the region. Soon, the scenery boasted horses, cows, and even a tractor or two.

Sedric turned the car down an unevenly paved road and began to slow down. Ahead of us was a lovely little house, complete with wrap-around porch and a stable in the back.

The car came to a stop in front of the red-and-white For Sale sign in the yard. I got out and hopped up the porch steps to ring the doorbell. The last visit had me feeling more optimistic about the search. Maybe my mate was as nice as Garson. No answer. I rang again. Nothing.

I tried to peer through the front window, but the burgundy curtains hanging inside obstructed my view. My hands rested on my hips and I turned around, defeated. I caught Sedric's eye in the car, but he looked down at his paper almost instantly. He'd been watching me. Enough.

"No one's home." I slammed the door shut and sat sideways in the seat, staring at him.

"What?" he asked.

"Stop."

"Stop what?"

"Acting like this. Like a spoiled child."

He didn't look up from the news. "*I'm* acting like a spoiled child? Really?"

I hated how calm he sounded. He never got heated. Nothing ever riled him. "I'm sorry if I hurt your feelings, but I didn't know what else to do."

"You didn't hurt my feelings."

"Bull shit. You've been acting like a wounded puppy ever since the thing at Bonnie and Caron's."

He turned the paper over, glancing at the headlines on the back page. "Oh, so first I'm a spoiled child, now I'm a wounded puppy. What next, a jealous sister?"

"Why can't we be friends?"

"We are."

"That's not how you've been acting," I said.

"I've been driving you around, haven't I?"

I rolled my eyes. "And you've been so happy about it."

He finally looked aggravated. "I'm not happy all the time. You sure as hell aren't, how can you expect me to be?"

I crossed my arms over my chest and slumped back in my seat. "Fine. Let's just go to the hotel. You don't need to come with me to meet families anymore. I'll do it on my own."

"If that's what you want." He started the car and backed out of the long driveway.

"I was perfectly capable of doing things for myself before I met you. You aren't like my savior or anything."

"Good. I don't want to be."

"Coulda fooled me."

He slammed on the brakes. Tiny pebbles flew up around the tires, making ping noises as they hit the underside of the car. "Damn it, Honor. You're a real piece of work, you know that? Most normal people say thank you, and tell the truth most of the time, and accept help when it's offered, and don't try to push away the people who care about them."

"Hmph. Who wants to be normal?" I hated the word.

"Not you. You've made that abundantly clear." He eased off the brake and the car inched forward. Once it was off the uneven pavement, he picked up speed until we were flying way over the posted limit.

We rode in angry silence. Him at me, me at myself. And at him a little bit, too, but mostly at myself. He swung into the hotel's parking lot and pulled into the drop-off zone. I placed a hand on his arm. He flinched, but didn't brush it off.

"I care about you, Sedric. I really do. And I do appreciate everything you've done for me. But-"

"It's too hard."

I shook my head. "No, it's not hard. It's easy. For now. Easy to forget there used to be someone out there intended for me. I've hurt for so long, it's nice to think you could make me forget that. But sooner or later, it's not going to be easy anymore. You're going to get hurt. Or I am. And then what? Are we supposed to smile and carry on like nothing happened? Like everyone's been expecting me to do since my accident, and since my lifegivers died, and since my pull stopped?"

"Why are you so convinced it's going to end?"

I took his hand and turned it over, putting my wrist next to it. "We aren't a match. Have you ever met people who weren't matched who made it work? Because I haven't."

Three abrupt taps on my window startled us. I twisted my torso and rolled the glass down. "Yes?"

"I'm sorry, ma'am, this area is for people unloading luggage."

"We're just about to." I rolled it up before the bellhop could respond and turned to Sedric, but he was already out of the car. I waited for the attendant to move so I could open my door without banging his shins.

Our luggage was out of the trunk and seated on the curb by the time I reached the back of the car. Sedric grabbed both bags and headed inside. At least his chivalry wasn't dead.

Bonnie actually answered when I called her from my room that evening. "How are you?" she asked.

"I've been better. Sedric's acting really pissy."

"Sedric, pissy? That doesn't really sound like him."

"That might be too strong a word, but he's definitely upset with me."

"Why?"

I'd never told Bonnie about the almost-kiss between Sedric and myself at her house. I half-expected a lecture on how to act while watching her child, and I really couldn't deal with that on top of Sedric's attitude.

"What did you do, Honor? Did you, um, do what I warned you about?"

"No, I told you I don't see Sedric that way." Except, of course, that was the only way I'd been able to look at him since Priamus. "I don't know what his problem is."

"And what's been going on with your little search?" she asked.

"The first family was horrible to me – threatened to call the police."

"What?"

"But the second lady was very nice and helpful. No dice, though. I wish… but, it doesn't matter. No one was at the last house we went to. It was out in the sticks, too. A wasted drive. Looked like a farmer or horse breeder lived there. Pretty place, though."

"That sucks. Are you going to go back and try again?"

"If there's time. He was low on the list, though. We couldn't find any evidence that he traveled to any of the other cities on my list. So, three down, fifteen to go!"

She chuckled. "You're surprisingly upbeat."

"At least I'm doing something. It's better than standing still, you know?"

"Yeah, I do."

"How's Caron? Any pregnancy news?"

"She's o-kay." Bonnie looked quickly over her shoulder towards their bedroom.

"What's wrong?"

"Nothing. We went to the doctor's office yesterday, and he put her on bed rest."

"No wonder you answered."

"Not funny."

"Sorry. What happened? Is the baby okay?" I asked.

"Their heart rates have been elevated at every appointment. The doctor thinks Caron has been putting too much stress on her body. Other than that, everything looks healthy."

"How is she handling being all cooped up?"

"She's been a nightmare." Bonnie laughed, so I started laughing, too. The idea of Bonnie thinking her mate was a nightmare was beyond hysterical to me. Bonnie practically worshipped the ground Caron walked on. It worked both ways, actually. Plus, Caron was one of the kindest, sweetest, most easy-going people I'd ever known.

"I just hope you never have to go on bed rest," Bonnie said, "because as much as Caron's been annoying me, I know you'd be absolutely insufferable."

I laughed again. "Maybe if that ever happens I'll be someone else's responsibility."

"Like the staff at a mental institution?"

"Exactly."

A loud knock on my door interrupted us. "Must be room service," I said.

"I've got to be getting back to Lang, anyway. With Caron in bed, it's like I'm a single lifegiver."

"Good luck."

"You, too."

I clicked the screen off and answered the door. It wasn't room service. "Can I come in?" Sedric asked.

"Sure." I stepped aside and he went straight to the window, pushing aside the curtain and peering down into the parking lot.

"Have you eaten yet?"

"Waiting on room service," I said.

He faced me and wrung his hands together. "Let me do this quickly, then."

"What?"

He wiped his palms on his jeans and took two broad steps across the room. One hand cupped my neck while the other arm snaked around my waist and drew me to him. His lips landed softly on mine and when I didn't pull away, pressed harder.

My head spun, or was that the room? His fingers were in my hair. I opened my mouth slightly; I wanted to breathe him in.

"Honor," his mouth whispered against mine, the fluttering of his lips causing my heart to speed up. They moved to the side of my mouth, then my jaw line. I opened my eyes and reached up, taking his face in my hands.

"You're insane."

"Takes one to know one." He kissed me again, now both arms around me, lifting me up to meet him. I wanted to remind him he was my boss and, technically, I could report him for sexual harassment, but my desire for him to continue harassing me overrode my rational thinking.

"I don't care about our larks," he whispered in between kisses to my neck. Shit. That killed the mood. Because I cared. I wished I didn't, but I did. Especially after today. I pushed on his chest and took a few steps back. He tried to follow, but I held up my palm.

"Stay right there." I leaned against the wall, with the bed between us.

"Why?"

"This is fun now. You say you don't care about your lark now, but how are you going to feel in the morning? Like you betrayed Zara?"

"Zara is dead. She isn't coming back. Do you really think I shouldn't move on with my life?"

"Yes, you absolutely should. Get new hobbies, make new friends. But don't replace your mate. I don't want to be second place to her."

"You won't be."

"Of course I will. And you'll be second place to mine."

He winced as if I'd slapped him. "You don't even know him. Are you telling me you'd rather find out who your mate is and live tethered to a ghost than take a shot at a real relationship with me?"

"But it won't be real. We won't be bonded. Say we stayed together for five years, ten years, hell, twenty, and something happens to one of us – the law won't recognize that we were together. Our families won't even recognize it. Society won't care that our mates died. No one gets a second chance at love. That's not how the world works."

"I think you're wrong."

"Most people do."

He crammed his hands into his pockets and rocked back on his heels. "How about we make a deal? I'll continue helping you find your mate. I'll go with you to visit every family, and stand by your side, and hold your hand when you need it. And after you learn who he is, we revisit this."

"To what end?"

"You are going to change your mind."

"I don't think so."

He smiled. "Maybe I will, then."

"Did you just lie to me? I think I've been a bad influence on you."

"I'm not complaining."

A loud knock caused us both to turn towards the door. A man's voice announced, "Room Service."

"Think about it?" he asked.

I looked down at my hands, then my wrists. It seemed like a lifetime since I'd found out my mate was dead. If I'd never met Sedric, would I have ever come to the right conclusion? Ugh, I was what if-ing again.

Sedric was more than a friend. I had to stop telling myself he wasn't. We both knew it. But he was asking for more than a moonlit walk on the coast and a few tumbles in the sack. He wanted all of me. For the life of me I couldn't figure out why. Did I want all of him? I didn't know. I knew I wanted the life I was supposed to have with my mate.

He watched me, patiently, waiting for some kind of answer. Finally, I nodded.

"Good night, Honor," Sedric said, letting the waiter in and letting himself out.

Chapter Twenty-Five: In a Different World

Technically, I hadn't agreed to Sedric's deal, but when we arrived in Trenalda the following week, he was all smiles as he drove me through the city. There were four potentials to check out, and I was ready to cross each one off my list. I had begun preparing myself for the possibility that I might never have the answer; that I was crazy to think I could track down someone I didn't know, without a name, a career, or anything to go on except the possible city of his death.

At times I wondered if he really was dead. Maybe we'd both stopped responding to the pull for another reason. I couldn't come up with what that reason might be, though.

Sedric created a map of our targets and a route to use our time most efficiently. We started close to the airport and worked our way into the city, toward the hotel.

No one home at the first stop. "Promising start to the day," I grumbled as we got on the road for the next place.

"We can come back on our way out of town. Or one night this week," Sedric said.

At the next house, a pair of gentlemen kindly explained that though their son had died in the city I'd been drawn to, he was bonded at the time of his death. Strike Two.

Third try. The gentleman in question had been a tenant of the couple who owned the house. They didn't know much about his history, but they did have a box of his personal items they'd gradually been selling off in yard sales. No one had ever come to claim it after his death.

"Do you mind if we go through it?" I asked.

"Well, it belongs to us, now," the old man said.

"We'll buy the box from you." Sedric retrieved his wallet from his back pocket and drew out a twenty note.

"It's a pretty big box, we could probably get fifty for it if we keep putting it in yard sales."

"How long will that take you? It's already been five years. It's twenty now, or fifty over a decade. Twenty now sounds pretty good to me." Sedric waved the note in front of the man's face.

He grimaced. "Forty."

"Thirty."

"I guess that'll work." The old man snatched the twenty and held out his grubby fingers for the rest. I reached into my purse, but before I could produce a ten, Sedric had one pressed into the landlord's hand.

"Follow me."

We went down a narrow alley situated between the house and a storage shed. Once in the back, out of sight from traffic, the man selected a rusty key from his full chain and inserted it in the padlock holding the door closed.

"Stay here," he commanded, then disappeared into the shed.

"You'd think we were trying to steal something after paying him for a box of crap." I crossed my arms over my chest and kicked up a stone in the dirt. It bounced off the wall of the shed and landed next to Sedric's shoe.

"Paranoid old loon," Sedric said. He nudged the rock back towards me.

I kicked it again, but this time it bounced on the other side of me, where neither of us could reach it with our feet. "I'll pay you back."

"No need."

"I don't want to be your charity case."

"How about you treat me to dinner one night this week?"

The shed door swung open and the landlord shoved a dusty box into Sedric's arms. "All yours, sonny. Now get off my property."

Sedric nodded, I sneered. The man walked inside his house. Sedric hauled the box onto the trunk of the car and started pulling out its contents. A few tattered books, an ashtray, cds, a poster.

"Any pictures?"

"This could be something." He handed me a leather-bound book, a string wrapped around to hold it closed. I worked the string off and flipped it open.

"It's his journal." I scanned the first few entries. "He did not like living here. No wonder he traveled a lot."

"Anything about his lark or his pull?"

I read through a few pages in the middle of the book. "Doesn't look like it. I'll have to go through it back at the hotel to be sure. Anything else in the box?"

"Dust bunnies aren't very helpful."

"It's sad that no one came for his stuff," I said, watching Sedric dump the box on the curb for the trash collector.

"That's not going to happen to you." His hand gripped my shoulder for a moment, then released.

"I know. Val or Bonnie would pick up my junk, which is good, because half of it's probably theirs."

"Are you a thief in addition to being a liar?"

I chuckled. "Pretty much. I only take stuff they don't need, though."

"A kind robber is the best robber."

"That's my philosophy."

He cracked half a smile. Pria, it felt good to joke with him.

"One left. Let's get going," he said, unlocking and opening my door for me.

"It's close to the hotel, why don't we go another day. Let's blow off some steam and do something fun tonight."

"Is the ballet in town?"

"Something else fun."

"I know what I'd like to do, but I'm pretty sure you're going to say no." He closed my door and went around the car to his side. He was grinning like a little boy who'd done something naughty and was waiting to get caught.

As he got in, I tried not to match his smile, but I'm not sure I fooled him. "Let's keep it family friendly."

"Whatever you say. If you change your mind, though, feel free to let me know."

"They call me one-note Honor, I don't change my tune."

"Alright, alright."

We dropped our bags at the hotel, and the concierge told Sedric about a festival in the downtown area held every other Sunday. "Apparently all the stores open their doors, the restaurants set tables outside, the galleries have free admission, and there are all kinds of street vendors out peddling their wares," Sedric explained, steering the car down a narrow road.

"Peddling their wares? Are you from the fourteenth century or something?"

"Would you prefer hawking their goodies?"

"Slightly better."

"Do you want to check it out?" he asked.

"Nothing would thrill me more."

"I could think of a few things."

Where was this flirtatious man coming from? It was entertaining and flattering, but was it really him? I'd always taken Sedric at face value because he never seemed to have anything to hide, but maybe there was more to him than met the eye.

The concierge had given directions to a parking deck a few blocks from the busiest area. The streets were cobbled brick, but looked as if they'd been installed to give the area the illusion of age. An illusion easily seen through. Remnants of fallen leaves cluttered the edges of the road and a brisk wind blew through the bare trees. I shuddered and pulled my jacket closed.

Sedric offered me his coat. "At least it's not overcast."

"I'll warm up as we walk," I said, declining it. We turned a corner and the festival came into view. Hundreds of people wandered the long street, haggling with merchants, sipping hot chocolate, and observing the performers. The low buildings enabled the sun's beams to heat the area so it felt more like early fall than winter.

"Do you like cotton candy?" Sedric strode to the first vendor, forcing me to jog to keep up.

"My lifegivers said it will ruin my dinner."

"I won't tell if you don't." He handed me a fluffy pink mound of spun sugar atop a white paper cone. The salesman chose a blue one for Sedric, who paid and immediately bit off a huge piece.

A juggler walked by us, a tip can chained around his neck, jangling in tune to his steps. "It's like we're at the circus."

"If you see a unicycle, I call first ride," Sedric said.

"What's gotten into you?"

He pulled another chunk of cotton candy from his cone and stuffed it in his mouth. "Beautiful weather, good company, and a street fair. It's an amazing day to be alive."

"Is there liquor in that candy?"

He laughed and took my hand. "Learn to let go, Honor. You're going to have fun today if it kills you."

"That's an awfully big price to pay for fun."

"Try your cotton candy."

Dropping his hand, I pinched a portion off and held it up for his inspection, then plopped it onto my tongue. "Tastes like childhood."

"Can't beat that."

"It's pretty good." I linked my arm in his so my hand was free to pick at the treat as we continued walking through the fair.

On one side of the street, a parade of terriers and their owners parted the crowd and caused many young children to drag their lifegivers over to pet and play with the dogs.

"I'm thinking about getting a puppy," Sedric said, bending down to greet a feisty one who'd escaped her owner.

"How would you take care of it, with all the traveling?"

He took hold of the dog's leash and started walking to the other side of the street. A young woman rushed forward to claim the rascal. "Thank you!"

"You're welcome." He watched as the woman and dog rejoined the terrier parade, before returning to me. "We're almost done meeting all my clients, and my job doesn't require as much travel as yours. I'll only be gone a few weeks every season, unlike your half a year."

"We won't be traveling together much longer?"

"You'll finally be rid of me."

"My prayers have been answered." I took the last bite of my cone and threw the paper into a nearby trashcan so I could grip his arm with both hands. He tossed his empty cone in as well, turning to face me in the process. His thumb grazed my cheek and moved along my lower lip.

"You had some sugar," he said, sucking the pad of his thumb into his mouth.

A skinny man with dreadlocks and a basket on his arm tapped Sedric's shoulder. "Would you like to buy a flower for your mate?"

"He's not... we're not bonded," I said, dropping his arm.

"How much?" Sedric asked.

"One for a note, or a dozen for ten notes."

"I don't need a flower."

"I'll take one." Sedric traded one note for a wilting pink rose. The peddler walked away and Sedric playfully patted my nose with the soft petals. I went to take it from him, but he moved it out of my reach. "It's not for you."

"Oh, really?"

He stuck the stem in his shirt pocket and took my hand, lacing his fingers around mine.

"When did you become such a goofball?"

"A couple weeks ago, I guess. Though I suspect I've always had it in me."

Who talks like that? New and improved Sedric, apparently.

"Oh, look." He pointed ahead of us to a small ensemble playing classical music on their violins and cellos. A crowd gathered in front of them, and a few people started to dance. Sedric tugged me forward until we were in the center of the twirling couples and put his right arm around my waist. Lifting our already clasped hands and pressing them against his heart, he said, "You showed me your type of dancing, let me show you mine."

We swayed slowly, keeping in time with the music, but not doing much else. "I'm not impressed."

He laughed. "I was just getting warmed up." With that, he guided me two steps back, a step to the left, and two steps forward. Keeping a firm grip on my hip, he led me as if I were a puppet and he the master puppeteer. The other pairs fell away and a haze surrounded Sedric and I as we waltzed.

The song stopped and a new one, even slower, began. Sedric drew me closer. He was too tall to dance cheek-to-cheek with, but my temple rested against his jaw. Nice didn't seem like a good enough word to describe it, but it's all I could think. *This is nice.*

"Don't go getting any ideas," I whispered when he turned his head slightly, causing his lips to brush against my skin.

"I'm not thinking at all," he murmured.

We continued to dance, with him occasionally spinning me away and then back as the song increased in tempo, but mostly we remained pressed together. I could smell the aftershave on his neck – sandalwood and pine. Sort of like the one Hero had worn when I was a little girl.

"What are you thinking about?" he asked. I realized I was smiling.

"My lifegiver, Hero."

"Not exactly what I was hoping you'd say."

"He was a good man. You remind me of him sometimes."

"High praise," he said, softly.

"Yes, it is." When the current song ended, I stepped back. "We should move on. See what else is out there."

"I couldn't have said it better myself."

"I meant the fair."

"Of course you did."

Advancing without him, I sidestepped a group of teenagers playing some sort of game with a beanbag where they kicked it with the sides of their feet or tops of their knees. "I'm starving."

"There's a cafe across the street," Sedric said. We crossed over and checked in with the hostess, who said there was a thirty-minute wait for outdoor seating, or she could seat us immediately inside.

"Not worth the wait," I said. She showed us to a corner booth at the back of the room, right next to the bathroom.

"Maybe it would've been worth the wait," Sedric said, the sounds of toilets flushing greeting us as we slid into opposite sides of the booth.

"You mean the stench of urine doesn't enhance your dining experience? Snob."

He laughed and handed me a menu. "Remember, it's your treat."

"I didn't forget."

Small talk commenced while we looked over the menu and placed our order. Once we got our food, Sedric asked, "How's your nephew doing? Did they ever get an answer on the two larks thing?"

"I talked to Val a couple of days ago. Handor hasn't found the second mate yet, but he still wants to. Nevin, the mate he already met, has been trying to talk him out of it, which hasn't been easy on him. He feels guilty for wanting to look and guilty for not wanting to."

"He doesn't want to leave the other mate wondering where he is."

"Yep. Plus, it's pretty inevitable that they'll find each other eventually – if he can ignore his pull because of Nevin, that doesn't mean the other one would be able to do the same thing."

Sedric took a bite of his sandwich, nodding his head. I pushed my pasta salad around the plate with my fork. It tasted fine, I just wasn't hungry anymore.

"How's your family?" I asked.

"They are… fine."

"That fine sounded anything but."

"No, everything is great. I guess I just didn't expect you to ask about them after the semi-disastrous party."

"I'd call it full-blown disastrous."

"Oh, trust me, things could have been a lot worse."

I put my fork down and put both elbows on the table. "Can I ask you a question?"

"Sure."

"At your lifegivers', Junie said something, and I didn't want to be rude and ask, but-"

"When have you cared to be polite?"

I screwed up an eyebrow, but didn't respond to the bait. "Junie said you wanted kids, but Zara didn't."

"Is that a question?"

"It seems odd, that's all. Why didn't she want kids?"

"Zara was," he stopped and picked up his napkin, wiping each finger individually as he thought through what he wanted to say. "Zara was a decent person, but she wasn't exactly nurturing. It's probably a good thing she didn't want kids, because I don't know if she would have been a very good lifegiver."

Whoa. That was kind of harsh, especially for Sedric. I must have looked surprised, because he shook his head and said, "I know that sounds horrible coming from me, but it is what it is. I'm not saying she would have been a *bad* lifegiver. She wouldn't have been abusive, or negligent, or anything like that."

I didn't say anything, but picked up the fork and took a small bite of my pasta. He pushed his plate toward the center of the table. "You think you are selfish, but you haven't had the opportunity that some people have to be truly selfish. Zara did. And she was."

"What?"

"I don't want you to think I'm ungrateful or that I didn't love her, because I did, but she was not an easy person to live with. She used up the hot water in the shower almost every day. She didn't consider me in important decisions, like quitting her job to stay at home."

"Without kids?"

"Yeah. That's one of the reasons she complained about my traveling. She got bored being by herself." There was a sting of bitterness in his voice I'd never heard from him before. It occurred to me that, though mated, perhaps he hadn't been very happy with that match. I couldn't think of anyone I knew who wasn't happy with their lifemate, but maybe I'd never bothered to see it.

"Did she know you wanted kids?"

He cleared his throat. "Yes."

"Do you feel cheated?"

It took him a moment, but he eventually answered, "No."

"You're a better person than me, because I sure as hell do."

"Life isn't fair, but its equal opportunity in its unfairness. Zara was my mate, and we were happy most of the time. Don't look at me like that. We were. There were plenty of things about me that got on her nerves, too. I shouldn't have told you that stuff. Now you think I think she was a bad person."

"I don't."

"You do, I can see it in your eyes."

I looked down. "Maybe that's your own guilty conscience for speaking so ill of the dead."

"Not everything has to be a joke."

"But life's more fun when it is. I shouldn't have brought it up. You were having such a good day, were in such a good mood, and I've ruined it."

"You didn't. It's this dark corner. And the bathroom sounds. I blame the restaurant."

I pounded my fist on the table. "Me, too!"

He dropped his napkin onto his plate. "Let's get out of here."

I put a twenty note and some ones on the table to cover the check and a tip and we rejoined the crowds outside. Sedric didn't regain his goofball persona, but his warmth increased. We spent the rest of the afternoon roaming through the fair, staying as far away from the topic of our mates as possible. In a different world, we could have been something special, but in this world I knew our happiness together could only last a short time. It would be gone too soon, just like all other things too good to be true.

Chapter Twenty-Six: Answers

Every night that week, after we finished my workshop for the day, Sedric asked if I wanted to check out the last two potentials in the city. I always said no. Our day together at the street fair had me wishing my lark would disappear, not so the sympathetic looks would stop, but so I could pretend it didn't matter that my path in life had been chosen for me. On the last night, though, I couldn't act like it didn't matter anymore. I was still the girl with no mate, and I still wanted to know why.

The street Sedric turned down was long, stretching beyond the horizon. We drove for fifteen minutes past cookie-cutter houses – all two stories, with grey shingles, deep brown-stained fences, two-car garages, and freshly mown lawns. I noted the numbers going by: 200, 212, 220, 236. Around the six hundreds, the shutter color changed to mauve, and in the thousands to beige.

When we passed 1200, a pricking sensation began tormenting my wrist. "What was the address, again?" I asked.

"1432 King's Boulevard."

The outline of my lark darkened as I looked at it and my stomach lurched. Sensations like a thousand needles pricking my skin crept up my toes and scampered through my legs, straight to my heart. If he didn't stop the car soon, my body was going to leap out and hit the pavement running.

"Holy shit," I whispered, now clutching my lark and taking large gulps of air into my lungs to attempt control over my actions.

"What's wrong?" He pulled the car along the curb and unlatched his seat belt, turning with concern towards me, but I couldn't wait to tell him. I dashed out of the car, and my feet carried me a few yards, to a path leading straight to the front door of number 1432.

A searing pain like I'd never experienced tore through my wrist, causing my legs to buckle. Sedric barely caught me before I hit the ground. When I pried my hand away from my wrist, the lark was no longer incomprehensible: a bird, wings outstretched, soaring through the air. Her wings actually looked like they were beating – feathers rustling as they carried her through the wind.

"Oh, Paolo," Sedric muttered, lifting me and steadying me with an arm around my waist.

"This is it," I breathed. "This was his home. We found him."

"How... I mean, he's got to be... he can't be..."

"I have to go inside." I stepped out of Sedric's hold and stumbled to the porch. My hand shook as I rang the bell and my wrist still burned like it was on fire, but happiness oozed from every cell in my body. I'd finally have answers. I'd finally know the path the Gods intended for me.

A middle-aged woman with a short dark bob and kind eyes opened the door. "Yes?"

"Hi, um, my name is Honor and um, I think..." my voice was scratchy and I couldn't seem to get the words out. I thrust my wrist out to show her my lark. She looked confused at first, but after a few seconds, her hands went to her mouth.

"Oh, my. Luther!" She turned and hustled down a small hallway. I looked to Sedric to see what I should do, but he was hanging his head, examining the specks of dirt on the welcome mat.

The woman was back, dragging a rotund, bald man with her. "Luther, her wrist."

The man pulled a pair of spectacles from his shirt pocket and adjusted them on the bridge of his nose before examining my lark. "Hmmm. Come in, please."

"Thank you," I mumbled, shuffling across the threshold and turning back for Sedric. He leaned against the doorframe and locked eyes with me.

"Maybe I should wait in the car."

"Please," I said. He stepped inside without another word.

"What was your name again?" The woman asked, guiding me to the couch. She sat to my left, the man to my right.

"Honor. And this is my friend, Sedric. He's been helping me look for my," gulp, "mate."

"I'm Cassandra Blake and this is Luther. We're Zachary's lifegivers."

"It's nice to meet you." My hands shook. I gripped my knees tightly to stop the tremors.

"We never expected to meet you."

"I'm very sorry about Zachary."

"Thank you. How did you find us? Were you still feeling your pull all these years?" Cassandra took my hand in hers and continuously patted it. I wondered if she was trying to comfort herself or me.

"No, it stopped immediately when he, um…"

"That must have been very confusing. How old were you?" Luther asked.

"Twenty-five."

"He was three years older, then," Cassandra said. My hand was starting to go numb.

"I was wondering what he was like. We found an article in an Eribank newspaper about the car accident, but it didn't say much about who he was."

Luther rubbed his temples. "He was our son, so we loved him, but he wasn't the brightest kid."

"Don't say that!" Cassandra squeezed my hand in between pats and I began mentally planning the extrication of my fingers from her death grasp. "He was smart, but he didn't share Luther's goals in life."

"He fiddled around with those drums and that stupid band for years, when he could have gone further in school, gotten a degree, and a real career."

"What kind of music did his band play?"

"Loud," Luther said, starting to chuckle. "They used to practice in our garage, and the neighbors would come and complain. I'd shut them down, but the next night they'd crank it louder."

"I'm not sure what the genre's called, but the local paper wrote a couple of reviews. Let me get them." Cassandra stood and went to a bookshelf on the opposite wall. I wriggled my fingers. "Here we go." She handed me a scrapbook. News clippings and photos were spilling out of the pages. I selected one at random. The headline stated *Local Indie Rock Band 'Lantern Light Night' Sells Out*, and went on to describe their first show at the Trenalda Theater. Music critics called them "fresh," "raw," and "unhinged." A picture showed the lead singer, lips to a microphone, sweaty hair hanging in his face.

"Look at this, Sedric." I handed over a copy of the band's tour schedule. We had looked online for performance dates, but could only find a few. The paper matched my timeline city-for-city.

Another article talked about a possible record deal, a third announced the release of their self-funded debut album. A few positive reviews of the album, followed by several negative. Negative was really too kind a word – they were brutal. "Why'd you keep these?" I asked, showing Cassandra one that compared the album to a flaming bag of dog shit.

She cringed. "I didn't. Zachary said the bad reviews were the best ones. Their audience was more likely to buy albums the critics hated."

"Oh."

"Here's Zachary with his drums." She flipped to the center of the book and pointed. The drum set hid most of his body, but his face and arms were visible. His mouth was open, singing, and his fist clenched the drumsticks so tightly they appeared ready to splinter apart. He wore a blue sweatband on his left wrist, covering his lark. Sweaty strands of dark hair also fell over his forehead. I wanted to reach into the photograph and push it back so I could see the color of his eyes.

"He looks like he loved it, playing music."

Cassandra nodded. "More than life itself."

I perused a few more pages, stopping at a picture of Zachary with his arm around a young woman. She had bleached hair, with streaks of pink framing her face. "Is this his sister or one of the band members?"

Luther peered over my shoulder and grunted. "No."

I glanced between the two of them; they were exchanging a look which clearly said *don't tell her.* "Who is she?"

Cassandra hopped off the couch and faced us with arms open. "Can I get anyone anything to drink? Water, tea? I could make coffee."

"No, thank you," Sedric said.

"Why won't you tell me who she is?"

"That is Kresta," Luther said.

My voice quivered. "And Kresta is his cousin, or a friend, or an agent, right?"

"There's not really a word for who she was to him," Cassandra rushed to answer before Luther could.

I put the scrapbook on the coffee table and rubbed my hands over my thighs, trying to process. "Did he look for me?"

"He was very busy touring with the band."

"Did he *want* to find me?"

Cassandra was frantically glancing around the room, as if the answers to my questions were hidden somewhere and she just needed to locate them. Luther stared at my lark. "I always wondered what it would look like, when it filled in," he said after a few seconds of avoiding my question.

"Yeah, me too. Since I was old enough to understand what a lark is. So what, twenty-five, twenty-six years? I looked for him. I followed my pull for years, wondering why it was so sporadic and spread all over the place. I wondered what I'd done wrong to displease the Gods, that they hadn't let me find him. Are you telling me he didn't care at all that I was out there, waiting and searching?"

"We tried to tell him that. We encouraged him to follow his pull. We told him she wasn't his match. We wouldn't allow him to bring her here. He wouldn't listen to us. He said the lark was wrong, that he loved Kresta."

My heart sank into the pit of my stomach and barely any noise came out when I croaked, "He loved her?"

"Honor..." Sedric said.

"Don't," I cringed. My mate was not only dead, he didn't want me. He hadn't thought about my feelings, he hadn't considered the fact that being with this Kresta woman meant completely rejecting me without even bothering to find me and tell me. Or hell, without bothering to get to know me to see if he could have loved me. The Gods thought we were right for each other, but that little shit thought he knew better.

"I've got to get out of here." I rose, moving towards the door, but Cassandra stepped in front of me.

"Please, don't leave yet. We'd like to get to know you."

"What's the point? Zachary decided I wasn't good enough."

Her mouth opened and immediately closed. Luther stood and joined his mate. "It's not the way we raised him. We taught him the lark story and told him how happy we've been together."

"He had a mind of his own." Cassandra's eyes pleaded with mine to understand. "Anything he could do to rebel, he did it."

"Then I guess my walking out isn't the worst thing to happen to you." I flung the door open and ran to the car, needing to get there before they could stop me. I heard steps chasing me. The passenger door was locked when I jerked the handle, but I kept yanking, willing it to miraculously pop open. But suddenly, there were arms pulling me away from the door, turning my body, pressing it against another.

"Honor, I'm so sorry," Sedric said, smoothing my hair away from my face.

I pounded my fists on his chest. "Let me go! Get away from me!" I screamed, but he only held tighter. "Please, let me go." And then I was crying. Tears rolled down my cheeks, onto his shirt. Snot dripped from my nose. Massive sobs clogged my throat.

"It's not fair," he said. "Scream, cry, you deserve to be angry."

Was I angry? Hell yes. But it was worse than anger. Disappointment, jealousy, rejection, and humiliation stormed through me. Tears weren't enough to purge the sadness.

Sedric wanted to talk about my feelings, but all I wanted to do was punch something. Luckily, the hotel had a gym on the first floor. There was a red punching bag hanging from the ceiling in a corner, but a beefed up man was already using it when I walked in.

"Hey," I said, "I desperately need to use the bag."

"Sorry lady, I'm going to be another twenty minutes at least."

"You cannot begin to imagine the day I've had. I need to hit something hard."

He ignored me and threw a hook at the bag. I paced around him for a few minutes, hoping he would get annoyed and give up, but it only seemed to spur his resolve to be the biggest jackass on the planet.

The weight center was free, so I walked over and started curling two ten-pound weights, alternating arms. I stared at the punching bag, giving the meathead my deadliest glare. Thirty minutes later, he finally removed his gloves and reached down to pick up a towel. I hastily put the weights on their shelf and trotted over. The punching bag was still moving. It swung towards me just as he straightened up and I planted my foot dead center, propelling it into his chest and knocking him over.

"Bitch!" he cried, jumping to his feet.

"That was an accident, but I'm not sorry. I told you I wanted to punch something. You should have let me get it out of my system. Enjoy the rest of your workout, asshole."

Back in my room I packed my suitcase, flinging shoes, toiletries, and dirty clothes in without bothering to organize any of it. What did it matter if shampoo spilled over everything? When I was sure I'd gotten everything in the bag, I put it by the door. Now what? All purpose seemed lost. I fell onto the bed and curled up, clutching a pillow to my chest.

Sedric and I wouldn't be traveling together much longer. Maybe another week or two. And I'd accomplished what I wanted – finding out who my mate was. What did I have left? Knowing was worse, so much worse than I could have imagined. And the idea of not seeing Sedric every day on such a friendly and informal basis actually hurt.

The screen buzzed, alerting me to a call. I looked over to see who it was. Bonnie. I wasn't ready to tell her yet, and as soon as she saw me, she'd know something was wrong. Better not to answer.

I hugged the pillow tightly, thinking how long it had been since I'd shared a bed with anyone. About four years. Not the longest dry spell in the world, I certainly wasn't going to break records anytime soon, but it made the thought of Sedric in the next room awfully tempting. Clutching the fluffy, white cushion, I willed myself to sleep, needing to be out of my conscious brain for a little while.

A bird flew towards me. I angled my wings so I could join him, but he bolted past me, swooping to the earth and landing on the shoulder of a little girl. She whistled a pretty tune and he mimicked her. I tried to follow them, but my wings were glued together and I couldn't change direction or pick up speed. I was trapped. Stuck in mid-air. A cloud broke above me, letting warm rays of sunshine descend and melt away the glue on my wings. I could fly again, but the bird and little girl were gone. I didn't know where to go, so I turned my face toward the sun.

Chapter Twenty-Seven: Choices

ang. Bang. Bang. I bolted out of bed, needing to know where the hammering was coming from. I searched the dark room, twisting about in my sheets before realizing the only logical place the sounds could be coming from. The door. Sedric stood behind it, his fist raised, ready to knock again.

"You woke me up," I grumbled. "What time is it?"

"Sorry. It's almost midnight." He lowered his hand and tucked it behind his back, rocking slightly on his heels, waiting for me to step aside. Which I didn't.

"Whatever. What do you want?"

"To talk."

I crossed my arms and leaned against the doorframe. "You always want to talk."

"It's a normal human desire to communicate with one's fellow man."

"Sure, when there's vodka or wine around."

"Will this do?" He revealed a bottle of tequila that had been hiding behind his back.

"Yep, that'll do." I took it over to the desk and unscrewed the cap. Sedric switched the light on as he stepped in and produced two *I heart Trenalda* souvenir shot glasses from a small plastic bag.

"Didn't take you for a collector," I said. I poured to the rim of each glass and gulped mine down. "Ugh, that's disgusting."

He tossed his back as well and grimaced. "The liquor store down the street was poorly stocked, and they wouldn't let me buy a bottle at the bar."

"After a couple more of these we won't be able to tell how low-shelf it is." I refilled my glass and pounded it. Sedric nudged his toward me. "Is this going to be our thing, then?" I asked. "Getting drunk when something shitty happens to me?"

"Hopefully nothing else shitty is going to happen to you."

I laughed. And laughed harder. Until tears were in my eyes and my stomach hurt from the effort. I laughed until I had to sit on the edge of the bed, so I wouldn't fall on the floor. Sedric filled his glass and drank it while I recovered.

"Don't you see? Shitty things happening is apparently the path the Gods have chosen for me. I ignored my pull for a few years so I could train." I paused and looked down at my feet. "I've never really admitted that to anyone."

He poured more tequila into my glass.

"Then, I got injured and couldn't dance. I started taking my pull seriously and it stopped. I find out who my mate was, and it turns out, he wasn't looking for me at all! I imagine I'll get hit by a car next, just like good 'ole Zachary. Then our karma will be complete." I drank the shot. My head was starting to feel fuzzy. I became very aware of my teeth and hands.

"Oh, look at that. My lark is back to normal." I pushed my wrist into Sedric's face. He took hold of my arm gently and guided it away. "I shoulda known it wasn't going to last. Can't have a complete picture when you don't have a complete life."

"Cut the bullshit, Honor."

"What? Isn't this what you wanted? For me to talk about my feelings? Am I acting differently than you thought I would? I thought you knew who I was."

"And I thought you were a strong, intelligent woman. Paolo, you don't realize how lucky you are."

"Excuse me?"

He began pacing the length of the room, seemingly unable to control his energy. His fingers ran through his hair, then he wrung his hands together, then stuffed them in his pockets. He removed them after a few seconds and wiped his palms on his jeans, and finally reached up to adjust a tie he wasn't wearing. Basically, every nervous tick I'd ever seen from him in a span of thirty seconds. "You're taking the entire lark thing way too seriously," he said. "Look at what it's gotten you. Or me. Hell, even Zachary. The lark shouldn't dictate our lives."

"But it does. That's how the world works. Or have you been living under a rock?"

"I wish I had the opportunity you have right now."

"What opportunity is that?" I asked, completely irritated and ready to kick him out of the room.

"To choose, without regard to what an ugly mark on my body says about who I should love. You have no idea what it's like, being thrust into a situation where the universe says, 'here you go, this is your mate *for life*,' and you get absolutely no say in it.

"I loved Zara, you know I did, but I loved her because I had to, not because I wanted to. Loving her wasn't easy. We didn't have time to get to know each other. It was intense. Meeting, to living together bonded within two weeks. Just a couple of kids. And after that, every waking moment revolved around each other. From big decisions, like where I was going to work, to small ones, like what to have for breakfast, I immediately thought, *what would Zara want?*

"It's not an easy way to live. Even now. She's been dead for almost four years and I still have that thought when I pick out my shirt in the morning, or when I see your smile." He laughed awkwardly and took another shot. I put my arms across my chest, ashamed, dizzy, and confused.

"She wouldn't have liked you, you know," he said.

"Most people don't."

"She wouldn't have liked that we are friends, and she wouldn't have liked your dancing or your baking."

"Sounds like a bitch."

"She didn't like much. Hell, I'm getting a little drunk, why don't I lay it all on the table for you. For us both. I wouldn't have picked her. If I could have been strong like Zachary, I wouldn't have fallen into the lie that we can only be with who our larks tell us we should be with. I would not have chosen her."

I filled my glass again, but didn't drink it. Was this really happening – was he really saying what I was hearing?

"And you know what?" He pointed his index finger at my face. "It's a good thing Zachary didn't try to find you. He loved someone else. You would have been miserable together. Yes, he would have loved you, too, but you'd know you weren't his first choice." He snapped his fingers. "Nayja – you remember Nayja? From Tap & Bap?"

I nodded.

"She hated her mate. Hate isn't even a strong enough word. Loathed him. They fought constantly about anything and everything. She'd been in love with someone else before she found her mate. She gave the guy up and regretted it every day. She kissed me one night, because she wanted to see what it felt like to be with someone by choice. She would have tried to take it beyond a kiss, but Zara walked in and saw us. She never spoke to Nayja again."

My hand shook as I poured another round into his shot glass. "Why are you telling me this?"

"Remember before, you said we'd be second place to each other, and I said we wouldn't? It's because I know, I know Honor, that the person you choose to love, that's the person who is first in your heart. You're shaking your head, trying not to believe me, but I can see it in your eyes: you know it's true. Tell me, honestly, if you could have decided for yourself – in a world where larks don't exist – is that the man you would have chosen?" He stopped his pacing and stood in front of me, looking at me so earnestly I wanted to run out of the room and out of his life forever so he wouldn't have the pain of dealing with me anymore.

"I don't know! I don't know anything about him. What kind of person would you have chosen?"

He pulled the rolling chair out from the desk and positioned it in front of me, then seated himself and placed both hands on my knees. Looking directly into my eyes, he said calmly, "Someone smart and witty. Independent. A woman who understands loyalty. Who thinks about when she's wronged someone and how to make up for it."

I shook my head and started to speak, but he stopped me. "I'm not saying those things because they describe you. When I was seventeen and I really started feeling my pull for the first time, I thought a lot about the person I'd eventually find."

"And you thought she'd try to make up for the people she's wronged?" I scrunched my nose and he grinned.

"Not exactly. I wanted someone who handled mistakes gracefully. Someone who makes mistakes. Flawed people are so much more fun."

"You're not very flawed, but you're fun."

"I'm plenty flawed. You're just not paying attention, again. You should really work on that." His hands slid ever-so-slightly up my legs as he laughed. I let my fingers fall on his.

"If I were to choose my mate… when Bonnie and I were growing up, we played this game a lot, but I haven't considered it in years. I thought my mate would be strong, not like strong in character, but physically strong, which is so against the rules of feminism, I know, but Hero would always open pickle jars and lift heavy boxes for Gizella, and I loved that. I thought it was so sweet."

"What else?"

"He'd make me laugh, and we'd never run out of things to talk about."

"And?"

I smiled, remembering our day at the street fair. "And he'd dance with me, even if he was no good or couldn't carry a beat to save his life."

"Sounds like a good guy."

"Yeah, it does."

He stood and pushed the chair back into place. "Don't look at today as a bad thing. I know it wasn't pleasant, but think of what you've gained. Freedom. To be your own person and make your own choices."

I nodded. He headed for the door. "Get some rest; we've got a long flight tomorrow."

Okay, I figured out Sedric's flaw. After helping me see he was exactly the guy I'd always hoped my mate would be, he completely backed off. Breakfast and the drive to the airport were lessons in politeness. He reminded me more of the I-just-met-him Sedric than we-should-get-to-choose Sedric. I knew what he was doing. He was giving me time and space to process everything. If he had held my hand, or kissed me, or pushed me against a wall and ripped my clothes off with his teeth, I would have been completely his.

I didn't want to make the choice, though. I'd lived my entire life under the assumption there's only one path each person gets to take and it's the one assigned by the Gods. But the past several weeks had turned everything upside down. I wanted it to go back. Why did I have to find the answers about my mate? Why couldn't I have been satisfied knowing he was dead, and we would never meet, and left things at that? Sitting next to Sedric on the plane and not touching him would have been so much easier.

I went into work Monday still completely confused, wanting someone to just tell me what to do already, but when I walked by Sedric's office and heard his voice, something clicked. He wanted an independent woman. Someone capable of thinking for herself. And that's who I was til my ballet accident caused a complete breakdown. If I hadn't found out about my dead lifemate and decided to go on an idiotic quest for closure, maybe I would have eventually reclaimed who I once was. I'd lost myself while trying to help myself. No more.

Ignoring the sixty-two new emails in my inbox, I pulled up a chat screen on my monitor and called Val.

"Hey, Honor. Can't talk long, I've got a board meeting in a few minutes."

"That's okay, I just need one thing. Can you give me Mrs. Keye's number?"

"Shyla's dance coach?"

"Yeah. When I was visiting, her mate mentioned she was looking for a teacher."

"Are you thinking about moving here and teaching at Shyla's studio?"

"Maybe. I want to discuss my options with her."

"Oh, wow. Um, I don't have it here, but I'll get it from Mabry and call you later, or email it."

"Thanks."

"What prompted this?" he asked.

"If you've got a meeting soon, we don't have time to get into it, but I'll tell you all about it someday soon. Tell Handor to call me later. I don't care when, I'll make the time for him."

"Okay, I will. Talk to you soon."

"Soon. Bye, bro." I closed the screen and shut down my computer. I was grabbing my purse off the floor when Felix walked up.

"It's been so long since you've been in the office, Honor."

I bit back my ready, *not long enough*, retort and did my best to smile at him.

"Did you hear the newest theory?"

"What's that?"

"We haven't had a visit from the Dessert Fairy in a couple of weeks."

Oh shit.

"Not since before Alyscia left. We think she was the one bringing them."

Morons. Didn't they realize the desserts had been showing up long before Alyscia started working there? "Wow, that's an excellent theory, Felix. You should be a detective."

He grinned broadly, patted the wall of my cubicle and moved down the hall. I headed for the exit.

"Where are you going, Honor?" Felix called.

"Anywhere but here. I quit."

A few heads popped up from the different cubicles that filled our floor. Sedric stepped out of his office. I didn't say anything else, just waved my hand behind me as I descended the stairs. Good riddance.

Chapter Twenty-Eight: Settling Details

Bonnie told me to come straight over when I called her from my house to tell her I'd quit my job. I packed some baking supplies in a tote bag and headed back out.

"What happened?" she asked, opening the door and attempting to restrain Skitzo. When he saw it was me he calmed down, but didn't stop trying to sniff the contents of my bag.

"Nothing, I just couldn't work there anymore. I've always hated that job, and suddenly it seemed really silly to stay."

"So you just left? No notice or anything?"

"Yep."

"Oh, Honor, you should have at least given them a couple of weeks." Bonnie guided me to the kitchen, shaking her head the whole way.

"They don't want me there any more than I wanted to be there."

"But what about when you're looking for jobs? You're going to need to put them down as a reference."

"Actually..." I put my bag on the counter and started emptying it. "I have one lead already, and they won't care about a reference from Taylor & James."

"What's the job?"

"Teaching ballet at Shyla's dance studio."

"Teaching!" she squealed, throwing her arms up. "You'd be such a good dance teacher. It's your passion. Wait." She grabbed my arm. "Shyla's studio – you're moving?"

"I'm thinking about it."

"But, how can you leave me?" Her arms flew around my neck. I started laughing and soon she was, too.

"I'll miss you like crazy, Bon, but I promise, we'll still see each other all the time, even if it's just on the screen."

She let go. "Not good enough."

"I know. Not for me, either. But I think I need to be near Val and his kids for a little while; get back to my family roots, rediscover who I truly am. When I'm with them, I remember Gizella and Hero so much clearer. I need that right now."

"When are you going?"

"I don't know. It's not even a sure thing, yet." I pulled a carton of eggs out of her fridge and cracked two in a bowl. "Plus, I have to let my landlord know and find a place there."

"What are you going to do if the teaching job doesn't come through?"

I poured several cups of flour into a second bowl. "This, maybe."

"Baking?"

"Yeah, why not? I'm good at it, and I enjoy it. Someone once told me I could open my own place."

"You definitely could, but I guess I never thought you wanted to operate a business."

"I never thought I wanted to either, but it's a possibility. I'm keeping all of my options open right now." I pulled her mixer out of the cabinet.

"What happened to create this life-affirming attitude?" she asked.

"I found out who my mate was."

"And you waited ten minutes to tell me! Oh Pria, Honor! Tell me everything."

"His name was Zachary Blake. He was a drummer in a mildly successful, indie rock band I'd never heard of. And, he was in love with someone else. He didn't want to find me."

Bonnie's face fell. "What do you mean?"

"Exactly what I said. He had a woman he was in a relationship with, they weren't each other's mates, but they didn't care. He didn't 'believe' in the lark, I guess."

"Are you okay?"

"I wasn't, but I'm feeling better." The batter was smooth, but I kept beating.

"How?"

"Sedric."

"Here we go. I told you to be careful. I told you he liked you. What did you do?"

"He kissed me, but we didn't do anything else. He just helped me see that maybe it's okay my mate didn't find me, and maybe it's okay for me to think about someone else."

"I don't like this."

"You don't have to. I'm not asking you to understand it. It is what it is, though."

"What does he say about your leaving?"

"I haven't told him yet."

"Are you planning to?" she asked.

"When I have all my ducks in a row. I need to know exactly what I'm telling him. I don't know yet how much I want him involved in my future. Some moments, I want him to be the person I grow old with, but other times I'm worried that those moments only exist because I've never thought of growing old alone, or with anyone other than my mate, and Sedric is the only man who has ever been an option."

Bonnie circled around the kitchen, straightening the towel hanging above the sink and closing a cabinet door. "I'm confused, can you even love someone you aren't mated to?"

"Zachary said he did."

"But..." she looked towards the room where Caron was sleeping.

"But you've only ever loved your mate. I know. And that's awesome for you. But it doesn't work that way for everyone. Apparently. You want to help me fill these wrappers?"

We stood shoulder-to-shoulder, spooning batter into the bright papers lining the cupcake tin. "Oh, I almost forgot," Bonnie said, completing a turquoise one. "We're having a boy."

I dropped my spoon and hugged her. "That's amazing! Congratulations!" This time, my support was one hundred percent genuine.

Handor called the next day as I was making myself lunch. "I can call back," he said.

"No, I want to talk to you. Let me turn the stove off." I moved my pan of sauce to a cool burner and flipped the knob. "I'm not really hungry," I said, coming back into the living room.

"What's up?" he asked.

"How are you doing?"

"Fine."

"How's Nevin?"

Handor shrugged.

"We don't have to talk about him if you don't want to."

"Good."

"I wanted to tell you what happened to me last week." I proceeded to detail the events leading up to finding Mr. and Mrs. Blake, and finally discovering who my mate had been. "I thought I'd finally understand my purpose in life or something; that knowing who he was would somehow make a difference in who I am."

"That's stupid."

I pursed my lips. "I always forget how sensitive teenagers can be in regards to other people's feelings."

"Sorry."

"My point is, finding him showed me how completely irrelevant he is to my life. That might have been different if we had found each other before he died, but we didn't. He didn't want to find me. He chose another path."

My nephew looked puzzled, but had taken my previous chiding to heart and said nothing.

"I think you should find your second mate, so you have a chance to get to know both of them. And then, I think you should make a choice with your heart – not your larks. In the end, you make the decision who to love."

"What are you talking about?"

"Listen to me, kiddo. Your fate is in your hands and your hands alone. The only thing you owe to the people who turn out to be your mates is the courtesy of letting them know your choice. Got it?"

"I guess."

"Alright, then. How's school?"

We talked for another twenty minutes or so, before Val made him get off the screen to come to the dinner table. When he was waving goodbye, he said, "Thank you," so I think he got what I was trying to say. Or, at least, he understood that I was looking out for him.

I spent the next two weeks settling details. I worked out an employment contract with Mrs. Keye, informed my landlord I would be vacating by the end of the month, and answered a few ads for room and apartment openings near the studio in Esterland.

Packing my little house actually brought up nostalgia I didn't know I had. The pictures on the wall had been the first and only items of décor I'd bothered with, but I'd specifically gotten them framed when I moved in so I could keep Val, Hero, Gizella, and the kids close to me when they seemed far away.

Emptying the pantry was like going to a dear friend's funeral – I was devastated I'd never see it again. I put my palm on the door and said goodbye, then closed it. The kitchen looked like a different place.

I donated the contents of the storage shed to a charity a few blocks away. There was nothing of value to me in them anymore.

Once my life finally seemed in order, I drove to Sedric's.

Chapter Twenty-Nine: Saying Goodbye

His car was in the driveway, but no one answered the door when I rang the bell. Winter was in full force — the air smelled like snow. I walked around the back of the house and checked out the woodshop. No Sedric, but it was full of things to look at. In addition to tools of all shapes, sizes, and varying degrees of *I'd hurt myself if I tried to use this*, were half-finished and almost-completed projects.

A rocking horse without a face or mane, but a bridle and saddle. A music box that didn't play a tune. What appeared to be a coffee table, but I couldn't tell if it was finished, or just begun and would end up being something else entirely. A small set of shelves. Another grandfather clock.

I stood in front of the clock for several minutes. He hadn't installed the mechanisms yet, so it wasn't working, but it was beautiful. Mahogany wood and carvings of songbirds and music notes — fewer towards the base, but multiplying upwards, closer and closer to the face of the clock. My fingers grazed over one of the birds. Its wings stretched out and its beak pointed north, like it was about to fly out of the wood and straight to the sun.

After a little while, I started feeling awkward about being in the workshop uninvited, so I closed the door behind me and went to the front of the house. I sat on the stairs, three steps high, and waited. My breath puffed out like little smoke clouds, and I rubbed my hands together to warm them.

About ten minutes later, I saw a tall man moving down the street in my direction. He was holding a leash and walking a tiny dog. I waved. Sedric paused, then waved back and increased his pace.

His little terrier beat him to me and sniffed my feet calmly. I patted her head. "You got a dog."

"Yeah, I was feeling a little lonely."

"I'm sorry I haven't called."

"You don't owe me anything."

"I know. I'm still sorry."

He sat beside me, and the dog leaned her head into my hand. I began scratching around her ears and she settled at my feet. Sedric reached over and unhooked her leash. "She likes you."

"Who doesn't?" I bumped his shoulder and he laughed.

"We've just been to the zoo."

"They let you bring dogs to the zoo?"

"That's what I call the dog park. It gets really crazy around there. There's this one short little bully, a Chihuahua. You'd think he owned the place the way he terrorizes the other dogs."

"Why do you go, then?"

"Constance likes it."

"Constance." I picked the dog up and set her in my lap. Her furry face tickled my arm as she bent her head to lick my hands. "I like that."

"It seemed a good fit. Dogs are loyal. Constant companions."

"I'm glad you won't be alone anymore."

He nodded his head and kept it down, like he knew I was there to say goodbye.

"How have things been at the office since I left?"

"You would have appreciated the chaos. Felix has been running around like a chicken with its head cut off, trying to reassign your clients and pacify the angry ones."

"Angry?"

"Yeah — your clients were not happy you left. A lot of them thought the company had done something to you — fired you or treated you unfairly, like passed you over for a promotion or something. They couldn't believe you left without personally telling them."

"Really? Wow, they didn't know me very well, did they?"

"They knew the you you showed them. Speaking of which, I'm happy to give you a letter of recommendation or to be a reference if you need it."

"That's really kind of you, but I don't think I will."

"Have you already found something?"

"Yeah."

A bird whistled over our heads. I looked up and spotted him in an oak tree whose branches shaded the front porch. He whistled again. I may have been wrong, but he seemed to look me right in the eye, telling me to be brave.

"I'm going to teach ballet," I said.

Sedric swung his head towards me. "Should I find something sharp to stick in your eye?"

"Not yet. I'll let you know."

"Is it stupid if I say I'm proud of you?"

I took his hand, letting our fingers intertwine. "No, it's really, really nice."

He leaned over and kissed me. I could feel tears forming behind my closed lids. I needed to go out, wander, try this new life, but I wanted to do it with him. When he pulled his mouth away, he brought his free hand to my cheek and rested his forehead on mine. Constance jumped up, her paws on my chest, and alternated licking our cheeks. "Down girl," he said without any conviction. Then, "Where are you going?"

"How'd you know?"

"If you were sticking around here, would you have taken so long to come and tell me what was going on?"

"I don't know, maybe. I didn't know if you'd still want me to be a part of your life after the way I left things."

He let go of my hand and put his arm around my shoulders, drawing me into him. He was warm and I snuggled closer. Across the street, his neighbor stepped out of her house and stared at us. I wanted to make a rude hand gesture at her, but Sedric waved calmly. "Hello, Mrs. Catsopolis."

She hurried to her car and backed out of the driveway without another glance at us. "Off to her job at the city dump?" I asked.

He chuckled. "Be nice."

"Does she know? About your lark and Zara?"

"A little. The neighborhood threw me a welcome party when I moved in."

"She thinks you're cheating or something."

"But I'm not."

"I know." I tilted my head up and kissed him again. "But nobody else is going to see it the way we do. No one else is going to understand. I told Bonnie a little bit and she doesn't."

"Since when do you care what other people think of you?"

"Touché."

He laughed again, his chest rumbling against me. I pressed my face into his neck, wanting to breathe in that woodsy smell he always carried about him. I wanted to steal a bottle of his aftershave or cologne, whatever it was that made him smell so damn good.

"Go ahead and spit it out," he said. "I'm a big boy, remember? I can handle it."

I didn't move, but murmured into his neck, "Esterland, near Val. Shyla's studio has an opening for a teacher, so I'll get to mentor my niece."

"And always have your family close at hand."

"Not my whole family. Bonnie, Caron, and Lang are still here. And you know, someone else."

He closed his free hand around the one on my shoulder, turning so the hug could encompass our entire upper bodies. "When do you leave?"

"End of the month. My house is all packed up and I turn in the keys tomorrow. I'm staying with Bonnie until the thirtieth. I wanted to spend as much time with them as possible."

"Do you want to have dinner here, with me?"

"Yes."

He stood and offered his hand to help me up. I set Constance on the ground and took it. "Hey, look at that," he said, turning my wrist over.

"What?"

"Your lark. It's faded since I last saw you. More pieces are missing."

I held it up and instinctually started to trace it. My finger tripped at the break in the pattern it was used to. "I didn't even notice."

He grinned. "Because you weren't paying attention to it. For once, that's a good thing."

I took his hand and examined his palm. "Is yours different, too? I can't tell."

"Every day, little by little, it's changing. Disappearing. Slowly accepting the fact that it holds no power over me anymore."

I looked back at mine. For the last couple of years, I'd wanted it gone and it was finally listening. "It's so, so... What is it?"

"Freeing?"

"Exactly."

He led me in the house, Constance scampering after us. While he made dinner, I ambled around taking stock of little things he'd improved or added since I'd last been there. New hand towels and guest soap in the downstairs bathroom. A lighting fixture in the dining area. Some new photos along the wall of portraits. I stopped in front of the one of him and Zara. He did look happy, but his smile was off. What about it was wrong? His eyes. They weren't laughing, not like when he laughed with me. I moved on. Zara wouldn't haunt my feelings for Sedric anymore.

In the master bedroom, I took a second to open his drawers and rummage through his socks and underwear. It was a little naughty, I guess, but I didn't think he'd care. It was all so neat and tidy, expertly folded. I made a mental note to ask if he ever worked in a men's clothing store when he was younger.

Moving into the bathroom, I sought out the medicine cabinet and found what I really wanted. The green bottle. It *was* aftershave. I went back to his dresser in the bedroom and took a handkerchief out of the top drawer. Back at the sink, I poured liquid onto the cloth and let it soak into every fiber. I hoped he wouldn't mind, but again, didn't really think it would bother him. Hell, if he didn't mind the slight stalkerish aspect, he might even be flattered.

I screwed the top on the bottle and placed it in the cabinet, then laid the handkerchief on the counter to dry. I shut the bathroom door behind me, clicking the switch for the exhaust fan so the smell wouldn't permeate through the house.

His bed stood in the center of the room. It didn't look so sterile anymore. No, it was strong and soft, just like Sedric. I slipped my shoes off and lay down, burrowing into the pillows and pulling the blanket at the foot over me.

"Hey, where are you?" Sedric's voice called. It sounded like it came from the bottom of the stairs, but I wasn't positive.

"Up here! In your room," I shouted, turning over to face the door. He appeared in the frame a few seconds later, his forearms pressed against the wood, elbows bent, and leaned into the room.

"You sure know how to make yourself at home."

"Yeah, sorry about that." Except I wasn't sorry at all and he knew it. I patted the mattress. He sauntered toward the bed and bowed over me.

"I like the look of you, so comfortable, in my bed."

"It's a really nice bed." I sat up, letting the blanket slip off, and put my arms around his neck, pulling his face to mine. He climbed onto the mattress and gathered me in his arms.

"I wish you weren't leaving," he whispered.

"Maybe I won't be gone forever." I lifted my shirt over my head and started unbuttoning his while he kissed my shoulders and throat. His hands fumbled around the snap and zipper of my jeans.

"It's been a while," he laughed.

"For me, too." I slipped his shirt off his shoulders and he wiggled his arms out of it. It fell to the floor and he stood to take off his trousers. I shimmied out of my jeans and he climbed back onto the bed, hovering over me, planting light kisses on my stomach and breasts. I could feel the frenzied beating of our hearts in time with one another.

"Dinner might burn," he said.

"Who cares?" My hands caressed his arms, his neck. I giggled as his chest hair brushed against me. His fingers danced down my thighs. "Hey," I said, touching his face. He shifted his weight so his body was almost completely covering mine and our eyes locked together. "I know the answer, but I think I need to hear you say it. Do you believe it's possible to love someone whose lark doesn't match your own?"

He rolled slightly to the side and lifted my arm above my head. With his left hand, he covered the brown spots on my wrist, so our larks were skin to skin. There was no pull, but there was a definite spark. His lips descended, but didn't connect. "Yes," he said. And then he kissed me.

The End

ACKNOWLEDGEMENTS

Thank you, thank you, thank you to my family and friends who continue to support me and my writing. I know sometimes you have no idea what I'm talking about, but you smile and nod all the same. Thank you!

Once again, I owe a million thank you's to Jaclyn Parks, of Twin Dog Designs, for the beautiful cover. I didn't know how we were going to create a cover for *Honor's Lark* that fit it as wonderfully as *Twenty-Five*'s did, but you knocked it out of the park.

Writing a book is never a solitary process, at least not for me. This book is a product of National Novel Writing Month – every November, millions of writers around the world attempt to complete a 50,000 word novel in thirty days. I wrote about 15,000 words of *Honor's Lark* before the month started, then another 57,000 to complete the first draft. The community of amazing writers NaNoWriMo has introduced to me has been invaluable in the writing and shaping of this book from a small idea into a full-bodied story. Thank you to the thousands of employees and volunteers who make NaNo happen each year. I can't wait for the next one!

Editing a book is not a solitary process, either! A huge thank you goes out to all of my beta readers – your comments and insights have made this a better book: Monica Frazier, Megan Ennes, Phil Locey, JQ Abbey, Jaclyn Parks, Jennifer Robinson, Hannah Long, Jaime Herman, Crystal Gonzalez, Tami Hamm, and Ashley Shanlever.

ABOUT THE AUTHOR

Rachel was born in Buffalo, NY but grew up in Burlington, NC. Raised by northern parents in the south, she likes to say she got the best of both worlds. Her writing is inspired by classic authors like Jane Austen and Charles Dickens, as well as contemporary ones like JK Rowling and Claire LaZebnik. She loves to read and has been known to spend an entire weekend engrossed in the adventures of her favorite characters.

Rachel now lives in Raleigh, NC, but someday hopes to make it to London. She's pretty sure (if reincarnation exists) she was British in another life.

ALSO BY RACHEL L. HAMM

TWENTY-FIVE

Abigail Bronsen is sure her life is going nowhere when she turns twenty-five and realizes she hasn't done anything on a list of goals she made for herself as a teenager. Ben Harris is looking to find "the one" after his last girlfriend cheated on him. When they crash into each other, it appears they've both found exactly what they wanted. A year of firsts follows: first date, first kiss, first "I love you's." The first fight is inevitable, but neither of them saw a breakup coming. When Abigail is offered a job overseas, they'll discover that no relationship is perfect and even true love sometimes finds itself separated by time and distance.

www.ingramcontent.com/pod-product-compliance
Lightning Source LLC
Chambersburg PA
CBHW020556180626
46810CB00007B/2525